NEW YORK TIMES & USA TODAY BESTSELLING AUTHOR

SHANNON McKENNA

EDGE OF
Secrets

OLIVERHEBERBOOKS

PUBLISHER'S NOTE: This is a work of fiction. Names, characters, places, and incidents either are the product of the author's imagination or are used fictitiously. Any resemblance to actual persons, living or dead, business establishments, events, or locales is entirely coincidental.

Edge of Secrets, previously titled Tasting Fear Copyright 2009, 2025 © Shannon McKenna

Cover Design by Kim Killion

Published by Oliver-Heber Books

This title was previously published.

0 9 8 7 6 5 4 3 2 1

Introduction

The three D'Onofrio sisters—Nancy, Nell, and Vivi—are in a bind. They're already grieving their foster mother, Lucia, who was killed in a home invasion. Now they're convinced that what happened to Lucia wasn't random. It's somehow connected to a secret from her past—something to do with her family's art collection, and whoever attacked her is convinced that Lucia's daughters have the answers. Which sadly, they do not. Lucia never shared her secrets.

And this situation is quickly becoming very dangerous for the D'Onofrio girls.

Nancy was the first to fight them off, with the help of her fiercely protective new lover, Liam Knightly (*Edge of Whispers, Book 1*). But Nell and Vivi are still out there on their own—scared to breathe, constantly looking over their shoulders.

Because Lucia's killers are still on the prowl, and unanswered questions follow the D'Onofrio sisters wherever they go, whispering like secrets in the night ...

Chapter One

I'd been waiting for my crush to show up at the café all day, even though I didn't admit it to myself. Then the bell over the café door jingled, and he stepped through. And there he was at last, in my face. Mr. Tall, Dark, and Hyper-focused.

I stepped behind the dessert display case, seizing the opportunity to ogle him from over the pecan fudge brownies and under the Napoleon pastries. Looking at that man gave me such a rush. It was dumb, childish, embarrassing, inappropriate. I was making my own self cringe. But the rush was impossible to resist—at least right now.

I had to have that little buzz. It was the only thing that even momentarily eased the dull ache in my middle. I'd been carrying that heavy feeling around ever since my world imploded a few weeks ago with my mother's death. Maybe I would be carrying it forever—always dragging those tight, forced, shallow breaths into that cramped, burning space around my bruised heart. No respite from it, ever.

At least not until I saw Mr. Hyper-Focused. The moment I laid eyes on him a few weeks ago, I got an effervescent rush through my body. It lasted only as long as it took for the guy to order, eat his lunch, pay up, and go—so, not very long. But oh, it was such sweet relief. Even for that brief interval.

The sickening awareness of what had happened to Lucia, my adopted mother, was never far from me. The home invasion. The alleged heart attack. Violence, fear, loss—it was always right there. Just pushed a little bit to the back so I could function in the world. More or less. I could dress a salad, pour coffee, clear away plates.

But when my crush walked out the door, grief slammed me back down even harder than before, as if to punish me for trying to evade it.

He checked to see if his usual table by the window was free, which it almost always was. Today was no exception. The lunch rush was over by the time he arrived—three-fifteen, regular as clockwork. That gave me a buzzy little hum of hopeful anticipation to carry me through all the hours of my shift that came before. Yay, me. Win-win.

He took off his jacket, tossed it on the chair, and seated himself. Then he pulled out a laptop, opened it, and set to work with all the grim concentration of a power drill.

For weeks he'd been here, every damn day. And ever since that first day, I'd been working all the lunch shifts—even though I would earn more tips with the dinner shifts, whenever I could schedule them around my teaching job.

But no. Broke and busted as I was, that fleeting rush I got from seeing Mr. Hyper-Focused was worth more to me than a pocketful of tips. How freaking silly and sad was that, considering the man was oblivious to my very existence.

I took my glasses off and swiftly polished them on my apron. *The better to see you with, my dear.* I perched them back on my nose and fished the order I'd just taken out of my short-term memory before it disappeared into the churning abyss, then promptly dished up ratatouille for the table of women under the aquarium—gawking at my crush all the while. I shot quick, surreptitious glances as I drizzled vinaigrette with a practiced flick of my wrist and tossed grated beets and roasted pumpkin seeds on their salads.

I loaded the tray and chose a path through the restaurant that brought me right past his table, close enough to smell the detergent his crisp white shirt was washed in. The next pass was to refill the water glasses. That run made me conclude that he'd asked his dry cleaner to put extra starch into his collars and cuffs. Another sneaky pass through the tables with the coffee pot got me a greedy whiff of his aftershave. Mmm, nice. Woodsy, notes of citrus. And those shoulders, flaring out—so broad, thick, and solid looking. I wondered what it would feel like to sink my nails into them.

He wasn't movie-star beefcake handsome—not with that rough, angular face and those deep-set, laser-sharp dark eyes—but something about him just got to me. I had studied his features, reviewing them over and over in my daydreams and sexual fantasies.

His face was rugged. Olive skin, that big, bladelike nose with the crooked bump on it, the black, slashing eyebrows set at a sharp upward angle. His cheeks were lean, with grooves flanking his mouth, and he had crinkled lines around his eyes, as if he'd squinted into the desert sun for a long time. His mouth was flat and unsmiling. His black hair was cut short, and stuck up wildly every which way.

The resulting look worked for me. No way would that guy affect such spiky, messy hair on purpose. He couldn't be bothered with such petty considerations. He did not give a rat's ass if anyone was looking at him. He didn't care about his hair. For some random reason, that was a turn-on for me. Go figure.

I dared a peek at his computer screen from behind his broad, muscular back. I could make out his prodigious muscle definition even through the fine cotton of his dress shirt. The screen was thick with code—which was all Greek to me, besides being none of my damn business. I walked away, chin up, resolute. Mature. Ignoring him.

After one last, hungry peek.

Behind the counter, my boss, Norma, looked over from the marinated mushrooms she was grilling with a smile. "He's here again, eh, Nelly?" she said. "Can't get enough of that strip steak sandwich, I see. Before I lose you in a romantic daze, honey, I need to ask a favor."

Oh, God. My crush was that obvious? I grabbed the bread knife and began slicing. "Ask away," I said grimly.

"Easy does it, hon. Don't maim yourself. Couldn't help but notice that you never take your eyes off the fellow. Can't say I really blame you. He's definitely a hottie. Those big, thick shoulders, mmm. If I were twenty-five years younger ... hell, maybe even just fifteen ..." Her voice trailed off, a teasing gleam in her eyes.

I was too mortified to be a good sport today. I just kept slicing bread.

"Workaholic, though," Norma went on in a musing tone. "Always tappity-tapping away, never a glance for the cute little waitress serving him. You're wasted on him, sweetheart. Take it from an expert. Leave that guy alone. He'd be good for nothing but a bunch of plate-throwing arguments about emotional availability. And believe me—I know whereof I speak."

"Thanks for the advice." I apportioned the sliced bread into a bunch of baskets. "But I don't need it. I'm not getting anywhere near him, or any other man. Believe me. I have enough drama in my life these days. Any more would break me."

"Whatever you say, honey. Hey, are you free to work an evening shift? Kendra just called in sick. Again. That girl's driving me crazy. Always at death's door."

I gave her an apologetic look. "I'm so sorry, Norma, but I'm teaching a discussion section tonight for the American poetry course."

Norma clucked her tongue. "I was afraid of that. Oh well. We'll be shorthanded, but we'll survive. Maybe I can get Pete to come in, if he's between boyfriends. Go on, get some coffee for that hardworking fellow before he starts feeling put upon. Do you absolutely have to wear those glasses, Nelly?"

I snatched the glasses in question off my nose and polished them again, defensively. "Unless you want me to bump into tables, yes! What's wrong with my glasses?"

"They just make you look so, I don't know. Bookish, I guess."

"Norma, I've got news for you. I *am* bookish! To the marrow of my bones! It's my most defining personality trait!"

"Aww, now, don't get your knickers in a twist. Your eyes are so big and brown and pretty, I just want the world to see them." Norma tucked a hank of curly black hair from behind my ear so that it dangled ticklishly around my chin, then tugged down the front of my apron to show a little more of my chest. "For God's sake, Nelly. Youth is wasted on the young. Go on, scram! Get the man's order!"

I poured the cup of black coffee he always wanted and scurried out with my order pad, self-consciously tugging my sunset-tinted apron bib back up over my cleavage, annoyed and agitated. Norma was very old school when it came to directives on mating behavior. She was also an immensely kind woman and a really good boss. I was lucky to have found her, and I knew she meant well, so I couldn't get huffy with her for crossing the line. Besides, I got too fluttery to stay mad when I took Mr. Hyper-Focused's order anyway. God alone knew why —we'd never so much as made eye contact. I could take his lunch order stark naked, and he'd never notice.

I placed his coffee on the table. Without shifting his eyes from the screen, he reached for it and took a sip. "Thanks," he said, in that deep, resonant voice that made me go all shivery and stupid. "The usual, please."

"Okay." I concentrated fiercely on keeping my voice from going breathy and high-pitched. "We have three soups today: chicken noodle, French onion, and three-bean. Which would you prefer?"

A small frown furrowed his forehead, but he didn't look up. "I don't care. You pick."

"Okay. One bowl of I-don't-care, coming right up." I stared, almost transfixed, at the cowlick at the crown of his head—a wild, spiky vortex. There was raffish stubble on his tense-looking jaw. His starch-stiffened cuffs were turned up, revealing tough, ropy muscles and black hair that lay flat and silky against the golden skin of his forearms.

"Is there a problem?" His voice was distant, but his fingers still tapping that constant, rapid-fire staccato.

"Um, no. Of course not." I fled, flustered, jamming my hip into a nearby table edge.

Ouch. I suppressed yelp of pain. Crap. The bruise that would show up tomorrow would serve as a stern reminder of what happened when one gave in to adolescent urges. Cripes, even Norma had noticed my condition. I'd let this silly crush get way out of hand.

I put the order in and began assembling his lunch. Norma glanced over with professional interest. "The usual, I assume?" she asked.

"Unsurprisingly." I popped a roll into the toaster grill, and scooped an enormous serving of Knorma's Knockout Coleslaw onto a small plate.

"You're ruining me with those portions, hon. Trust me. The fella's not worth it."

"Give it a rest, Norma," I snapped, arranging thick slices of tomato, radish rosebuds, and carrot curlicues onto his plate. I tossed on a handful of alfalfa sprouts, hesitated for the barest instant, and cut a substantial slice of sweet onion. I added it with a flourish—his breath was neither my responsibility nor my problem. I scooped some oven-roasted rosemary potatoes onto the plate, then added a few more.

The toaster pinged, and I pulled out the roll, still avoiding Norma's gaze.

"What soup did he want?" Norma inquired.

"He doesn't care. I'll give him the three-bean. It's good today."

"Really? I don't know, hon. Chicken might be safer. You know ... gas?"

I snorted as I ladled his bowl full of soup. "He can learn to express a goddamn preference if he doesn't like it." I hefted the tray, and the soup slopped dangerously close to the edges of the bowl.

"Easy does it, Nelly. He's not going anywhere without his lunch."

I gave her a withering look and carried out his soup.

When I brought out the rest of Mr. Hyper-Focused's lunch, the only place to put the sandwich plate was the extreme edge of the table, which looked precarious. He hadn't even touched the soup yet. His big hands chattered ceaselessly on the keyboard. I had to hand it to the guy. Nothing distracted him. It seemed almost pathological.

"That'll be all." His voice was cool and distant.

I backed away, still staring. I'd been summarily dismissed. Now that I'd brought his sustenance, like a silent and dutiful handmaiden, the time had come to melt silently and unobtrusively into the walls. God forbid I disturb the grand master at his important work.

His refusal to look at me was really bugging me today. I was getting genuinely pissy about it. I headed back to the kitchen, mentally ticking off the various issues I meant to cover in tonight's discussion section on Emily Dickinson's poetry. The plight of women in nineteenth-century America. Powerlessness. Arid celibacy. Secret, unrequited love. Constraint. Corsets. The life of the imagination. Agonizing sexual frustration.

Things could always be worse. But this reflection did not comfort me.

"Did everything go smoothly?" The smile in Norma's voice drove me nuts.

"Smooth as silk." I loaded ice water onto a tray, marched past Norma with my chin up, and tripped over the edge of the plastic mat.

Crash. Glass broke, heads turned, water sloshed and spread, ice cubes rolled.

I took a breath to contemplate the extent of the damage, then grabbed the dustpan and started picking up glass shards and ice cubes. Eyes down, mouth tight.

"Nelly. Honey." Norma put her hands on her substantial hips, her eyes full of dismay. "You have got to get out more."

"Norma, I am in no mood for a lecture," I said through gritted teeth. "My sister was almost murdered by a slobbering maniac. I'm short on rent because of all the lost work afterward. My thesis adviser is on my case night and day to get the damn thing finished. I can't get any sleep. And Lucia ... oh, God. Just let me be, okay?"

My face was dissolving. Norma tugged me up to my feet and wrapped me in a big, smothering hug. "Oh, honey, I'm so sorry. What happened to Lucia was so shocking and horrible for you girls. I didn't mean to stress you out. And your sister getting attacked was really scary—but things have worked out, am I right? She's got that big, tough-looking guy looking after her now, and he's down for watching her like a hawk day and night, so things seem to be calming down a bit. I'm sure Lucia would want you to have some fun, move on with your life! You know she would!"

I put my glasses back on, sniffling fiercely. "I'm not in the mood for fun, Norma, no matter what Lucia might have wanted. And I don't mean to be rude, but I don't have time for this lecture, either. I need to get dessert for table six, table eight needs their check, and Monica's taking another cigarette break."

"Yes, yes. I'm sorry. Forget I said anything. But truthfully? I'm glad to see you taking a healthy interest in a likely-looking man. All in all, that's a good sign."

I grunted something bad-tempered in response and headed out to dump broken glass into the trash. I struggled to compose myself before going back out on the floor. My eyes were red and puffy, but who cared? Mr. Hyper-Focused would never notice. When I refilled his coffee, I asked, "Care for dessert?" I was just throwing it out there, because what the hell. If the sky fell, he'd barely notice.

"The usual," he said flatly. Not looking at me.

I hesitated for a moment, then let 'er rip. "Are you sure you don't want to try something new? We have fresh strawberry shortcake on sweet, hot butter biscuits today, and the pecan fudge brownies are wonderful, too—served with whipped cream."

His hands froze over the keyboard. "I'm sure they're all

good. Give me the usual." *'And no back talk'* was the subtext. He was impatient with me. Huh. That alone was more attention than I'd gotten from him thus far in the past several weeks.

I sighed, and went to get him his goddamn apple crumb pie with vanilla ice cream.

As always, when he finished, he closed his laptop, dropped bills on the table that covered the check along with a very generous tip, and left without a backward look. The guy had the imagination of a cement block. The manners of a molting snake. To hell with him. I was embarrassed for myself. Crushing out on a meat-headed, insensible, uncurious, indifferent, soulless, gearhead dweeb.

At least he tipped well, so there was hope for him as a human being.

The rest of the shift was a tired blur. I helped Norma start the dinner prep, then went to the bathroom to freshen up before going uptown to my discussion section. I took off my glasses, leaned close to the mirror, and squinted at myself—a critical once-over.

Norma was right. The round glasses were very eighteenth-century. I think I'd been going for a Brontë sister vibe when I picked them out, but it was not a look that flattered me in the third millennium. And my long, thick mop of black, curly hair was juvenile and nondescript and dowdy. And very heavy.

I twisted my hair up into a knot, letting curly wisps fall down around my ears and jaw. Marginally better, but I didn't have the technology to make it stay up there. My eyes were my best feature—big and dark, with long lashes and thick eyebrows that I had to pluck regularly, or else they staged a *coup d'etat* and took over my whole face. A nice mouth, I conceded, if a little large for my jaw. Norma and Monica kept nudging me to wear lipstick, but I always ended up wiping it off whenever I tried. All that bright red, ka-boom. My mouth took over my face. It literally scared me.

I should be braver. With the lipstick. With my clothes. And maybe I should try contact lenses. And do something, God knows what, to my hair.

Most importantly, I should get my ass moving or be late to my discussion group.

I splashed water on my face, hefted my heavy shoulder bag, and headed for the downtown bus. Why stress over my looks? What difference did it make? Who cared?

I had more pressing things to worry about ... like staying out of the clutches of our nemesis, who Nancy had named Snake Eyes.

And who knew if I could pull that off.

Chapter Two

Nell

The class went more or less as expected. A healthy two-thirds of the group actually attended, and of that number, only three appeared to be sleeping. Not half bad, statistically speaking. We had a rousing discussion about Emily Dickinson's love poetry, and one very serious young man with lank, stringy hair asked earnestly, "Like, how do you know Emily Dickinson never had, you know, sex? Some of those poems are scorching! I can't believe she could feel like that if she never got any."

"Believe it," I said grimly.

I regretted the thoughtless statement amid sideways looks and muffled chortling. Then I noticed that the young blond man and I wore the same type of glasses.

I was overcome with a sudden, almost desperate urge to change my style.

"Let's wrap it up for tonight," I told them. "I expect a five-to-ten-page paper from everyone by Wednesday at five."

"But I can't!" one of them said. "I have a physics midterm to study for!"

"And I have a philosophy paper to turn in on Monday!" another lamented. "Can't we have till Friday?"

"Wednesday. Five o'clock." My pitiless mandate was met with a chorus of groans.

I trudged through the bustling, congested city campus toward the English Department offices. The office door opened as she approached, and Marielle, a fellow grad student, came out holding a sheet of paper, looking bemused. "Hey, Nell. This just landed in my inbox. Weirdest job posting ever."

I took it, and looked it over.

WANTED Writer-Editor-Proofreader for a fantasy video game project
MUST BE EXPERT IN <u>POETRY</u>
Good Pay Flexible Hours
Ask for Duncan

A phone number followed the name.

"Weird, huh?" Marielle commented. "I'd follow up myself, but I'm in the middle of writing my thesis right now. And this Duncan is probably a total weirdo. So ... nah."

I stared down at it. "Interesting."

"Thought you might think so. Good luck with it. Later, Nell."

I bade her an absent good night, still staring at that weird posting. What would a video game want with poetry? Particularly now, when cheap doggerel was so easy to generate with those infernal AI programs that were rotting my students' brains.

I scribbled the number, wondering what "good pay" meant to Duncan. It was an extremely subjective concept, but my standards were high. I often picked up temp legal secretary jobs at night when I was extremely low on funds, but working nights exhausted me. I was always on the lookout for gigs that paid well enough to actually consider quitting the Sunset Grill job and living a life that resembled ... well, normality, if such a thing existed. Which was to say, working only one or two jobs, not three or four. Getting a full night's sleep occasionally. Having time to cook a meal or do my laundry. Leisurely, luxurious activities like that.

But a 'normal life' was pie in the sky for me, considering all the terrifying things that had happened, starting with the day that Lucia was killed.

I didn't dare think about Lucia for long, or I'd start to cry again. I reached up and fingered the jeweled ruby pendant she had given me, hidden under the fabric of my blouse. It had become an automatic gesture, reaching for comfort. My sisters and I had decided that we should keep them hidden, but I didn't feel like leaving mine anywhere, not even in a safe deposit box. Plus, it made me feel closer to Lucia to have it on my person. The necklaces had been her final, posthumous gift to us.

The beautiful golden pendant, studded with small rubies, was a reproduction of a Renaissance Italian-style pendant. My foster mother, Lucia, had commissioned three unique necklaces in that style for me and each of my two sisters, Nancy and Vivi. Nancy's was decorated with sapphires, and Vivi's with emeralds—our respective birthstones. They looked like the kind of bling a haughty Florentine duchess with a lace ruff and a brocade gown might wear. They were extravagantly beautiful.

Lucia had bestowed them upon us, commissioning them right before her violent and untimely death. They had become talismans of love and power for us. The jeweler delivered them to us on the very day of her funeral—a gift from beyond the grave.

But a shadow clung to them. Lucia had given them to us for a very specific reason, according to a fragment of a letter we found in Lucia's garbage. We didn't have enough information to figure out that reason, just that the pendants were the key to a puzzle Lucia had devised. One that the three of us had to solve by working together.

And there the matter stood. Lucia could give us no more clues from the other world. We'd already lost one of the necklaces to Snake Eyes, so the key to Lucia's puzzle was lost forever. Which made us all wild with frustration.

My fingers tightened around the gold pendant. Snake Eyes had ripped Nancy's pendant off her throat when he'd tried to abduct her. The angry red welt the chain left had still been visible on her neck the last time I saw her.

We could never solve it now. We had to swallow that bitter pill. And it was risky, stupid, and childish to wear my pendant —a blatant provocation to that bastard. *Come on and take it, dickhead. Go ahead. Try me.* That was what I said by wearing it around.

Like I was prepared to go *mano a mano* with Snake Eyes. *Hah.*

Still, I felt stronger when I wore it. I had run my own risk/benefit analysis, and I had opted to continue wearing it. It was a power object. I needed all the power I could get.

I'd compromised by tucking it between my boobs, well out of sight. I kept pepper spray in my bag now, too. And I fully intended to sign up for a self-defense class, as soon as I could establish one free night a week when I didn't have to work.

Who knew, maybe I'd even learn to use a gun. I'd never dreamed I would ever do such a thing, but after what happened to Nancy, all bets were off.

Then again, just knowing how to use a gun meant very little when all was said and done. I had to be willing to point the gun at someone and actually pull the trigger.

That terrifying thought propelled me straight to my closet-sized office to call my sister, desperate for the comfort of a familiar voice.

Since Nancy's wild adventures in the past weeks, I'd begun to come around to the concept of cell phones, and I was eating crow. I'd made such a big fat deal of how much I hated them all these years. All my pompous tirades about potential brain tumors, the sinister loss of privacy, the looming shadow of Big Data, how I hated to be constantly on call, how they impeded reaching deep levels of concentration, how important it was to tolerate boredom, etc., etc., blah-blah-blah. I had my tail firmly between my legs after what happened to us.

Privacy had completely lost its charm. When evil killers with unknowable agendas lurked in the shadows, eating crow didn't seem so terrible anymore. The world was weird and dangerous, and it was very good to be only an electromagnetic frequency away from the people I loved and trusted most. An actual smartphone was outside my budget at the moment, but I had bought a flip phone, and I was glad to have it.

Vivi picked up promptly. "Hey, babe. Everything okay?"

"If you keep the bar low," I said. "Nobody's abducted or murdered me lately. How about yourself? No duels to the death?"

"Not so far today. I'm still working. Busy day. I moved lots of stock. I'll wrap up in about an hour, then I'll break down and take off straight for Wilmington after I grab a bite. I feel twitchy if I stay in one place. I prefer to be a moving target. Is that silly?"

"Hell, no. Sounds smart to me. Drive carefully. Did you talk to Nancy?"

"Yeah, she's with Liam in San Francisco, hanging with his dad. They're coming back tomorrow. Thank God we don't have to worry about her, at least. That guy is like a Doberman lunging at the chain. Very comforting. Got a customer, babe. Gotta go."

"Okay. Later." I slid the flip phone into my purse, stared at the flyer again, and shrugged inwardly. What the hell. I might as well give it a shot. I dialed the number.

"Burke Solutions, Inc., can I help you?" said a youthful, reedy male voice.

"Yes, please. May I speak to, um ..." I consulted the flyer again. "Duncan?"

"May I ask what it's regarding?"

"It's regarding the writing job I saw advertised."

"Oh, okay. Just a sec. Hold on."

I drummed my fingers and fretted about whether I was wasting my time or not until a deep, resonant male voice came on the line. "Hello. This is Duncan."

"Hello, Duncan. My name is Nell D'Onofrio, and I'm a grad student of literature at NYU. I'm interested in the writing job I saw advertised."

"Do you have writing and editing experience? Are you familiar with poetry?"

His curt tone got my back up. "Of course," I said. "I'm writing my thesis on nineteenth-century women poets. I lead a discussion section for a summer poetry lecture course, and my graduate seminar focused on Christina Rossetti."

"Ah." There was a thoughtful pause. "Well, then. I'm supervising the creation of a computer game. It's a mystery quest, and it has clues encoded in maps, books, poems, etc. I need a writer for the texts. And I want good texts."

"That sounds doable," I said cautiously. "I'm a big fan of

good texts myself. I noticed that the flyer says flexible hours. How flexible? And is this remote work?"

"I imagine so, at least some of it. I don't know yet. I've never done this kind of thing before." He sounded irritated. "This is actually my brother's project. I have meetings all afternoon, so come to the office tomorrow at six. I'll interview you then."

His master-and-commander tone bothered me. "I won't be free until seven-thirty," I said, although I could have probably done six with a little finagling. But I'd be damned if I'd go out of my way for a guy that bossy and presumptuous.

"Seven-thirty works. Tomorrow, then. My receptionist will give you directions."

I wrote down the directions the receptionist gave me, committing them to memory. Huh. Who knows. If the hours were flex, this might have potential, even if Duncan seemed grumpy and irascible. Depending on the money, of course. Besides, tomorrow was Friday, and I had nothing better to do after my restaurant shift than go home and jump at shadows.

I shoved a pile of midterm essays into my bag. They would keep me too busy to work myself into a paranoid frenzy over every little sound I heard—or else climb the walls all night with sexual fantasies about Mr. Hyper-Focused, which was my other classic option. That one had a better short-term payoff, but neither was very restful.

I armed the alarm as soon as I went into my apartment. A breach of the door or window would be instantly reported to the police, but the new alarm didn't make me feel much safer. I heated up a dinner of three different types of takeout leftovers cobbled together. I did cook occasionally when Vivi stayed with me, but I usually didn't bother when I was alone. Who had the energy?

I was finishing up a stale Oreo that I'd found forgotten in

the cupboard when the buzz of my phone sent me zinging up into the air.

I picked it up with shaking hands, heart thudding wildly. "Hello?"

"It's just me," said my sister Nancy. "Relax, sweetie. You sound nervous."

I sank onto the couch, knees trembling. "No, not at all," I lied. "I'm good. Great to hear your voice. How are things? Vivi told me you guys were still in San Francisco."

"We are, with Liam's dad and his lady friend, Joanne. I have news. Remember when Liam's friend Charlie Witt told me about that elderly guy with the designer clothes? The one they found in Jamaica Plains, with his throat snapped?"

"The one they called the clotheshorse? That was right after Lucia died, right?"

"Right. The time of death was estimated to be roughly the same time Lucia died, although they couldn't be sure."

I doubled over, pressing my hand hard against the nervous twisting in my stomach. "I see," I said. "What about him?"

"Well, after what happened to me in Boston, Detective Lanaghan finally deigned to take all of this a little more seriously." Nancy's voice had an ironic edge to it. "She had his prints compared to the ones found on the coffee cup in Lucia's apartment, as I requested they do weeks ago. But no one ever got around to it, evidently. Until now."

"And they match?"

"Yes. They match," Nancy said quietly. "Lanaghan just called and told me."

We sat silently, for almost a minute. Then I let out a slow breath. "The clotheshorse must be Marco," I said. "Lucia's long-lost husband. That poor guy."

"Yeah," Nancy said. "It has to be him. He came to find her,

and got himself murdered that same night, by the same person who killed Lucia. Maybe even at the same time."

I squeezed my eyes shut and pressed my hand against my cold, clammy forehead. "That poor guy. After not seeing the love of his life for, what, fifty years? Finally they reunite, and then ... oh God, Nance. It's just so damn sad."

"At least they're together now," Nancy said softly. "And she loved him to the very end. She stayed single all those years. With all those men beating down her door."

"You could look at it that way, I guess. If you believed in love and eternity and all that good stuff, dusted with bright, hazy sparkles." I hated the edge in my voice.

"And you don't believe it?" Nancy asked.

"Not right now, I don't," I admitted. "Sorry to be a downer, but you're in love. You've got hazy sparkles by the bucketful. In my world, they're a rare commodity."

Nancy paused. "I'm sorry. I was just trying to cheer you up. I really love you, sweetie. I'm sorry you're having a hard time. I know exactly how you feel."

I felt guilty. Look at me, scrooging on my poor sister, whose only crime was getting lucky in love, and after a dry spell every bit as long as my own. "I love you, too," I said. "And I'm sorry I'm being such a sourpuss. I'm glad for you. Really. Did you tell Detective Lanaghan about the letter in the picture frame?"

"Yes, and she said it's a great lead, but since all we have is the guy's first name and the name of his town, it's going to take a while. She has to contact the local police in Italy, find an interpreter, et cetera, et cetera. So I started to think, in the meantime ... since you studied Italian ... you know?"

"You want me to call the cops there? In Italy?"

"Would you?" Nancy asked eagerly. "Just to facilitate things? To speed things up?"

I looked up at the clock, calculating time zones. "I could try tomorrow morning, before I leave for work, I guess," I said. "But don't get your hopes up. Bureaucracy is bureaucracy, no matter what country you're talking about."

"I understand. Where are you now? Are you still up in Silvana's apartment?"

I gritted my teeth for what I knew was going to be a big fat overreaction. "Ah. About that. Actually, no. I'm back in Brooklyn, at my own apartment."

"Nell! What the hell? You promised!"

"I know, I know, but Silvana's fiancé came to visit, and I was clearly cramping their style. I did put in the new locks and the new alarm. And when Elio leaves, I can go back up there and stay with her again. It's just a couple of weeks."

Nancy carried on, I soothed and cajoled—all familiar conversations after our recent adventures. Then we went through our now near-obsessive routine of admonishing each other to be careful. When we finally hung up, I stared at the wall for a long time.

I was grateful for a job to do, something that might yield some answers. But I was going to have to brace myself. Any answers I found were not going to be comforting.

A sheaf of student papers later, I laid down the red pen, rubbed my eyes, stretched, and flopped onto my bed with a groan. There wasn't much room there, since the surface of my bed was covered with books. There was a strip the exact size of my body to sleep on. It was a poetic metaphor for my life. I couldn't take a lover. Where would I put him? Between *The Riverside Shakespeare* and my twenty-pound annotated Dante's *Divine Comedy*? Would I perch him on top of the seventeenth-century religious poets? Drape him over Chaucer's *Canterbury Tales*? It sounded uncomfortable as hell.

Mr. Hyper-Focused popped into my mind, predictably enough. He was my default mode, whenever I needed to steer around an uncomfortable thought. I wondered why my brain had latched onto him so intensely. I'd never been the type to fixate like that.

Maybe it was not in spite of, but because he was so oblivious to me. He was completely inaccessible, and what could be safer for a scaredy-cat like myself? I knew nothing about him. Only that he had a truly stunning capacity for concentration, and he really, really liked strip steak.

But thinking about him was better than thinking about that poor old man whose body lay in the morgue in Jamaica Plains. Nameless, unclaimed, unmourned.

The bleakness of it made me roll over and shove my face into the pillow.

Maybe tomorrow I could put a name to the man who may or may not have been Lucia's husband. I could give the man the dignity of recognition, at least.

That was the best I could offer, and it wasn't too goddamn much.

Chapter Three

"What's she doing now?"

The old man's sharp tone, loaded with implied criticism, made John Esposito flex his fingers until his knuckles popped. Murderous fantasies flashed through his mind, red-tinged, and dark and hot. Like fresh blood.

He did not turn his head from the monitor, and kept his voice rigidly even. "She appears to be reading papers."

"Papers? What papers?" Ulf Haupt came hobbling over, his cane tap-tap-tapping against the floor. He leaned down to peer over John's shoulder. John suddenly pictured jabbing an elbow deep into the decrepit shithead's guts, hard enough to cause an internal hemorrhage. He would crush the guy's liver in one blow, and then he would put up his feet and smoke a leisurely cigarette as he watched the old bastard gasp on the floor while his abdominal cavity slowly filled with blood.

"Student essays," he said, through clenched teeth. "Poetry. She's a teacher, remember? She's getting her doctorate."

"Essays?" Haupt leaned lower, his head bobbing far too

close to John's face. He leaned away maintain some space and avoid the guy's sour breath. "Keep watching. She might get another phone call. You must let nothing slip through the cracks. Nothing. Tomorrow, she will make that call to Italy and possibly put a name to Barbieri's corpse. This is already a disaster, John. Already a disgrace. You have failed me."

The old man's shrill, accusing tone put John's teeth on edge.

"Why?" he demanded. "It'll tell them nothing. It will change nothing. I need to take a piss. The stupid bitch hasn't moved in hours. Watching her is about as useful as watching water evaporate."

"I'm not paying you to be entertained," Haupt retorted. "Keep your eyes on this one at all times, John—since you lost the other two."

"I did not 'lose' anyone!" John said, stung. "I know exactly where they are at all times. The youngest is in Pennsylvania, working at a crafts fair, and the older one is with her fiancé in San Francisco. If you want me to take the youngest one, I could take off right now and drive to—"

"No. Stay where I can direct you, blow by blow. I don't like the results when you are left to your own devices."

John ground his teeth. He loathed having his employer looking over his shoulder. By the end of this, he might just cut the whiny old bastard's throat. And punish the D'Onofrio sisters just for having been such pains in his ass.

He stared at Antonella as she tossed an essay onto a pile and grabbed another. The camera was hidden in her smoke detector, so he was staring down at the top of her head. A great angle for cleavage—of which she had plenty. She was a bigger girl than either of her scrawnier sisters, with some tits and ass to her. He liked that. Something to grab onto. Something that jiggled.

The pendant he was going to take from her sparkled in the plump cleft of flesh bulging from the neckline of her gray tank top. She had peeled down to loungewear—gray cotton stretch shorts hugging her round, curvy hips. Taut, pinchable nipples poked through her tank. A cock-teasing outfit, like she knew he was there and was trying to lure him into doing something rash and stupid. Dumb slut.

He thought of her older sister, the one who'd slipped him twice. Rage grabbed him deep, twisting, hot and painful. He glared up into Haupt's eyes.

"I'll go get the bitch for you right now, if you like," he offered. "She's alone in her apartment. I have the code to disarm her alarm. Then she won't make that call to Italy."

Anything to get this goatfuck moving.

"No," Haupt said coldly. "Wait. They will identify Barbieri anyway. It's only a matter of time. Discipline, John. She's finally getting back to her normal schedule, in her own apartment. And once you take her, you'll have to move fast to collect the other sister."

"I have backup for that. And for following Antonella tomorrow."

"I hope they'll prove more competent than that idiot you hired last time. I want this done without mistakes that end up on the evening news, if possible," the old man lectured. "We lost precious weeks waiting for the noise to die down. Keep watching." He hobbled stiffly out of the room.

John looked back at the screen. Antonella was stretching, tossing her head back. He admired her strong, curvy, flexible, luscious body. He could imagine it writhing desperately beneath him. He licked his lips. She massaged her temples, a tiny frown between her brows. A headache. Awww, poor baby. Working so hard. She needed Big John to give her a neck rub.

After which, he would rip those cock-teasing panties off

her, stuff them into her mouth, and make her forget all about her poor head.

It was the least he deserved, after all this fucking aggravation.

Chapter Four

Nell

"Grazie per la telefonata, signorina," said Osvaldo Tucci, the person at the *commissariato* who had fielded my call. "I do not believe that we have any pending missing-persons reports from Castiglione Sant'Angelo. And to be sincere, without a surname for reference, it will take a long time to—

"But that's just my point, Inspettore," I argued. "If he got on a plane for New York weeks ago, then why would it have ever occurred to anyone to declare him missing? Perhaps you can cross-reference. I know that he was a resident of the Palazzo de Luca, and I know that he was married to Lucia de Luca, sometime between 1957 and 1968, I think. Her father was the Conte de Luca. Doesn't that help narrow it down?"

"Not really, *signorina*. I am not familiar with all the *palazzi* of the noble families in Castiglione Sant'Angelo," Inspettore Tucci said, his voice heavy with professional patience. "I did not grow up here myself. I was transferred here from Calabria.

But I assure you, we will look into this, and we will get in touch with Detective Lanaghan as soon as possible."

We closed the call with a polite round of pleasantries, and I hung up, tense and unsatisfied. Not that I'd expected anything to be so easy.

Unfortunately, all Inspettore Tucci had heard was an unhinged American woman asking weird and inappropriate questions about things that probably weren't any of her business. I should've waited for the official channels, language skills or not.

Lunch prep at the Sunset was crazy, but that was just as well. It kept me too occupied to dwell on Marco's tragic fate. Or to entertain the awful possibility that Lucia had been forced to witness her long-lost, still beloved husband's murder before her own. The thought horrified me: that someone so fine and kind as Lucia had to die that way.

At three-fifteen, I felt a familiar tingle in the nape of my neck and looked up from the banana kiwi smoothie I was blending. Well, look at that. Here he was. My own personal coping mechanism, standing right there. Nice.

I welcomed the restorative thrill, vaguely guilty for indulging myself. But I didn't have much to thrill about. I'd take what I could get. The guy would never know or care.

He looked at his favorite table, but it was occupied. He chose another, frowning with irritation as he pulled out his laptop. Monica jerked her chin in the direction of his table, although the man had seated himself in her section, not mine. Even Monica knew.

Norma tapped my shoulder. "Get that strip steak ready pronto, Nelly," she murmured under her breath. "That big, tall, strapping drink of water looks hungry."

"I don't want to give him the strip steak," I said rebelliously. "Always the same damn thing, day after day. It can't be good for him. To say nothing of the nutritional implications and all that saturated fat, a person needs stimulation, variety, change! Or else they're as good as dead!"

Norma snorted. "You're a fine one to talk, sweet cheeks. I have a suggestion for you. Go tap him on the shoulder and tell him he needs a change, and so do his arteries. The tofu cashew stir-fry. The curried chickpeas. Or a candlelit dinner with you."

"Norma! As freaking if! He doesn't even know that I exist!"

"And whose fault is that?" Norma shot back, exasperated. "You'd be gorgeous if you played yourself up a little bit, and I'm talking the absolute minimum! You'd cause car accidents when you walked down the street! Go on, get the man coffee!"

I marched out onto the restaurant floor. I was so damn sick of being lectured and hounded. And why would a person want to be responsible for car accidents on the street? For fuck's sake. I wasn't interested in stupid power games with anyone.

I plopped the coffee on the table beside the guy, slapped a menu down, and whipped out my order pad. "The usual? Again?" I demanded. Monica passed with a tray of soups, making smooching sounds. I gave her a narrow look. *Don't you dare, girl.*

He frowned at his screen. "Why ask? You know what I want."

I took a deep breath. "That's a good question. One to which I have perhaps given more thought than it actually deserves, but I am prepared to answer."

His fingers slowed their incessant tapping on the keyboard, then stopped, and reached for his coffee. He took a slow sip, still watching his screen. Still not looking at me. "Okay," he said, his voice guarded. "Let's have it, then."

My heart thumped. "Although I know that you always want the strip steak, the one day I don't ask will be the day that

—out of sheer perversity—you decide you want the bulgur pilaf."

"I promise you, that's not going to happen." He looked up at me. For the first time ever, I had his full, direct attention.

Whoa. It was dizzying. Like standing in a strong wind. He looked straight into my face, his eyes narrowed and thoughtful. They were dark, penetrating, intense. Gorgeous. He had unbelievably long lashes.

"Therefore," I continued, "by saying, 'the usual,' I'm killing two birds with one stone. I acknowledge that you have a relationship with us, and that we will cater to your preferences. But asking at all pays homage to the fact that life is full of surprises, and people do change." I poised my pen over the pad. "Your order, sir?"

He stared at me for a long moment ... and blinked. I waited, belly fluttering.

"The usual," he said blandly.

I turned tail and ran.

Back behind the counter, Norma gave my cheek an approving pat. "Good start! Not what I told you to say, but boy, did he take notice! No, no, don't look now! He's still looking at you. Wow, he's practically staring! For goodness' sake, act nonchalant."

"Yeah. Like, play it cool, girlfriend," Monica advised. "Like, you could take it or leave it."

"Leave me alone. You're embarrassing me to death. Monica, would you take over his table? I can't face him again," I begged.

"Not in a million years," Monica said, heartlessly. "He's all yours, chica. Knock yourself out."

"I'll dip up his coleslaw," Norma said in a businesslike tone. "Put the roll onto the grill, and tuck that hair behind your ears. Monica, get a bowl of soup, and pass me those veggies! And give the man some extra potatoes. There's a lot of him to nourish."

Norma and Monica smartly assembled his lunch and passed the tray into my cold, nerveless hands. The guy pushed his computer to one side of the table and watched as I laid the dishes down. His gaze on my face made my skin tingle and burn.

I straightened my spine and forced myself to look into his eyes. "Will that be all?" Damn. My voice sounded so wispy and tremulous.

His eyes traveled down my body. Slow, cool, assessing. I wished desperately that I hadn't called attention to myself. If he kept looking at me like that, I was going to melt, burn, combust. Fly into a million pieces.

"For now," he said. His voice was so scratchy and deep and low.

I retreated to the kitchen, where Norma and Monica hooted and cheered in whispers. "He's eating you with his eyes, honey! Don't look! Get the coffeepot and do a round," Norma directed. "Let him look his fill."

"Yeah, chica, you did good. Tomorrow wear something sexier. Say, like, a tight ribbed turtleneck. Sleeveless, 'cause you got good arms. If you don't have one I'll lend you one of mine," Monica offered.

"Ladies, do you mind?" I hissed, grabbing the coffeepot.

I did as Norma suggested, refilling all the coffee cups to steady my nerves.

I didn't really have that much experience with men. I'd dabbled with sex in college, but this guy was in another league from the callow literary types I'd discussed poetry and philosophy with over cheap wine and takeout.

God. Such a brief, inconsequential encounter, but I'd almost had a seizure.

The moment he finally took notice of me, a feeling stabbed through me, part excitement, part stark terror. I couldn't tell if the feeling was pleasurable or not. I had never felt so vulnerable. So female. And all he'd done was ogle me intensely.

I would be hopelessly out of my depth with Mr. Hyper-Focused. Now I was backpedaling at a hundred miles an hour, like a dithering coward.

I went back to the counter to refill the coffeepot and dared a sidelong peek. Yup. He was still looking right at me. Fixedly. Hungrily. Those keen, scorching dark eyes, following my every move. My stomach jumped up and crowded my lungs. Now what?

Norma presented me with a plate of apple crumb pie with vanilla ice cream. "You've got to see it through," she said sternly. "Just gotta. Come on, girl. Buck up."

"Norma, I can't. I just can't."

"You must, or I'll fire you," Norma threatened.

"Go ahead. Fire me then. Do your worst," I said, putting the coffeepot on the warmer and putting my hands over my hot cheeks. "I don't care."

"If you don't do it, I'll start talking real loud about how you have this huge crush on the hot guy by the window with the computer. I swear to God I will." Monica's voice rose in volume then and there.

I shot her a furious look and snatched up his dessert plate, forcing myself to approach his table. I laid it beside his computer and turned to go.

"You didn't ask if I wanted the usual dessert," he said, freezing me in place. His resonant voice sent a shudder of excitement down my spine. "I feel cheated of my agency. Robbed of options, freedom, and spontaneity. How could you do that to me?"

"I think you'll live," I informed him. "I've taken enough

risks today." I gathered up dishes just to keep my hands from shaking. "Next time, maybe we can take that leap together. I haven't given up hope of persuading you to try the pecan fudge brownies."

I walked away—back very straight—and as I moved, I could feel his gaze burning against my back. It was a very stimulating sensation.

I watched with my peripheral vision as he sat there staring at me for a few breathless minutes. Then he dropped a couple of bills on the table, got up, and walked out.

When the door closed behind him, I exhaled and sank down onto a chair.

Monica punched my shoulder gently in approval. "Good job, chica! That was some flirting to be proud of!"

"I wasn't flirting!" I protested. "I merely tried to persuade him to order something new, and I failed in the attempt. Failed miserably. That's all that happened. That's it."

"So why are you hyperventilating?" Monica asked.

"Because I'm stupid, okay?" I yelled. "Dumb as a rock! Everybody on board with that assessment? Anybody need more clarification?"

"Oh, calm down, Nelly." Norma bustled over and squeezed Nell's shoulder. "Monica's right. You did great. Couldn't have done a better job myself in my heyday, and that's saying a lot, if I do say so myself. He's obviously intrigued. Come in early tomorrow and let me fix your hair."

"Norma, please!"

"It's true," Monica said sternly. "It's time. The hair needs help."

"I am not playing this game with you two!" I glared at both of them.

"Oh, honey, indulge a fond old lady!" Norma wheedled, pinching my cheek.

"I'm gonna bring that shirt I was talking about tomorrow. And I'm putting some makeup on you, too," Monica said, looking her over with a critical eye. "What's your shoe size? Got any heels?"

"For waitressing?" Nell asked, aghast. "Under no circumstances! Ever!"

"Babe." Monica cracked her gum. "One must suffer in order to be beautiful."

"That is not my creed, nor will it ever be. I reject it on every level of my being." I heaved myself up onto unsteady feet. "I'm going out for a cigarette break."

Monica's eyebrows shot up. "But you don't smoke."

"If I smoked, now would be the moment that I did." I marched out the back door without taking off my apron, and walked down the street through blaring traffic, my face feverishly hot.

I was so flustered. So discombobulated. God, I was close to thirty years old, and all I had done was serve the guy lunch. Imagine if he and I were actually to ever ... well, no. Better not imagine it at all if I wanted to keep functioning. I was already in a state of total emotional and sensory overload.

It had been years since I'd fooled around with a guy, and the more time that passed, the harder it got to contemplate. My sister Nancy had at least gotten out there and tried. She'd gotten burned a lot, but she'd finally landed a winner in Liam. Grit, persistence and guts had paid off. Vivi and I were so proud and pleased for her.

But that was Nancy, all over. She had courage and perseverance to burn. I didn't have the stomach to run the risk, or face the kind of feelings that I knew lay in wait for me if I made a wrong move. The way I'd feel if I got used. Hurt, humiliated, rejected.

Not if. When. It was a sure thing, statistically speaking.

Anyone who jumped into that particular shark tank had to face the odds. Nobody got through it unscathed.

Elena, my birth mother, had never feared men. She had just used them. Coolly. Expertly. Elena Pisani had been an extremely beautiful woman, and as a practitioner of the world's oldest profession, she had used her beauty as currency, with ruthless practicality. Elena had always looked flawless, no matter the circumstances. Sexy clothing, shoes, makeup, and hair—seduction and allure. Those were the tools and weapons of her trade. She had always looked, felt, and smelled fabulous.

Which was probably why I avoided makeup and favored baggy, shapeless dresses, frumpy shoes and nerdy glasses. Dressing down blurred my startling resemblance to my mother. Looking like her frightened me. A good therapist would be able to diagnose all my fixations with ease. They were probably all described in the standard manuals.

I had been an inconvenient surprise to Elena, a pregnancy she had unaccountably decided to bring to term. For the first ten years of my life, I watched my mother being kept by a series of rich men in various lavish apartments around the country. When it was convenient, Elena brought me along. When it was not, which was most of the time, I stayed in a series of boarding schools. I was taught to call her Elena, not Mom. She thought that emphasizing her maternity made her seem older. Unsexy.

I'd just gotten old enough to get an inkling of the nature of Elena's arrangements with this long string of "uncles" when she died suddenly of an undiagnosed brain tumor. There had been only twelve terrifying days from the onset of her crushing headaches to her death under the surgeon's knife.

There had been no relatives to contact. No savings or life insurance policy to keep me. My mother had no friends to speak of, and her current lover had swiftly vanished.

I had entered the foster system at the age of ten, and three very dark years followed—years that I tried hard to forget. Then Lucia found me.

And that had been my salvation. Lucia, Nancy, and Vivi. A family of my own.

Yes, I had plenty of reasons to be reticent about sex and romance, if I thought about them, though I flinched from self-analysis as from a poisonous spider. I preferred to analyze books rather than my own sad and silly self. Books were much more fun.

One thing I knew for sure. My particular childhood trauma had forged me into a hopeless and insatiable devourer of books. My choice had been brutally simple: romantic escapism or brutal cynicism. Romance was clearly the better choice.

Books were havens, other worlds to escape to. Other feelings to experience. As I got older, I discovered tales of love and passion, and got hooked on those as well. An even more potent haven, with even higher, thicker walls.

It was so much better to spend my time wallowing in the highest, purest sentiments of which human hearts were capable, and if it was all blather and bullshit, who cared? It was beautiful blather and bullshit, and I would dedicate my life to it. Reading it, studying it, teaching it. Hopefully writing it, too.

There was only one problem. My body didn't care about my high ideals. My body wanted the real, flesh-and-blood thing, faults and all. And a real, live, flesh-and-blood guy with all his foibles and flaws and his ridiculous male nonsense would never live up to my fictional ideals.

Particularly not a guy with no manners, no imagination, no way with words. And deep-set, intense dark eyes that burned with fascinated lust when he looked at me.

I didn't want it to be about just lust. I had seen what sex purely for sex's sake looked like. It was cold, sterile, and sad. I didn't need to see it ever again.

Though Mr. Hyper-focused's scorching gaze had not felt neither cold, sad, nor sterile. Not in the least.

Enough of this. I had tables to clear, rent to pay, and Snake Eyes to stay alert for. A job interview to mentally prepare for, too. Here I was, stumbling through the crowded streets without even paying the slightest attention to the hordes of people teeming around me. I had to sharpen up, or I'd get stuffed in the trunk of a car, like Nancy. Thank God Liam had come charging to Nancy's rescue like an avenging angel.

I didn't have one of those following me around.

After my shift, I changed into my most professional-looking suit and put on some lipstick that Vivi had given me. It was frighteningly red. I stared doubtfully in the mirror. I twisted my hair into the tightest knot I could manage, with all that curly volume, but the sheer weight of it pulled the knot down from the crown of my head to bounce at the nape of my neck in a matter of minutes.

The receptionist's directions were easy. It was just a twenty-minute walk uptown. I entered the lobby of a large Midtown office building, took the elevator to the sixteenth floor, and found the door. Burke Solutions, Inc., was stenciled on it.

It was a large, attractive office. The receptionist was a fresh-faced young man with rather bulging eyes and a bow tie. He gave me a big smile as I approached, hanging up his phone. "Can I help you?" he asked.

"Yes, please," I said. "I'm here for an interview with Duncan Burke."

His eyes widened. He blinked at me. "Another poet?" His tone suggested that I was a rare bug that might sting him.

"Sort of, I suppose," I said. "I'm a grad student in literature."

"Okay. You wouldn't believe some of the weirdos who have

been coming in. You look relatively normal, comparatively, but you never can tell. I'll tell Duncan you're here." He pushed a button. "Hey, Duncan, I've got another poet for you ... yeah. Right away." He stood up. "I'll take you to his office. Follow me."

I followed him down the hall to the corner office. He knocked on the door.

"Come in," a deep voice said. A voice that prickled my senses. I knew that voice.

The receptionist gestured for me to enter, and the professional smile on my face froze as I saw the man who rose from his desk to greet me. Oh. My. God.

Mr. Hyper-Focused stood right there in front of me.

Chapter Five

Nell

My mouth was open. I forced myself to close it. He stared at me silently, eyes narrowed in furious concentration as he tried to place me.

I lowered my outstretched hand, my stomach cartwheeling. I pressed my hand against it, then realized how weird that looked, and forced myself to drop the hand.

My hand twitched and swung, unsure of what the hell to do with itself.

"Wait," he said slowly. "I know you."

I ginned up some instant bravado. "Yes, you do, in a manner of speaking. Strip steak sandwich, soup of the day, and apple crumb pie with vanilla ice cream. And coffee. Lots of coffee."

"You're the waitress. At the café where I get lunch." His tone was accusing. He seemed so much taller here, but of course, in the restaurant he'd always been sitting down. He studied me, his eyes puzzled and suspicious. "You look different."

"I'm not wearing an apron or holding an order pad. Not that I need one for your order." I resisted a near-overwhelming urge to button up my jacket. There was no need to scream my discomfort and self-consciousness to the four winds. I had buttoned my blouse to the top, hadn't I? Hadn't I? *Do. Not. Check. Just don't.* I was also acutely, intensely aware of the lipstick I'd painted onto my mouth. I regretted it bitterly.

"Wait. So you guys know each other?" The receptionist's eyes were goggling.

"Derek, that'll be all."

Derek blinked innocently. "Can I make you some coffee? Or bring in some—"

"Get out, Derek," the man said, with an authority that was both flat and absolute.

Derek sidled obediently out the door. Mr. Tall and Hyper-Focused and I looked at each other in absolute silence for a moment. The weight and pressure of his full attention was as bewildering and disorienting as it had been earlier today at the restaurant. I had to brace myself, as if I were standing in a hurricane wind.

"You said you were an expert in poetry and a doctoral candidate at NYU," he said.

"And so I am," I replied.

"Excuse me for making personal statements, but you look too young for that."

Oh, for God's sake. I absolutely had to change my look. "I'll be thirty in October," I said. "I can show you my driver's license, if you'd like to verify that. Or my passport. Not that it's particularly relevant."

"That won't be necessary. Look, Ms. ... uh ..."

"D'Onofrio," I supplied.

"Ms. D'Onofrio, I sympathize with your desire to break out of waitressing, but I'm not the kind of employer who hires young women just for scenery. So if you're not actually qualified, don't waste my time. It would be unpleasant for us both."

I was stymied for a moment as I unpacked that complicated statement. The fucking nerve of him, to imply that I was lying or scamming. To say nothing of the fact that he'd just implied that I was ... well. Pretty enough to be considered scenery. Which was a compliment hidden inside an insult, or maybe it was an insult hidden inside a compliment. I wasn't quite sure which one it was. Or which one was worse.

Or, well ... better. As the case might be.

"I gave you my credentials," I said icily. "They were absolutely genuine. I did not misrepresent myself in the least. If you'd like to verify my references, feel free. Do it now. I am more than qualified for the work you've described. I'm interested because of the flexible hours and the possibility of working remotely. It's very difficult to find jobs that fit into a graduate seminar and teaching schedule."

"If you're a teacher at NYU, then why are you waiting tables?"

Ah, how innocent he was. I exerted all my self-control and did not roll my eyes. "It's impossible to pay rent on a grad student's stipend," I told him. "Though that, too, is irrelevant, and nobody's business but mine. I am an extremely busy person, Mr. Burke, but I'm the best you're ever going to find for this project. If you're interested in interviewing me, we can proceed. If you intend to insult and belittle me, I'll be on my way." I stared straight into his eyes.

He stared back for a harrowing moment, tapping his pen rapidly against his keyboard. "I never meant to insult or belittle you," he said.

I sniffed. "Very well. Apology accepted."

"Apology? Did I apologize?" he said, his brow furrowed.

I gave him a thin smile. "I sure hope so. Or else I'll just be on my way right now. Did I misread you?"

He chewed on that, still tapping. "No, I guess not," he said. "Let's proceed."

I rummaged in my bag and handed him a resume. He flicked his gaze over it and tossed it on his desk. "Pull up a chair," he said.

I looked around, at a loss, since both chairs were piled high with books and folders.

Burke got up, grumbling under his breath. His white sleeves were rolled up, and the muscles in his forearms bulged appealingly as he grabbed armfuls of paper and dumped them on the floor. "Derek was supposed to file this stuff," he growled. "Sit down."

I seated myself gingerly on the chair, nerves buzzing.

Burke studied me for a long moment. "We're creating a cutting-edge computer game," he said finally. "Puzzle solving, riddles, prophecies, secrets, treasure maps. Less blood and guts, but there's plenty of that, too. To move to the higher levels, the player must pass a series of trials each time, like following an enchanted map, breaking a spell, or figuring out how to enlist the help of some magical creature. That kind of thing. Instructions for the tasks and trials will be encoded in hidden texts that are stylistically in keeping with the game. I also desire texts that have actual artistic merit, although I'm no judge of that kind of thing myself. That's where you come in. Do I make myself clear?"

"Yes," I said. "Look no further. I'm your woman."

The words rang in the air between us. They sounded so suggestive and sexual. Dear God. What on earth had come over me to say something so in-your-face flirtatious?

He gazed at me for a moment, blinking. "You sound very confident," he said.

"Absolutely," I said. "I know my strengths, and this plays right to them."

He nodded. "We've been interviewing people for weeks, but I've been unsatisfied with the pool of applicants that have come our way. Several struck me as lightweights. Others took it far too seriously. It's a game, for God's sake. So I thought maybe the local universities might have people with the right vibe. Competent, yet playful."

"A sensible idea," I commented. "You said last night that you'd never done anything like this before? So this project is a first for you?"

"That's right. I'm not a game designer myself. I design cyber-security programs, data analysis programs, systems with real-world practical applications. The game is my brother Bruce's baby, so you'll be working with him. My mission is just to make sure everything stays on track. I've invested a fortune in game designers and programmers. I can't afford for this thing to fail. The one thing we haven't covered is someone to handle the written texts."

"I see," I murmured.

"Let me tell you exactly what I want from you." His intense gaze made his words sound seductive. I plastered on a politely interested smile and tried to breathe.

"For instance, to move to the second level, the player must find a hidden manuscript and get three clues out of it: a silver vial, a scrying pool, and a jeweled dagger. You pour the contents of the vial into the pool to figure out where to find the dagger, which leads you to the next level—the cursed labyrinth. Got it?"

"Uh, yes. I think so."

"Write me something that gives the clues but leaves the

player to figure out the details—while also alluding to the overall quest of the game."

"Which is?" I asked.

He shifted restlessly in his chair, looking vaguely embarrassed. "Um ... well," he muttered. "Actually, it's to, uh, rescue the captured princess."

Awww. I smiled, in spite of myself. That was pretty freaking adorable.

He flapped his hand impatiently to banish my amusement. "I know, I know," he said. "It's tired. It's been done to death. We know, we know."

"I'll say," I murmured. "For, like, all of recorded history."

He harrumphed impatiently. "I didn't come up with it. The princess was Bruce's idea. He's a very basic guy. Maybe we can come up with something snappier and more original later."

"No," I said. "Rescuing the captured princess is a winner. It works for everybody. It's an archetype that's programmed into our deepest childhood memories. Although I hope she won't be a dull, helpless princess with no agency, or a sleeping princess, or a princess in a coma. Those will definitely get you the stink-eye these days. Your princess might need some help, but she has to have something special up her sleeve that's all her own. She needs to participate."

"I'll keep that in mind, but we haven't gotten that far yet," he said. "We're still in the design phase. I'll be happy for your feedback about proactive princesses."

"Good," I said. "So it's a computer game for hopeless romantics. Even I might be tempted to play a game like this one, although I'm sure I'd suck at it."

Duncan Burk's tapping pen was a steady sharp staccato. "It's not for romantics," he said tersely. "It's mind candy for magic and fantasy freaks."

"You don't think that rescuing a captured princess is romantic?"

"That isn't the point," he said. "So? What can you do with the clues?" He leaned back in his chair and looked expectant.

I blinked. "You want me to write something for you right on the spot?"

"If you can," he said blandly. "Write me a poem with the elements I gave you."

I pulled off my glasses and polished them. It was easier to look him boldly in the face when he was a little blurry. "What type of poetry would you prefer? Early, mid, or late medieval? Renaissance? Classical antiquity? Homer, or Catullus, or Dante, or Chaucer? Spenser? Sidney? Heroic couplets, like Pope? Or something more, say, Miltonian?" I put my glasses back on, blinking as his dark, narrow, hawk-like face came back into focus. Wow. He was so fine. It was distracting.

He scowled. "How would I know? I don't do poetry. That's why you're here."

"It's not a matter of knowing anything," I explained patiently. "I just need a point of reference. A jumping off point. The more indications you give me, the quicker I can structure the piece. If you like, I'll just choose a style arbitrarily for the purposes of this exercise. How about a Shakespearean sonnet?"

"Fine, whatever. Go for it."

"Could you give me something to write on?"

He passed a legal pad and pen across the desk. I swiftly scribbled down the list of elements: vial, scrying pool, jeweled dagger, labyrinth, captured princess.

"Excuse my back," I told him. "I'll just turn around so I can concentrate."

"Absolutely. Feel free," he said.

I swiveled my chair until he was out of my direct line of

vision and got to work with the elements he'd given me, taking notes and structuring the piece as ideas bubbled up.

There was great pleasure in doing something I was made for, even under pressure. This was my happy place. Words, language, stories, myth, and magic. I let the fear and stress melt out of my mind: Snake Eyes stalking us, losing Lucia, my still-unwritten thesis, my unpaid rent, how badly I needed a few hours of uninterrupted sleep with no stress nightmares to shatter it. Even the charismatic and compelling Duncan Burke himself faded away as I descended into that inner space.

These were the brain waves that had saved me when I was a little kid living with Elena. I had urgently needed not to focus on what was happening in the next room.

That shielded inner world had saved me once again while I was being shuttled from foster home to foster home, back before Lucia found me.

The magic place had always been there for me. It was safe, it was home, and it never let me down. In that place, I was at my best—clear-eyed, smart, brave, generous, connected to my creativity. I could imagine myself as deeper, calmer, wiser. Better.

About twenty minutes later, I turned spun the chair around and realized that Burke had not moved or spoken for the entire time that I was working.

He'd just sat there and watched, and it must have been about as interesting as watching paint dry.

I wondered if he was one of those guys who loathed being ignored. But he didn't seem bothered by my having forgotten his existence. He looked curious. As if I were a puzzle that he was intent upon solving.

I ripped off all the drafts, scribbles, and notes and held out the legal pad with my final version. "Take a look," I said. "That'll give you an idea of how I work."

Burke took the pad, looking dubious. "Finished already?"

"It's a familiar exercise," I told him. "I make my students do it all the time. The best way to study a poet's style is from the inside out."

He read what I'd written, then read it again. He looked at me for a long moment, still tapping his pen. *Tappity-tappity-tappity-tap.* It was starting to make me nervous.

"Do you want the job?" he asked.

Chapter Six

Duncan

The sexy waitress had the wiles of a street merchant when it came to negotiating her pay. I escorted her to the door after eventually agreeing to give her far more than I'd ever anticipated. She had a very high opinion of how much her time and skill were worth, and she was absolutely willing to walk away if her demands were not met.

I admired that in a person, if it was backed up by competence. Which it clearly was, in her case. This woman was the real deal. High-quality production, under pressure, in real time, while I watched. That was the kind of focused, high-octane energy that I liked to infuse into all of my projects. It was expensive, but it was always, always worth it.

Except for one thing. One dumb, selfish, childish issue I was embarrassed to find myself sulking about.

Ever since that unexpected conversation I'd found myself having with her at lunch today, I'd been considering asking the hot, intriguing Sunset Grill waitress out. This fantasy had made my afternoon brighter than it had been for a long time. Now my cute, provocative waitress with the dark, flashing eyes had morphed into a key employee for this project, which made that scenario no longer feasible. Who knew for how long.

Derek had the poor judgment to approach me at that moment. "So, did you hire her or what?"

"Derek, do you remember when I told you to deal with all that crap piled around my office? Filed, recycled, disappeared?"

"Uh," Derek mumbled uncomfortably. "Yeah."

"Put the phones on voicemail for the evening, Derek, and do it."

Derek scurried away, and I stared out the window. What was the waitress doing being a goddamn academic, anyhow? She'd ignored me utterly while she was writing, which had given me a long, leisurely opportunity to study her profile—the sensual shape of her full lips, her smooth skin, the thick, wavy texture of her black hair. I wanted to tug on one of those fuzzy dark ringlets just to watch it spring back into shape.

She had that old-fashioned, pinup-girl type of curviness. Lush and sexy. It made my hands clench with the urge to touch her. Handle her. Hoist her up to wrap around me.

It had been a long time since I'd gotten any, I realized, doing some calculations in my head. I was actually pretty good at sublimating the need for sex at this point. Dealing with women was so exhausting. Their unspoken expectations, the fuck-ups I didn't remember having committed, the endless demands to demonstrate emotions I did not feel. It made me feel hunted and confused.

Talk of love gave me acid stomach. And the perennial need to know "where this relationship is going," which of course, was usually straight to hell.

I never had the stomach to lie to my hook-ups, as many of my male friends casually did. For some reason, I just couldn't pretend. I got the urge for sex as often as the next guy, but I could shove it under the rug when necessary. My usual stratagems were extreme exercise, overwork, cold showers, and my own right hand. I did okay, for the most part, but every now and then, the sex thing reared up, tossed the rug aside, and bit me hard in the ass.

I'd never been bitten like this, though. Today in the restaurant, when she provoked me, I felt the urge roar to life, and now, after thinking about her for a few hours, it felt like a big, dangerous animal—snorting and snarling, rattling the bars of its cage.

My dick had been hard on and off all afternoon.

I grabbed my jacket. I had plenty more work to do, but work never ended. I could keep myself busy until midnight or beyond, and often did. But tonight I needed air and movement. I could go pound a punching bag in the gym, but I'd already spent two hours there that morning, from five until seven.

I had to unload some of this excess energy before I did something stupid, like break my personal code. I repeated it silently in the elevator, grinding my teeth. *Don't fuck your employees.* I might as well just shoot myself in the head rather than pull a stunt like that. I'd save myself a lot of time and trouble.

I'd had the ideal scenario in my head before she walked in. It was a self-serving, horn-dog scenario that I wasn't particularly proud of, but I couldn't stop imagining it. A hot affair with a gorgeous, luscious girl—one old enough to be hungry and curious, but a little too young to be seriously husband-hunting. One who was still just trying things on for size, figuring out what she liked, not ready to settle down. I would offer myself up as one of her learning experiences and let her squeeze me like a lemon. A girl who would be content with nights of juicy, pounding sex, not a whole lot of conversation, maybe some nice gifts from time to time—flowers, jewelry, clothing, electronics, whatever. A woman who had no connection with my family, or my professional or social life. No one would know about her. She would meet no one, be vetted by no one, be judged by no one. A few nights a week, a car service would bring her to my condo, where I would peel off her clothes and make her come screaming. I would exhaust her with pleasure, and then, after a long, erotic shower, good coffee, and a hearty breakfast, a car service would take her away again to whatever else she did during the day. And I would get back to work. Refreshed and restored. My life still beautifully uncomplicated.

Sex was awesome. Nothing like it on earth. But only under controlled conditions— without repercussions, regrets or strings attached. Hard conditions to create, unless I turned to professionals. And that was definitely not my vibe.

So much for my pornographic fantasy. The snooty, smart-mouthed poetry professor was not that hot, curious, uncomplicated, sexually adventurous girl I had envisioned. Twenty-nine was plenty old enough to be husband-hungry. And Nell D'Onofrio was complicated as all get-out. Demanding. Too smart for her own good.

She would definitely be too smart for my good.

This one would not settle for being some sex-crazed meathead's undemanding fuck buddy. She would want to converse. She would try to connect with me on levels that I didn't even know existed. And my mind just didn't work that way.

It was sad but true. I had enough experience to know that I would disappoint that woman. Depressing, but better to just suck it up right now, from the get-go.

I was the kind of guy who preferred to know in advance what I would eat for lunch. I wanted uncertainty and drama in a sexual liaison even less.

The evening air was cool, and the street was wet with rain.

Traffic blared from the downtown avenues. I picked a direction at random as it occurred to me that she'd be working much more closely with my younger brother than with me. Bruce was a charming, flirtatious womanizer. We'd scheduled a meeting with Bruce for the following evening to discuss his project and introduce them.

Bruce was going to lick his chops when he saw her. He was good at talking to women. Connecting, conversing, being charming, being funny. Unlike myself.

That usually didn't bother me, but tonight, it irritated the living shit out of me.

I rounded the corner onto Eighth Avenue, stopped in my tracks, and retreated swiftly into the shadow of a restaurant awning when I saw Nell D'Onofrio standing at the curb a few yards away, arm up as she tried to flag a cab. It swept on by.

There was a constant stream of yellow cabs, but they were all taken. She kept on trying, and after each arm-flapping attempt, she turned to scan all the people swirling around her. We were on Restaurant Row, near the theater district, which was always crowded. I could read body language in a glance, having served for years as an NSA field agent abroad. I immediately recognized the indicators of stress her body betrayed.

She was afraid of something.

Curiosity ignited inside me. What could a girl like her have to be afraid of on a well-lit, crowded street? An asshole ex? That was an old classic.

I could rip the shithead's throat out for her if she wanted me to. I had the skills.

Whoa. That bloodthirsty thought had sneaked up on me while I struggled not to stare at the way that button strained over the swell of her tits. How sooty and long her lashes were. I loved the exotic, cat-like upward tilt to her eyes and brows. Hers wasn't a glossy magazine sort of pretty, and that was fine with me. I'd never gone for hollow cheeks or toothpick legs. I liked a nice round ass, and that deep inward curve at her waist that cried out for the grip of my hands. She had that Mediterranean milkmaid look: creamy golden skin, wide hips, full, bouncing tits. Dimpled knees, maybe. The skirt was just a shade too long to ascertain the knee situation. But a guy could hope.

She finally saw me lurking and gawking, and shrank in on herself, clutching her blazer closed. So she felt the animal rattling its cage, after I'd tried so hard to play it cool. So much for my best efforts. With this girl, they were sure to always fall short.

"Looking for a cab?" I asked.

"Not having much luck." Her gaze darted around, avoiding mine. "It's so hard to get one when it's raining."

I couldn't stop gawking at her—despite her discomfort, despite the fact that I had already drawn my conclusions about how I would handle this. Which was to say, according to my rock-solid principles and innate common sense. *Don't think with your dick. That's never been its forte.*

But it was late, and she was all alone, and the rain was pattering down harder now. I needed to know what she was afraid of, and if something could be done about it.

And, incidentally, if her knees were dimpled.

"I'll drive you home," I blurted out.

Chapter Seven

Nell

"Oh, no. Thanks, but I couldn't. It's okay," I babbled. I waved my arms wildly at the next cab that went by, even though its light was off. "It's far. All the way out to Williamsburg, and with all this traffic, too. It would eat your whole evening. I'll just walk downtown until I find a cab."

Or Snake Eyes finds me. My sisters and I had promised each other that we would take cabs as often as possible. Not that catching cabs had helped Nancy much. She'd been nabbed out of a crowded hotel restaurant, surrounded by all the people she knew.

"No." Burke's voice was low and authoritative. "You're not walking. It's late, and it's raining. I'll drive you."

I opened my mouth to politely slap him down to size. Who did he think he was, anyway—announcing what I could or could not do?

Then I looked into his eyes, and the anxious babble in my mind just stopped.

It was dark, wet, and no cabs were stopping. My neck was prickling in the worst way. The people on the street had all hustled for shelter, leaving the street dismal and deserted. Why not just accept his offer?

I tried to talk myself down from this silly clutch of panic. Burke was plenty intimidating in his own way, but he was no Snake Eyes. And I was no brainless bimbo, whatever he might think with his I-don't-hire-young-women-just-for-scenery comment.

I could handle anything this guy dished out and serve it right back. And have fun doing it, too, I realized. Being uppity with Duncan Burke was kind of fun.

I licked my dry lips without thinking and quickly regretted it when his gaze flicked to my mouth and stayed there.

"Um, thank you." My voice felt dry and scratchy. "I appreciate that. If you're sure."

"Great. I'm in a garage close to the office building," he said. "Just a couple blocks."

We took off down the sidewalk, side by side, in total silence. I was freshly strangled by shyness, and angry at myself for feeling this way. For God's sake, I had just accepted a job from this man. We had plenty of things to talk about, but my voice was huddled into a tight, nervous ball in my throat, like a twelve-year-old at her first dance.

He led me down into an underground parking garage near his office building. I stumbled on the steep concrete slope, clutching the folder that held the game outline I was supposed to study tonight. He caught my elbow and held on to it, all the way to the sleek silver Mercedes that answered his remote beep with a pert flash of lights.

He helped me into the car, which smelled luxurious and new. The soft, plushy leather seat felt like it was hugging me.

My mute and strangled state did not improve, even after

the necessary interchange about the best route to take to my Williamsburg address.

After a few minutes, he spoke up. "What are you so afraid of?"

That question took me utterly by surprise and left me floundering. "What on earth are you talking about?" I demanded.

"You looked scared when you were hailing those cabs."

His sharp perception made me feel naked. "Ah, wow. I didn't ... I'm not ... that is to say, I'm surprised you noticed that. I had no idea it was so obvious."

"Only to me," he said. "Why would you be surprised at me noticing?"

Yikes. Now he might think I was criticizing him, and only thirty minutes after hiring me. "It's just an unexpected observation," I hedged. "I think I cover pretty well, all things considered. Most people wouldn't see it. And ... well, it's very intuitive of you. I wouldn't have thought you were the type to notice."

He glanced at me with a puzzled frown. "What type? Why not?"

"I don't know," I said, helplessly. "You never noticed anything in your field of vision at the restaurant. You never made eye contact with me, or anyone else, for that matter. You always order the same thing. You seem to have an extremely narrow range of focus. Intuition requires ... well, openness. So that the data can go in."

His laugh had a touch of bitterness to it. "Hah. You and my family. That's Duncan for you. Thick as a brick wall."

"Not at all! I don't think anything of the kind," I protested. "Just very focused. More than most people could ever dream of being. I'm sure it's a sort of superpower. And like most superpowers, it's probably a double-edged sword. I have a few of those myself."

He was silent for an unnervingly long time. "It's true," he said finally. "I do have a narrow range of focus, when I'm in work mode. But there's a flip side. Whatever is inside that narrow range of focus? Oh God, do I see it. Every last goddamn detail of it."

I felt my face heat up. "Well, thank you, I guess, for noticing all these subtle and intimate details about me. I appreciate your intense interest, but—"

"But you still haven't answered my question. What are you afraid of?"

My chest jerked with nervous laughter. "Good God. You're like a dog with a bone!"

"Yeah. I'm like a pit bull, my family tells me," he agreed easily.

I shot him a nervous glance. "Family? So you're, ah—"

"Married? No. Absolutely not. I'm talking my mother, brother, and sister. I am one hundred percent single. So? Let's have an answer."

My loaded question and his matter-of-fact answer made my face burn hotter. It was impossible to sidestep a man this blunt and insistent. Not without being rude and brusque, and I did not have the stomach for that while cuddled up in the yielding leather seat of his Mercedes, feeling so warm and dry and safe. At least for the next half hour.

There was no reason not to tell him the truth. God knows, there was nothing to be ashamed of. But still, it was a dark, flesh-creeping tale, still frighteningly unresolved, and this guy had just become my new employer. I wouldn't want a person on my payroll with the kind of problems I currently had. No one needed that kind of trouble.

Plus, it was none of his damn business. But he clearly did not care.

He waited patiently. I could feel his relentless insistence in the silence. He just sat there, motor idling, in no hurry at all. Waiting for me to snap.

"It's a long, complicated story," I said warily.

"So what? We're stuck in traffic. Entertain me."

True enough. They were motionless in a gridlocked snarl. But still.

"It's not entertaining, unfortunately," I went on. "It's awful. Sad, ugly, violent, scary. You might be better off not knowing. I wish I didn't have to."

He glanced over at me, one eyebrow up. "I'll take that chance. Tell me, or I will literally die from curiosity right now. And you will be the one who killed me."

I let out a snort of laughter, pressing my hand against my belly. That sour ache, my constant companion, was still there, but it was less than before. It was therapeutic to sit in the dark, in a warm, luxurious car with Duncan Burke, with windshield wipers swooshing soothingly over the glass in that hypnotic rhythm.

"It started a few weeks ago," I began, my voice halting. "When my mother died. In a home invasion."

He shot me a startled glance. "Oh God. I am sorry to hear that. My condolences."

I acknowledged that with a nod. Then I told him the whole tale, as simply and sequentially as I could. The burglar, the necklaces Lucia had commissioned for us, the mysterious letters. The elderly clotheshorse the cops had found at the landfill, the luckless jeweler and his family being murdered, the attack in the stairwell, and finally, my sister Nancy almost getting abducted in that hotel in Boston. My long, winding, improbable tale—and Duncan's quiet, probing questions—got us all the way across the Williamsburg Bridge and all the way to my apartment.

He double-parked as I concluded, telling him about Nancy getting together with Liam, the only good thing to come out of this shitshow so far. At least Nancy wasn't all alone in the void, like Vivi and me. In the thoughtful silence that followed, I was intensely uncomfortable. He must think I was a paranoid, attention-mongering nutcase.

"So, anyway," I said. "That's it. That's why I'm scared. Me and my sisters. Whatever we do, it feels like the wrong thing. The stupid, boneheaded thing that's going to get us tortured and murdered. So, let's have it. Do you want to fire me now?"

He frowned. "What? Fire you? Why on earth would I want to do that?"

Before I had to come up with a reply, a guy opened the door of the SUV parked right in front of us, got in, and pulled out onto the street, leaving a parking spot right in front of my building. Which was unheard of. It simply never happened.

Burke pulled into it and killed the engine. "I'd better walk you up to your door."

Oh. How very gallant of him. If only my heart would stop trying to pound its way violently right out of my chest. "Oh, don't worry about it," I told him, with a breathless laugh. "It's a fifth-floor walk-up. I wouldn't wish those stairs on anybody."

"I'm fine with stairs. I always choose stairs over an elevator. You know. Cardio."

Cardio, my ass. I looked over at his body, strangling a crack of laughter and transforming it into a cough. Then I got out and led him into my building.

Up, up, up. Those damn stairs never ended. I stopped in front of my door, glad for a legitimate excuse to be that breathless and flushed. "I appreciate the ride, and the company, and walking me up the stairs, and the listening ear,"

I said. "You were very patient and kind. Thank you. It was good to lay it all out. It makes it seem less like, you know ... like this vast, shadowy thing looming over me. Even though it still is."

He nodded and kept standing there. A mountain, a monolith, just waiting for something from me.

But whatever it was, I just wasn't ready to give it to him. And it looked like he was going to make me just say it, right out loud. Damn the man.

"I'm not going to invite you in," I blurted out. "Not for coffee, or drinks. Or, ah, anything. Sorry. I don't mean to be rude, but ..."

"Of course you won't," he said. "You hardly know me. I wouldn't expect you to."

But he did not make any leaving words, or moves, or noises. "So?" I prompted. "Then why are you still standing there? What do you want from me?"

"Something that I just can't have, I guess." He touched the end of a fuzzy ringlet that had escaped my bun and was now dangling at chin level. "I got this really strong feeling from you today. At lunch, in the restaurant."

"Yes?" I felt my lips tremble. I pressed them sternly together.

"I got the feeling that you were trying to get my attention," he said slowly.

Duh. I swallowed hard. "Well, yes. I suppose I was," I admitted. "You were ignoring me so completely. I guess I sort of took it as a challenge."

"Huh. Well. Whatever challenge you took on, looks like you definitely won." He tugged the curl again, watched it rebound again. "I just want you to know that you've definitely got my attention now. All of it."

"Ah. Well ..." I laughed, a little nervously. "I'm not sure

what to say, then. Now that I have it, I'm not quite sure what to do with it."

"There's a lot you can do with it," he said. "It's multi-purpose."

"Um. Really." The door pressed against my back. There was nowhere to retreat.

"Yeah. You'd be amazed." He wound the curl around his finger, stroking the texture. "This is the thing—once you've got my attention, it's really hard to shake. I can be like a dog with a bone, they tell me."

"I noticed that," I said. "The way you stared at that computer at the restaurant, a herd of elephants could have trooped by and you wouldn't see them. But I won't be doing anything interesting or notable with your attention tonight. Thanks again. For the ride, hearing me out, walking me up all those stairs. It's nice to have a sympathetic ear." I hesitated, waiting for him to take his cue. "Good night," I prompted, pointedly.

"Is your sister here now?"

I considered saying yes, just to defuse the tension, but I had a feeling that if I lied to him, he'd see right through it, as closely as he was observing me right now. That would embarrass me to death. "No," I admitted. "She's driving to Delaware right now. She designs jewelry. Works the crafts fair circuit. She travels a lot."

"You and your sisters have a lot of nerve, wandering around all alone, just doing your thing like it's no big deal while an unknown stalker is out there gunning for you."

I bristled at that, since it hit far too close to the bone. "That's not fair. We don't have any choice. We both have to make a living."

"Yeah, okay," he soothed. "I get that. You do have an alarm, at least?"

"Absolutely. Top of the line," I said promptly. That, at least, was true.

He lounged against the wall, still in no hurry at all. "A dog might be a good investment," he commented.

I snorted. "Hah. Hardly. First off, I can't afford it. It wouldn't be fair to the poor dog, the way I work. And you have no idea how small my apartment is."

"Nope." His voice was a low, suggestive rumble. "And I guess I'm not going to."

I shook my head, licking my lips before I could stop myself. "Nope. Not tonight."

The words slipped out, and panic flashed through me, since the obvious corollary of my incautious statement was that he might well get lucky some other night.

The look in his eyes set off fireworks in my head, my chest, my thighs. He smiled as he pulled his smartphone out. "Let's exchange numbers," he said. "If you have any problems, anything at all, call me. Whenever. Any time of day or night. I mean it."

"Ah, wow. Thank you. That's very kind, but I'm sure it won't be necessary." I groped in my bag for the flip phone that Vivi and Nancy had insisted that I get, tapping around awkwardly until I opened up the address book function.

He smoothly took it from my hand. "Let me," he said. "I'll just put mine into your phone, and call my phone with yours."

He entered the number swiftly, and listened for the buzz of his own phone in his pocket. "I don't like to leave you like this," he said, frowning. "I feel like you're not safe here alone. I won't be able sleep tonight."

I tilted up my chin. "Well, that sounds like a 'you' problem, Duncan."

He grinned. "I guess so. Poor me. I'm just ... it's hard to leave. Goes against instinct. Leaving you unprotected."

"I'm sorry for your instincts and your insomnia and all your various discomforts, but it's late, and it's been a long day for me. Good night." I put all the commanding punch I could behind the word.

He still didn't move. God, the guy was tall. And broad. And he smelled really good, even at this hour of the night, many long hours from his morning shower. It filled my senses.

"You're not going," I remarked.

"No," he agreed.

I tried to look stern and forbidding. It was hard, with my lips trembling the way they did. "Why not?"

"Because you don't really want me to."

I laughed right in his face. The nerve of him. "Oh, no. Are you one of those guys who's going to tell me that you know better than I do what I want and need? Please, Burke. Don't be that guy."

"I'm sorry, but I can see it," he said, his tone utterly unapologetic.

"So you're a mind reader now?"

"Not minds. I read faces and bodies. Yours is saying something different."

I was blushing again. "You can read my face and body all you want, but keep in mind, buddy—my face and body do not make the executive decisions around here."

"Of course not." His voice was a velvety, rumbling caress against my skin, making me shiver as he leaned closer. "They have better things to do."

I was still groping for a comeback when he leaned forward and kissed me.

The wild rush of feelings that released took me by surprise. The startled heat, unfurling instantly through my body, the sense of sudden, voluptuous opening inside me, like a flower blooming wide. It spread out—sweet, fragrant—a feeling too delicious to resist.

I rose up on my tiptoes and leaned hungrily into his kiss, and that added fuel to the fire. I felt the very instant that it spun out of control. I was spinning in a vortex of pure sensation, pinned to the wall and writhing, kissing him back madly, greedily, my fingers clutching his coat, his shoulders, my nails trying to dig in. Forgetting everything except for how sweet it was, how good it felt. How much more I wanted.

Right ... freaking ... *now.*

He hooked my knee with his hand and pulled it up, inviting me to clasp his muscular thighs with my legs, leaning against me so that the big, hard bulge at his groin pressed right at that melting, aching spot between my legs, rocking with a slow, skillful, deliberate pulse that made me ache and squirm and gasp for breath.

His tongue slid inside my mouth, commanding and directing the kiss with relaxed, implacable skill. His hands cupped my bottom, stroking, lifting me up to just the angle I needed for ... I wasn't even quite sure what yet, but I started to shake, disoriented, as the energy changed, sharpening to something almost agonizing. Something was happening inside me and I couldn't ... I didn't ... oh God.

The heat, the light, the sweet ache—it was all coalescing, swelling into something huge and bright and terrifying.

It burst through me, and my startled cry was smothered against his mouth. He held me tightly while shudder after shudder of unbelievable pleasure wrenched through me.

My eyes fluttered open as reason returned, but it found no place to land. I did not recognize myself. Not in this undone, confused state, his gaze burning into my face.

My eyes were wet and my throat couldn't stop shaking. My heart still galloped wildly. I could barely breathe. I could not believe what I had just done—and with a virtual stranger, too, in my own stairwell. Any one of my neighbors could have come up the stairs at any time and seen everything. I had completely lost my mind.

My gaze slid away from his. I was too overcome to meet his eyes. So that was what an orgasm felt like on the far end of the scale. I'd thought that I knew, but this experience was infinitely more intense than anything I'd ever experienced. Over-whelming.

He stroked my cheek with a gentle fingertip. "Amazing," he whispered. "So. Any new executive decisions coming down the pipeline?"

Oh, that opportunistic bastard, messing with my head. I wanted to yank him inside my apartment and eat him alive, and he knew it. If this is how he could make me feel fully clothed, in my public stairwell, with nothing more than a hot tongue-kiss and some dry humping—well. I didn't dare to imagine how it would be in private, in the dark. Naked. With him all over me. Beneath me. Inside me.

But not tonight. I was too fragile, too compromised, unsure of both myself and him. I shook my head, and mouthed the word.

No. I didn't have the breath to actually say it.

"Got it," he murmured. "There's just one more little thing I really need to know."

I blinked at him nervously, still breathing hard. "Um. And what might that be?"

He reached down, pinched my skirt, and tugged it up just a couple of inches over my knees. Then he looked at me and smiled. "Mmmm," he said. "Dimples. Cute."

"What the hell?" I slapped his hand sharply away. "Stop that!"

He stepped back. "Sorry," he said. "I'm overdoing it, huh?"

"Yes!" I snapped. "Back off!"

He started down the stairs, walking backward like he didn't want to take his eyes off me. "You're sure you'll be okay alone?"

"Me and my chubby knees will be just fine," I said tartly. "Good night."

I stayed there until I heard the downstairs lobby door click closed behind him, far below. Then I fumbled with my keys.

Once inside my apartment, the alarm armed and blinking an angry red, I sank down onto the couch without turning on the light, still shaking. My throat ached and burned, as if a tuning peg were ratcheting the tension relentlessly tighter and higher.

I was so angry at myself. Not for kissing him, or for letting him make me come, but for depriving myself of the rest of the experience. Because I was chicken-shit.

As usual, there was always a compelling reason not to reach out and grab something good when it was offered. I could have been stark naked, being pounded deliciously against the wall by the hottest man I'd ever fantasized about, right now. But no. I was all alone, shivering in the dark, feeling sorry for myself.

Like a pussy-footing coward.

Chapter Eight

Duncan

I stared at the screen of the online version of *The Golden Thread Poetry Journal* and sent the relevant pages to print. The collection of short lyric poems by Antonella D'Onofrio were really hard to grasp. I wanted them to exist in a solid, physical form. As if being able to hold them in my hand might help me understand what was in them.

The pages churned out of the machine, and I tried reading them again, but no dice. It was the tenth time I'd gone through them and I still had no clue what the fuck she was getting at.

The poetry thing baffled me on so many levels. The poems themselves were gibberish, but it was the way they made me feel that alarmed me most. Like a cliff had suddenly appeared in front of me, and I was reeling backwards to keep from falling.

Except not in a bad way. Which made no sense. And I usually didn't like it when things didn't make sense. I always scrambled to fix it, order it, organize it.

This was different. This defied fixing, ordering, organizing.

I read the poems again, searching for that strange, vanishing feeling they elicited. It was like glimpsing something out of the corner of my eye, but having it disappear when I looked at it straight on. Or trying to spot a star so faint, I could barely sense that it was there. Just a tiny, teasing blur of light in the sky. The vague idea of a star.

I stared down at my stubborn boner with unfriendly eyes. I'd tried to deal with it in the shower, with the help of some extremely vivid water-sex fantasies: Nell—naked, soaked, and soapy, hair drenched, face rosy—pinned to the shower wall, her legs draped over my arms. Whimpering with delight at each deep, slick thrust.

I'd come so hard I practically knocked myself out, so why I still had a tent pole poking out of my sweatpants was beyond me. Maybe it was the poetry. Hah.

I couldn't believe how completely I had bulldozed through all my fine principles. I'd gone all alpha on her, grabbing her, kissing her, making her come. God. Peak experience. One that could totally fuck my professional life, depending on how she felt about it after the fact. I'd left myself wide open to attack. Thinking with my dick.

I'd been at the computer since I got home, too wound up to sleep. I'd used the time researching everything I could glean off the internet about the D'Onofrio crime saga. I was chomping at the bit to call my old buddy Gant, my NYPD source, to get some hard inside details. But it was still too early for that.

So I'd ranged further to pass the time. I'd tried reading the articles she'd published in a bunch of literary journals—pieces about Sara Teasdale, Emily Dickinson, Edna St. Vincent Millay, Sappho. Her paper for her graduate seminar. There was poetry she'd written and published herself. Entries on websites that catered to poets and scholars. Online poetry workshops she'd critiqued. It was outlandish stuff. Computer nerds were bad enough, but they had nothing on poets. This crap was from fucking outer space.

I glanced at my phone. It was almost five a.m. Good enough for me. My friend and ex-colleague back in our NSA days was now a detective in the NYPD. Gant owed me his life, after various bloody and memorable adventures in Afghanistan back in the day. If he wasn't awake by now, it meant he was getting soft and needed his ass kicked.

I dialed the number and waited as it rang twelve times before he picked up.

"Who the fuck is this?" said Gant sleepily.

"I need some info," I said.

"Oh, Christ. You. For fuck's sake, Burke. Couldn't it wait till daylight?"

"It's dawn." I stared out the picture window of my condo at the spectacular New York City skyline, silhouetted against the faint glow of breaking day. "I need the details on an ongoing police investigation in Hempton. It involves an elderly woman named Lucia D'Onofrio. She died of a heart attack during a burglary in her house. It happened few weeks ago."

"Yeah? Why do you want to know? What's it to you, Dunc?"

I leaned my hot forehead against the cool window glass. "I'm interested," I hedged.

"Interested, my hairy ass. You wake me up at this un-fuck-ing-godly hour because you're *interested*?" Gant paused for a moment. "This is about a woman, right?"

"None of your goddamn business," I told him.

"Bullshit. At this hour, it's definitely my business," Gant bitched. "I knew this would happen. Goddamn over-compensating freak that you are. You act like a fucking monk for years at a time. It was just a matter of time till you blew your top. So it's finally happened, huh? You're obsessed with some girl? Tell me you're not awake at this hour because you spent the entire night googling this woman's entire life. Go ahead, tell me that."

"I don't have to tell you shit," I said. "Don't be a dick."

"This poor woman has no idea what she's in for. What does she have to do with the old lady who had the heart attack?"

"She's the old lady's daughter," I said reluctantly. "Stop busting my balls and just get me the info."

"You'll have to wait. I won't call my people until it's a decent hour. That's known as basic common courtesy. Baseline, elemental social skills. Ever heard of those? Go to bed, Dunc. Better yet, go jack off, and then go to bed. Later."

Gant hung up. I tossed the phone onto the bed and spun the chair around to read Nell's poems again. I didn't understand what she was talking about, but who cared?

They made something shift and flex inside my mind as I read them.

It felt strange, but good.

Chapter Nine

Nell

"Stop right here, please."

The cabbie screeched to a halt, hit the meter, and took my money. I was spending a fortune on car services, Ubers, and cabs these days but, there was no help for it. At least I could walk to work from here afterward. The streets were busy enough now that I felt safe walking the rest of the way to the Sunset Grill.

Though I knew it was just a mind game. If Snake Eyes wanted to take me, he'd find a way. He'd found one with Nancy. Only Liam's heroic efforts had saved my sister.

I pushed that thought resolutely away and looked at the hair salon with trepidation as the cab drove away. I'd been circling the hair issue all morning. I had stood in front of the bathroom sink for an embarrassingly long time before winding my hair back into its usual thick, fuzzy braid and twisting it into its usual heavy knot.

I caught a glimpse of my reflection in the window of the

salon, slid my glasses up the bridge of my nose, and took a long look. In light of recent revelations, I couldn't lie to myself about this any longer.

I was hiding. Cowering behind the antique-looking glasses, the baggy dresses, the dowdy, frizzy hair, and the cowardly assertion that looking pretty was all vanity and nonsense, that I was a lofty scholar, too intellectual and above it all to care.

What a heap of steaming bullshit that was. Ten lust-charged minutes with Duncan Burke in the stairwell had demonstrated to me that I cared passionately. I couldn't stand being at a disadvantage with that guy. I needed every weapon possible at my disposal, to interact with him from a position of power and confidence.

That made me wince. There it was again—beauty as a tool, beauty as currency, beauty as a weapon, beauty as power. That crass, chilly, ugly association was programmed into me so deeply. I had deliberately chosen to be plain and unnoticeable because I just wanted to stay off the battlefield permanently.

But things changed. The battle had come to me. My choices were fight or run.

I was not running. Not this time.

I went into the salon, sniffing nervously at the unfamiliar scents of perfume, shampoo, chemicals. A slight, balding Latino guy with a gray pearl earring gave me a big, toothy smile. "What can I do for you today?"

"Do you take walk-ins?" I asked.

"When I feel like it." His dark eyes narrowed as he assessed me from head to toe. "I happen to have room on my schedule this morning. Looks like it was meant for you. What do you have in mind?"

"Ah, well. I'm not really sure," I said apologetically. I gestured at my head. "Just not, you know. This."

"Hmmm. Yes, I can see why you feel that way. This is

going to be fun. Get into the chair, and let's have a look. I'm Riccardo, by the way."

I was soon in a swiveling chair, swathed in a plastic cape, and Riccardo's expert fingers were plucking out hairpins, unraveling my hair, and fluffing it up with coos of appreciation. "Good material here," he commented, plucking off my glasses. "You ever consider contacts?"

I snorted. "I've been getting that a lot lately. Can you do something that's easy to style? I work as a waitress, so I need to be able to easily pin it up in the back."

"Oh, yes. I'm just going to shape this bit, thin it out here, lighten it up there. See?"

Of course I couldn't see a thing, but Riccardo inspired confidence, so I went with it. The shampooing part was relaxing. The snipping part unnerved me. Without my glasses, my reflection was just a hopeful blur in the mirror.

Later, when I finally retrieved them, I stared at the result, mouth agape. Riccardo had layered and shaped my frizzy, waist-length mop into a glossy halo of black ringlets that framed and flattered my face while still reaching halfway down my back in an artful taper. I kept putting my unbelieving hands up to feel the softer, springier texture of the curls. They felt so different, with all the goops and salves and waxes he'd massaged into them. Actual curls instead of frizz.

The price was staggering, but I passed over my credit card without protest. The only problem now were the glasses. With my new hair, they looked even goofier than before.

One step at a time, though.

My hair caused a sensation when I walked into the Sunset Grill. Monica wolf-whistled, and Norma spun me around, looking at me from every angle. "You look as gorgeous as I knew you would!" she exclaimed, her eyes wet. "I just wish Lucia could see how pretty you look. She'd be so happy to see you all primped up at last."

That made my eyes overflow. I hugged Norma tightly.

"Enough of this gooey sentimental stuff," Monica said briskly. "Let's get down to business. C'mere, Nell. I wanna put some makeup on you."

"Aren't we supposed to be prepping for lunch?" I asked plaintively as Monica dragged me to a chair.

"That's all right, hon. I'll pick up the slack," Norma said indulgently. "How did that job interview go?"

"Oh. The job interview," I hedged, as Monica tilted my face up and outlined my eyes with pencil. "Well, now. It was extremely interesting."

"How so?" Norma asked, picking the chairs off the tables.

"You will never, in a million years, guess who it was who interviewed me," I said.

Norma froze. Monica's pencil stopped moving.

"No way, chica," breathed Monica.

"You don't mean to say ... nah. You're putting me on, Nelly. I simply don't believe it," Norma said.

"Believe it," I said.

There was an incredulous silence. I turned around to find Norma and Monica grinning at each other like fools.

"Did he ask you out?" Monica tilted my head back and brandished my eyeshadow sponge. "Did he come on to you? Did you kiss?"

The steamy sequence in the stairwell played through my mind in a timeless instant, and my face went beet red. "As if I would," I lied. "I've barely met the man."

"Well?" Norma said. "So try, try again! Take the bull by the horns, honey!"

"It's not that simple," I said. "He's my boss now, and I'm meeting with him after my shift here to discuss the—"

"My goodness, you mean he hired you? Mercy! Things move so quickly in this world for an old lady. And just this morning Kendra told me that she has an auto-immune disease. I already forgot which one. But alas, all's fair in love and war."

"Norma, you don't understand." I wiggled as Monica wielded her mascara wand "Monica, that tickles!"

"Hold still, chica. You're making me smear. Lemme put some lipstick on you, and you can look at yourself."

I headed to the bathroom afterward, and my reflection made me gasp. My eyes looked big and shadowy and luminous. The lipstick was a deep, sexy red. All turned out and made up, with my hair fluffed into that luxurious mane of black ringlets, I looked ...

Exactly like my mother. I stared at Elena Pisani in the mirror and gulped.

"What do you say, chica? Are you stunning, or are you stunning?"

I put on a big smile for my co-worker. "Yes. You're an artist, Monica. Thank you."

I pulled my glasses out of her apron and perched them on my nose. Then I dragged out a hair clip to twist my hair into an updo. It was so much easier to do now. My hair was lighter, the twist higher, the curls on top were higher, and the bits that dangled around my chin now looked sexily tousled, rather than the frazzled scullery maid look I had sported before.

"Do you have to wear the glasses?" Monica complained. "It ruins the effect!"

"I'm afraid so," I said regretfully. "I'm blind without them, and the hair absolutely has to go up. No one wants my hair in their lunch, no matter how cute it looks."

"Oh well. You still look way better than before. Strip Steak's going to have a stroke when he gets a look at you."

"His name is Duncan Burke, and it's not going to happen.

Ever," I said, resolute. "He's my boss now. I would not compromise a paying job."

"Taboo!" Norma said, sticking her head in the bathroom door. "The tantalizing lure of the forbidden! Just look at you, honey. Good enough to eat. Strip Steak's jaw will hit the floor. Have you thought about contacts, Nelly?"

I swept past them, chin high, and the two of them giggled like idiots.

But three-fifteen came and went with no Burke, and the afternoon fell as flat as a failed soufflé. I still had the meeting after work to look forward to, though, and hanging in my garment bag was the oatmeal-cream sweater dress I'd bought for Nancy's engagement party, by far the prettiest thing in my closet. I pictured myself walking into Burke's office in that subtly clinging dress, imagined his eyes on me, and shivered.

Yikes. Stop it. He was my boss. He was rude, arrogant, bossy, presumptuous, and handsy. Plus, he suffered from a profound lack of imagination, judging from his lunch habits. And he seemed to have a weird, fetishistic thing for my chubby knees. Weird.

Ergo, nothing doing. I was not going to complicate my life like that.

So why had I spent money I could ill afford on my hair? Why was my face all painted up? Why had I brought my tightest dress? I'd tricked myself out for what?

The afternoon passed slowly. At the end of my shift, I slipped unobtrusively into the back to change, but I needn't have bothered sneaking. Both Monica and Norma were lying in wait for me outside the door. Monica grabbed my chin and freshened my lipstick by brute force. "Good luck, chica," she said. "Seize the day. Be bold."

"And be careful, honey," Norma said, her eyes misty.

"Oh! Speaking of careful! Don't you dare forget." Monica

held up a three-pack of condoms, and stuffed them into my purse. "Safety is key!"

"You guys! For God's sake! This is a professional project meeting, not an orgy!"

I had time to walk uptown, but I took a cab anyway, just to honor the promises my sisters and I had made to each other about safety. I dithered for just a few minutes outside the building before I had the nerve to take myself and my swirling flock of internal butterflies inside.

I took the elevator to the sixteenth floor and approached the door to Duncan Burke Solutions, Inc., gathering my nerve. As I reached for the handle, the door flew open.

I looked straight up into Duncan's startled eyes. My throat clenched. So did my toes—and various other intimate parts of my anatomy.

His eyes flashed down over my body, taking it all in. "It's you," he said blankly.

"Yes," I said, bemused. Did I get the appointment time wrong? Isn't it tonight that we were supposed to meet to talk about the project with your brother?"

"Yes, yes, of course," he muttered. "Come on in."

I was already regretting the dress. It didn't cling provocatively, but the way he looked at me made me feel as if I was reclining naked, draped in silk, like Bathsheba in an old Renaissance painting. *Come and get me. At your peril.*

Or my peril, rather.

"You look different. You changed your hair." His tone was faintly disapproving.

"Why, yes, I did. And so?" I said, instantly on the defensive.

He looked like he was about to speak again when a handsome young man strode out into the lobby. He flashed a big smile and shook my hand, continuing to hold it. "Wow.

Duncan told me you were an excellent writer, but he didn't say you were so pretty. Can I call you Nell?"

"No, you can't," Duncan said sharply. "Ms. D'Onofrio, this is my brother, Bruce. Please excuse his unprofessional behavior. It won't happen again. Will it, Bruce?"

Unprofessional behavior ...? For real? From *him*? Once again, that moment in the stairwell flashed through my mind, and I could tell it was in his mind, as well. His eyes met mine, then slid away, abashed. Hypocritical bastard.

"Uh ... I guess it won't." Bruce looked chagrined. "Sorry."

Duncan gestured toward the conference room. "Come on. Let's get started."

I marched into the room and sat down, pulling out my folder of notes just before the two men took their places across the table from me.

Bruce began. "Ms. D'Onofrio—"

"Nell is really okay," I told him.

"I prefer that he use 'Ms. D'Onofrio,'" Duncan said.

There was an uncomfortable pause while my mind revved and stalled in one of those what's-wrong-with-this-picture moments. That was swiftly followed by the what-the-hell-do-I-do-about-it moment, and at the end of the queue, the is-it-actually-worth-it moment.

Bruce tried again. "So, Ms. D'Onofrio, as I was about to say to—"

"No," I broke in.

The two men just looked at me in silent confusion.

"Um, no, what?" Bruce said carefully.

"In this context, I believe it is my own personal preferences which should determine how I'm addressed." I stared into Bruce Burke's eyes. "Can I call you Bruce?"

"Of course," he said swiftly. "In fact, I insist on it."

I turned to Duncan. "How about you? Since both of you

would be Mr. Burke, using your surname would be confusing, don't you agree?" I waited, holding his gaze relentlessly and letting him ponder that moment last night in the stairwell for himself. Like I was going to address a guy who had tongue-kissed me and brought me to orgasm by 'Mr. Burke.' As-fucking-if. What would he want next? Sir? Not in this lifetime.

He looked like he'd swallowed a rock. "Fine. Call me Duncan."

"Excellent," I said briskly, turning to Bruce. "Then you can call me Nell."

Bruce's gaze flicked nervously toward his brother, then to me. "Ah ... okay," he said. "So, Nell. Moving on. Duncan showed me your writing sample. I was really impressed. I take it you've looked over our game outline?"

"Of course." I'd been too rattled last night to review it, after the stairwell incident, but I had glanced at it this morning over my coffee, and had been pleasantly impressed.

"So?" Duncan prompted. "What do you think?"

I leafed through the folder, choosing my words carefully. "All in all, I think it's great. The story is involving, and the graphics are beautiful."

"Thanks. I sense the setup for a 'but'," Bruce said. "Let us have it."

"It's just that I think the choices the player needs to make to move through the game seem too, um ..." I hesitated, still reluctant to criticize.

"Too what?" Duncan demanded, his voice curt.

"Too rational," I said. "Too logical."

The two men looked at me, confused.

"If you want to appeal to people who love stories, it makes more sense to play up romantic, magical elements," I continued. "Ultimately, to win, the player should be required to grow in some way—like a protagonist in a story with a growth arc."

The frown that had creased Duncan's brow since he opened the office door for me deepened. His chair creaked in protest as he pushed himself away from the table.

I pressed on. "I suggest introducing plot twists toward the end based on leaps of faith. Acts of selfless courage and generosity. This could deepen the feeling of mystery, intensify a sense of wonder, and set it apart from almost every other game of its type. Also, the game's title. *'The Dagger and the Thorn'* strikes me as, um ..."

"Pointy?" Bruce grinned at me.

"Yes, exactly," I said. "Warlike, aggressive, hyper-masculine. You're want to market this game to women, too, right? To that end, I recommend a more evocative, mythical, dreamlike image for the title. When I read about the sixth-level forest sequence with the lake and the magical swans, I thought of *'The Golden Egg.'*"

"*The Golden Egg,*" Bruce mused. "That has possibilities."

"I like it," Duncan announced.

Bruce whipped his head around, incredulous. "Really? No shit, Duncan. You've never liked anything imaginative in your whole life!"

"Not the title," he said. "I mean her hair."

Bruce looked confused. I stared from one to the other, mortified.

Duncan looked defensive. "So? What of it? I didn't think I liked it at first. Now, I've decided that I like it. Is that so hard to understand?"

After a moment of uncertain silence, Bruce spoke up gallantly. "Well, ahh, fine. That was a sharp left turn in the conversation—par for the course when dealing with Duncan." He shot me an apologetic look. "I didn't have the pleasure of seeing how you wore your hair before, so I can't offer any comparisons, but I can certainly say that it looks lovely now. If you'll excuse the personal observation."

"Thank you," I said, my face hot. "I suppose. Strangest two-headed, backwards compliment I've ever gotten—but whatever. I'll take it."

"And if you got the approval of anybody as resistant to change as my brother, you better believe—it's a humdinger," Bruce added.

"Shut up, Bruce," Duncan said.

"You're acting unprofessional, Dunc," Bruce murmured. "Count your breaths, remember? Activate your parasympathetic nervous system."

"Don't start," Duncan ground out. "You're bugging me."

"Listen, gentlemen. My hair is beside the point," I said. "I'm not loving this sharp left turn. Let's get back on track. I'd much rather talk about what you think of my ideas."

"I don't like them," Duncan said.

I exhaled slowly. "I see." Well, shitstickles. This was going nowhere fast.

"I don't want an interactive fairy tale." His voice was impatient. "I want a fantasy adventure quest. What you're proposing sounds impossible to reason through—an exercise in useless frustration."

"But that's just it," I argued. "Reason isn't the only tool people use when they're problem solving. There are spells to break, dragons to defeat, a princess to woo. It should require using more heart, more soul, not just the head. It should be romantic, unexpected, moving. Surprising."

"Duncan hates surprises," Bruce informed me.

"Shut up, Bruce," Duncan snarled at him.

"Sheathe your claws, Dunc. You're scaring her," Bruce warned.

"Not at all," I said. "I don't scare easily." Which was true, actually. There was nothing all that scary about a brotherly spat, or even a few mild insults. Not after the Snake Eyes incident. The one good thing about a brush with mortal danger was the ruthless perspective that it afforded. One ceased to sweat the little things.

Duncan got up with an abruptness that knocked his rolling chair against the wall with a smack. He stalked out of the room, anger radiating from his broad, rigid back.

I watched the door fall shut behind him and turned to Bruce, bewildered. "What the hell is going on? Did I say something wrong? Is there something I don't know?"

"No, not at all," Bruce assured me. "He's just that way. Don't worry—he likes you. Really. I can tell from the way he acts. And your ideas are fascinating. It's all good."

"Uh, thank you," I said, confused. "But, ah ... that reaction did not bode well."

"I swear," he said. "It means nothing. Don't mind him. He's just twitchy because there's been so much turmoil in his company since we started working on this game. And there's an element of risk, too. Everything's shaken up. He'll calm down."

"But if he hates all my ideas, I really don't see the point in developing—"

"He doesn't hate anything," Bruce soothed. "He's just being a dickhead. It'll pass. Pay him no mind—he's just programmed that way. I think maybe because he always has his guard up. He used to be a spy, you know."

That startled me. "Really? I did not know that!"

"Yeah. Intelligence and analysis for the NSA. He spent a lot of time in nasty hot spots, sneaking around and monitoring bad actors. I'd like to say that being a spy made him a tight-assed bastard, but the truth is, he's been one since we were kids. So don't expect it to change anytime soon."

"I wouldn't expect anything of the kind," I murmured.

"He's a genius when it comes to cybersecurity," Bruce went on, warming to his subject. "His biggest client is the U.S. government—they love his stuff. He's made a fortune designing stuff for them. But everything's always so damn serious. National security. Terrorist threats. Blood and guts. Something frivolous like a video game drives the poor guy nuts. He'll feel better about it once the money starts pouring in. He likes money just fine. You just keep coming up with those brilliant ideas, and he'll calm down. Everything will be great. Trust me."

"Okay," I said cautiously. "I'm taking you at your word."

Bruce circled the table. "You can take it to the bank," he said as he sat down next to me. "So let me just tell you what I need from you right away, okay?"

We worked for the better part of an hour, detailing and prioritizing the texts that I needed to churn out first. I was pleasantly surprised to realize that this work might actually be fun. A hell of a lot better than paralegaling and typing up legal briefs all night long. I could even get a bit excited about it, even if I was probably going to have to skip pesky little details like, say, sleep, to keep up with Bruce's schedule. He needed what would amount to about twelve hours of work by tomorrow afternoon, and I had a long waitressing shift cutting right into the middle of it. I would be required to warp time and space in order to fulfill my professional obligations. So what else was new.

He started to wrap things up, but I held up my hand. "Wait a second. Doesn't any of this stuff need to be signed off by your brother?"

"No," Bruce said forcefully. "Ignore him. Suit yourself. But work fast, because I've got programmers and graphic artists working on the sixth level, and we need to catch up with the texts." He looked over his shoulder with exaggerated caution, and dropped a gallant kiss on my hand. "Our unprofessional secret," he whispered.

I was laughing when the door opened.

I pulled my hand back when I saw Duncan standing there, looking thunderous. "What the hell is going on in here?" he demanded.

"Work, Duncan," Bruce's voice was heavy with practiced patience.

"It didn't look like work," Duncan said.

My hackles went up at his tone, but Bruce just glanced from me to Duncan and back again with a thoughtful frown. "Hey," he said. "Duncan. Did I tell you lately about the new girl I'm seeing?"

"No," Duncan said brusquely. "It's not relevant. Nor do I particularly care at the moment. Since we're working. Tell me later."

"Her name's Melissa," Bruce went on, ignoring him. "She's a knockout. I've got to introduce you. Oh, and she's a poetry fan. The romantic literary type. Speaking of which, Nell, maybe you could give me a little advice." Bruce slanted me a sly smile.

I crossed my arms, wary of a trap. "What kind of advice?"

"Well, like I said, Melissa loves poetry, and I want to impress her. What would be a good poem for me to memorize? To, ah, you know, melt her?"

"That depends entirely on her tastes," I said. "But before I recommend anything at all, tell me one thing. What's your ultimate purpose in this exercise?"

"Isn't it obvious?" Bruce said, with a roguish wink.

"No, not necessarily," I said. "If you mean to genuinely court this woman, then I caution you against presenting yourself as other than who you really are, because she'll just be disappointed when she realizes the truth. Which she will. Don't fool yourself."

"I'm not a total Neanderthal, Nell," Bruce said, looking faintly miffed.

"How nice for you. But if, on the other hand, you're not serious, and you mean to simply use this woman to, uh ..."

"Slake his animal lust?" Duncan offered.

"Yes, exactly—to slake your animal lust, leaving her crushed and embittered—then you're a dirty dog, and you don't deserve my help. Either way, I don't want to participate in your wicked little games. Don't ask me for seduction advice, Bruce. Read some actual poetry yourself, for real. Expand your horizons. Take a night class. Go to the public library. I wish you luck. More to the point, I wish Melissa luck."

I slapped the file closed, and looked at him sternly over the lenses of my glasses.

Bruce stared at me for a second, then started to laugh. "You'll do," he said. "You're perfect for this wacko place."

"Thank you for sharing your opinion," Duncan said. "That'll be all. Get lost, Bruce."

Bruce choked off his laughter. "Uh, yeah. I'll just let you guys, uh, work your stuff out, then. Bye."

He left the room, still snorting with muffled laughter. The door clicked shut.

The luxurious conference room was so quiet. Faraway city sounds came into focus, floating up from the street. I stared out at the darkening cityscape, tongue-tied and intensely nervous to be alone with him. Bruce seemed like a good guy, and his enthusiasm was heartening, but I was afraid Duncan was going to be a problem. I simply didn't have the kind of self-confidence it took to ignore his disapproval, as Bruce had suggested. That took brash nerve, and I was coming up short on that quality with Snake Eyes circling me. I needed all of my brash nerve just to walk out my apartment door every morning. I didn't have any left to spare for wrangling sexy, difficult men. For God's sake, I could barely bring myself to talk to the guy.

Well, whatever. If this didn't work out, I would be no worse off than before.

Time to go home, heat up something from the freezer, write some epic poetry about goblins, demons, and holy quests. There were worse night jobs. I'd knew, having done a lot of them already.

I cleared my throat. "Well. I have a whole lot of writing to do, so I'll just, um, be on my—"

"Don't go yet. We need to talk."

My heart thumped. "We do? About what?"

"I'm sorry I was rude," he said, his tone gruff. "My brother was driving me nuts."

The apology took me completely by surprise. "I could see that," I offered tentatively.

"I shouldn't have taken it out on you."

"That's true. You definitely shouldn't have," I agreed swiftly.

A smile came and went on his face, so quickly, I wondered if I'd imagined it. "The whole situation just makes me so goddamn nervous," he said.

I cleared my throat. "What situation is that?"

He shrugged. "This project. This game. I design security software, and specialized data-sorting and analysis programs. I'm extremely good at that. I understand what they're good for, how to make them stand out, who to market them to, what they're willing to pay. Then Bruce bounces in with his big, shiny idea. I couldn't talk him out of it, and God knows where he would've gone for the money if I'd refused."

He stopped and turned to look out the window, shaking his head.

I took the opportunity to study his gorgeous profile. The slanting sunlight and shadows in the dim room accentuated the harsh angles and planes of his face. I wished I could draw like Vivi. He'd be an amazing subject.

"And now?" I prompted.

"I don't know shit about video games. So I don't like the situation I find myself in. At a total disadvantage." His voice was clipped. "This is not my scene, you understand? I am not the playful, lighthearted type. I like to have my facts in a row. No surprises. Minimized uncertainty."

"Strip steak sandwich," I said softly. "And apple crumb pie with vanilla ice cream. Forget the fudge brownie."

He shrugged. "I guess it's probably the same phenomenon."

I perched on the edge of the table, clasping my hands. "Well, consider this," I said. "The soup changes every single day, and you've bravely tried a new one every time."

"Yeah, but I've already ascertained that they're all pretty good. That's a minimal risk which has already been assessed and factored in beforehand." He took a step closer to me. "I didn't come to the Sunset Grill for lunch today."

"I know. We missed you." My voice felt breathless at his proximity. "There was a very nice curried chickpea stew that you could've tried."

One step closer and I could smell his aftershave. His face was in shadow now, backlit by the glow of the buildings outside. He had a gorgeous silhouette.

"I don't actually hate your ideas," he said. "Not at all. I'm sorry I was such a pain in the ass. I just automatically contradict everything my brother says. It's a programmed reflex, and it has nothing to do with you, or your abilities."

"Thanks for telling me," I said. "I get that. And he shouldn't tease you. Any man who runs his own business knows about taking risks. What's Bruce risking? He's using your business as a springboard. You're the one putting everything on the line."

In the startled silence that followed, I was embarrassed by my own vehemence. After all, the weird Burke family dynamics were none of my damn business.

I couldn't see his face, but I sensed that he was smiling. "Thank you for saying that," he said. "I appreciate your understanding."

The hairs rose on my arms as he came closer. I could smell the fresh, crisp scent of his shirt. I stared up at his inscrutable silhouette. "You're welcome," I whispered.

"I spoke to Detective Lanaghan today," he said.

I jolted back. Detective Denise Lanaghan was the investigating officer for Lucia's case. Hearing her name spoken in this context was jarring. "You did *what?* Why on earth?"

"I wanted to see what progress they were making on the case," he said.

His voice sounded so casual—like he had every right to rifle through the most painful details of my life. My shock was quickly replaced by anger. "I imagine you wanted to check and see if my story was just so much paranoid bullshit, right?"

He hesitated. "Not at all, actually." His voice was guarded. "A couple of minutes with a good search engine was enough to establish that."

My outrage grew. "So you checked up on me? You hacked into my private business?"

"I wouldn't call that hacking. I didn't get into anything private. I just looked at what was lying around in plain sight. Matters of public record."

"But why?" My voice rose in pitch. "Why poke into my life?"

I still couldn't make out the expression on his face, but his shrug looked unrepentant. "I was interested."

"Well, your level of interest is invasive and weird, and it's making me nervous," I said. "And I don't need anything else in my life to make me nervous. I am at full fucking capacity, Duncan! Do you get me?"

He nodded, but did not apologize. He just stood there, obdurate. Waiting.

"Good God, Burke," I snapped, exasperated. "It's all or nothing with you. Either you completely ignore my existence, or you pin me under a microscope and stare. Whatever happened to just, you know, flirting? Suggestive conversation? Casual chatting?"

"Not my strong suit," he admitted.

"I've noticed! So? 'Fess up. What did Lanaghan say? Not that she should have said anything about our business to some random guy off the street."

"I'm not some random guy. And she spoke to a cop friend of mine, not to me. She said pretty much what you told me last night. They haven't made much progress."

"No, they sure haven't," I said bleakly. "They are nowhere with it. The guy's really good. He left no trace. No prints, no DNA, nothing at all. Even the car that he used in Boston when he tried to kidnap Nancy turned out to be stolen just hours before."

He nodded. "Yeah. That's what I heard."

Thinking about it chilled me. I shied away from the subject, groping for something else to think about. "So, Burke? What else did you find on me out there on the internet?" I demanded. "Did you read my last term's graduate seminar paper on

Christina Rossetti? Did you dig into the archived transcripts from the message boards at the online poetry forum?"

"Yes, both. But my favorites were those five short poems you published in *The Golden Thread Poetry Journal* last January."

My mouth opened and closed in astonishment "Ah ... actually, I was, um, just kidding about you reading that stuff."

"I wasn't," he replied. "I read it. All of it. Several times."

After a few moments of my speechless silence, he gestured with his hand. "Don't get me wrong," he said. "It's not like I can discuss your poems intelligently. I absolutely can't. To be honest, I don't have a clue what you were talking about."

I was puzzled. "Ah. Okay. So how did you know they were your favorites?"

He fidgeted, clearly uncomfortable. "I don't know how," he said impatiently. "I just liked the way they made me feel."

I was oddly moved. "Wow. I think that might be one of the nicest things anyone's ever said to me about my work," I told him. "Thank you."

He kept drifting closer, like a shadow, until he stood right in front of me. His aura interfered with my brain function. Alarm bells were ringing, colored lights flashing in there. It was complete pandemonium.

"You're welcome." His low voice felt velvety to my ears. "First time in my life I ever got something like that right. And it was by accident. Just dumbass luck."

"It's not something that you get wrong or right," I said. "It's just a matter of paying attention. Telling the truth."

He touched one of my ringlets, winding it around his finger. "Those are strong points for me. I've got no problems with paying attention. Or telling the truth."

"You sure don't," I agreed.

He stroked the texture of my hair, pulling the curl, letting it spring back. "So, what's my prize for getting this right?" The deep vibration of his voice made my skin tingle. His breath was so warm. It smelled of coffee and mint. "Did I earn any points?"

"Don't reduce it to a game," I scolded, breathless. "It's not about scoring points."

His lips grazed my temple. "It's not?" Then my cheekbone. His voice was like a brush of sable over my jangling nerves. "Then what is it about? Teach me. I await your wisdom."

My head dropped back, and his hand was ready to support it, warm and strong, cradling my nape. "Do not make fun of me," I whispered.

"Never." He breathed the words into my ear ... and kissed me again.

True to form, my body went nuts. Delicious heat flushed every part of me. Some sinuous, muscular animal thing inside me was awakened—not afraid of him at all, not one little bit—and it knew exactly what it wanted, and that he had plenty of it to give.

I wound my arms around his neck, which provoked a satisfied rumbling sound deep in his throat. He positioned himself between my legs where I was perched on the table. He cupped my head with one hand and my bottom with the other, sliding me tighter against him. Close, but not enough. I wanted to wind my legs around him and yank him closer, closer, infinitely closer.

I'd kissed men before, and been kissed. I'd had sex before, too. Some, not a lot. I'd even enjoyed it, almost, but with some part of me always standing apart, critiquing, judging, comparing. I wanted to let myself go so I could experience the ineffable magic that poets wrote about, but it just didn't happen to me. I stayed flat, cool. Mind racing, hyper-aware of every single embarrassing detail about my body.

With Duncan, there was no problem with letting go. The

problem lay in holding back. I wanted to eat him up, strip him bare, ride him hard. He coaxed my mouth open, and I wound my fingers into his thick hair and moved against him, helpless to stop.

He bent me back on the table until I let go of his arms to prop myself up on my elbows. He grabbed my ankles, folded my legs up high until my skirt rode up and my gartered stockings showed. The ones I'd put on this morning, back when I had still been trying to fool myself into thinking that I wasn't going to wrestle this guy to the ground and have my wanton way with him.

Who had I been trying to fool? He was so hot. A smorgasbord of sexual delights. So big, so strong and solid and hot, and he tasted so damn good. I gasped and pressed back at each grinding shove of his erection against me. He circled against that crazy, hot, delicious, writhing sweet spot, and oh ... *God*.

Bursts of pleasure rocked me, jolting me into a new way of being.

When I opened my eyes, I found his hand clamped over my mouth. He was grinning. He looked absolutely delighted with himself.

"Wow," he whispered, slowly lifting his hand. "That was wild."

"Oh, my God," I squeaked, mortified. "Did I ... make noise?"

"Oh, yeah. So hot. Hold on a sec." He pulled away, wrenched the door open, and my legs snapped together as a blade of light sliced into the room and assaulted my eyes. Duncan poked his head out the door, peered around, and closed it, plunging us into darkness again. "They're all gone," he said. I heard the click of the door lock engaging. "Thank God. Not a sound out there. But just in case. Since you're a screamer."

A thread of cold unfurled in my belly. I slid off the table, tugged my skirt over my legs. He moved swiftly to block me. "Oh, God, no," he said. "Don't panic on me now." There was a pleading edge in his voice.

"I just ... the locked door, it, ah ..."

"I'll unlock it if you want. I just didn't want any surprise visitors, that's all." His hands slid under my skirt and gripped the tops of my thighs, sliding slowly up toward my mound. "Making you come is not a spectator sport."

"Uh, no, of course not. But I—"

"Shhh." He seized me, and we were off again, kissing wildly.

Oh, hell with it. I gripped his arms and gave in to it. Our mouths melded with the abandoned sureness of well-matched dancing partners, as if we'd known how to kiss each other senseless since time began. All the excitement of novelty, all the sureness and grace and ease of familiarity. I wanted to claw his shirt off, to feel every detail of that big, solid torso, to smell his sweat, to feel the texture of his chest hair, the shape of his nipples, the contours of his muscles.

And his cock. I wanted to grip it, test it, pet it, squeeze it. Make him gasp and moan and shiver. I pressed my hand against his flat belly and slid it down over his belt. His hand covered mine and pressed it against the bulge in his crotch. He stroked the gusset of my panties and a low murmur of satisfaction vibrated against my shoulder as he found me slick and wet. He kissed me again, his tongue venturing into my mouth to dance lazily around mine, and both of us moaned as he explored my tender folds with a gentle finger, sliding into my slick opening. I clenched around him in shocked delight.

"Oh, God," he said roughly. "I think my hand is going to come."

"You think you've got problems," I said unsteadily.

Then there was no more talking. Just deep, ravenous kissing while his finger delved my tender, secret places, and my hand appreciatively stroked and squeezed the hot, stiff shaft of his cock. My legs twined around his thighs for balance, and we shuddered and gasped, tongues twining, wrapped in a tight, trembling knot of desire. Tension rose, until the sweet, keening ache of anticipation shattered.

Molten pulses of delight throbbed through my body.

I sagged against him. I was made out of liquid now. I was a pool of glimmering moonlight. He'd undone the fastenings of my gartered stockings at some point and was tugging my panties off my legs, but I was too limp to react. I hung on to his shirtfront and tried to form words. "What ... ah, what are you going to—"

"I don't have latex. So I'll do this instead."

He dropped to his knees and put his mouth to me.

I almost screamed, the sensation was so intense. He murmured something soothing and incomprehensible against my thigh and rubbed his cheek against my skin, petting and nuzzling. He parted my sensitive folds, and I felt his tongue, warm and soft, fluttering, up, down, around, exploring me lustily. Tenderly circling my clit.

I collapsed back onto the table, and a tiny part of my brain stood apart for a moment, astonished at how my life had upended itself. Yesterday, I was the sad girl, celibate and crushing on an unattainable man. Today, I was spread-eagled and pantiless, getting marvelously tongue-lashed by that same unattainable guy.

It was an improbable sexual fantasy come to life. Too good to be true.

Yeah, and if I didn't attain him all the way, I was going to implode. Collapse into a screaming, writhing human black hole. The hunger bit so hard. I pushed his face away. He looked up in silent question, wiping his mouth. I saw his grin flash in the dimness.

"Mmm," he murmured. "Good. More?"

"What about you?"

His soft laughter tickled my mound. "I'll live." He paused for a moment, then added, "Somehow." He pressed his lips to me, fluttering his tongue around my clit in a way that made me cry out, writhing against his face.

I pushed his face away again, struggled up onto my elbows. "Make love to me."

He lifted his head, and I suddenly wished I hadn't used a silly romantic euphemism. It made my vulnerabilities so obvious. I should have just said, *Fuck me.* That would have been clearer, more honest. We'd both know where we stood. Or sprawled, as the case may be.

But I just couldn't. Such a blunt, crude phrase wouldn't come out of my mouth. Romantic, old-fashioned, poetry-addled idiot that I was.

He gripped my hips, fingers digging in. "No latex," he repeated.

"I have some," I whispered.

He froze. "No fucking way."

"Um, actually, yes. In my purse. My co-worker bought them for me today as a joke. She was roasting me. I never thought I'd—"

"Where's your purse?"

"On the chair, I think, on the other side of the—"

He'd already yanked it open and flung its contents onto the table. He found the little package, and seconds later, he was back, opening his belt and tearing open the wrapping with a show of manual dexterity that would have been dazzling if I'd been in any condition to appreciate it. I caught a glimpse of his big, thick cock as he sheathed it, and then he pushed me back down onto the table and folded my legs up high. No time to appreciate the view.

The bulb at the end of his cock seemed so big and blunt, pressing against my slick, sensitized opening. He slid it tenderly up and down my tightly furled seam caressing me until he was wet, and I was squirming against him, silently pleading.

And then he pushed slowly inside me.

Chapter Ten

Duncan

I counted back from ten, holding my breath. Please, God, not yet. I breathed my climax carefully down, but the second I opened my eyes and looked at her again, spread out beneath me, I was in trouble again.

She was so fucking beautiful. My body was on the verge of exploding. The tight, eager grip of her pussy was a sweet torment. Each stroke was another excellent lick of that excellent, silken lash.

I was glad I'd gotten her good and wet, or I'd never have gotten inside. As it was, each stroke was slow, pushing against the plushy resistance of her gorgeous body. She enveloped me —her pussy hugging me—the swift, heavy beat of her heart throbbing around my cock. Again ... and again ... and finally, my tight, careful strokes began to relax, and we found our slick, wet rhythm of deep, rocking thrusts, punctuated by my labored breathing, her breathless gasps. She was working up to another climax.

And my own orgasm was crashing down on me like a falling meteor—the sky was in flames—but God knew how, I held it off just until she took flight.

We soared together, through that inner nowhere. Fused.

I collapsed over her, panting. My mind was wiped clean. I'd never imagined feeling so close to anyone. The essence of her was burned into my mind, a twisting, pulsing glow. I felt like I would always feel it, no matter where she was.

My eyes fluttered open. I was pinning her soft body onto the hard table with all the weight of my torso. Crushing her. That couldn't be comfortable.

I lifted myself up. Her face was turned away. She couldn't meet my eyes.

A strange feeling of shyness hit me, too. I felt humbled, uncertain. I didn't know if she'd felt what I'd felt—and the post-coital crash of doubt chilled me.

I pulled out of the tight clutch of her body.

The condom was a problem. No way in hell was I leaving it in the trash can in the conference room. I rummaged on the table for the drugstore bag the box had been in, peeled the condom off, sealed it up. Tongue-tied as a thirteen-year-old boy who'd just had his first lay. I hastened to shove my still-hard dick back into my pants and fasten them, with some discomfort, before I dared to even look at her.

She'd straightened her own clothing in the meantime. Her panties were back on. Her stockings were up, her skirt tugged down. She was fastening her garters.

And she was waiting for me to speak first. For fuck's sake. Women were always the talkative ones. This was the first time in my life I'd ever actually wanted one of those long, awkward silences to break.

"Are you, uh, okay?" I ventured.

She nodded.

So much for that brilliant attempt. "That was incredible," I offered.

"Yes," she agreed.

I felt a spark of hope. "I didn't mean for things to happen so fast," I offered.

She stifled a soft, whispery giggle. "Me neither," she murmured.

So far, so good. Thank God, she wasn't getting all emotional on me. Maybe she was actually reasonable. "Well, there's no going back now," I said.

She crossed her arms. "Meaning?"

"Meaning, I think we're on to something here. It'll be complicated, but it's worth it to me. Let's get some dinner, and we can hammer out the details."

"Details?" she repeated, her voice slow and deliberate. "What details?"

"The details of our mutually beneficial arrangement," I explained. "It'll need to be secret, for obvious reasons, but I'm sure we can make it work. I'll take you to my condo. We'll order some dinner in, and I'll show you just how beneficial it can be."

The second she flipped the light switch on, I blinked. The sheer, blazing fury on her face rocked me back on my heels. The *fuck?*

She started shoving things into her purse. "I don't fucking think so," she said.

I frowned. "Nell—"

"That's Ms. D'Onofrio to you." She stuffed the last of her things into her bag. "You can take your mutually beneficial arrangement and shove it right up your ass."

She slung her purse over her shoulder and stalked out, black curls bouncing with each furious step.

I lunged after her, grabbing her shoulder to spin her around. "Nell! Wait! At least tell me what I—"

"Don't touch me." She flinched away. She vibrated with rage.

"You didn't complain about me touching you ten minutes ago," I pointed out. "Are you fucking with me? Because we both know that was mutual."

"No, I am not fucking with you." She spat each word out. "It looks like we were fucking with each other, but we're done with that. Definitively."

I still was not getting it. "What the fuck? Just tell me if I need to call my lawyer."

She let out an explosive breath. "No, Burke. I'm not setting you up for a lawsuit. I'm not an extortionist or a con woman. If you want me to sign and notarize a piece of paper saying I came six times, I'll—"

"Eight," I corrected.

"Do not push me," she said, biting the words out. "The sex was great. You're amazing in bed. Actually, that's a misnomer. I'm sure you're amazing on the floor, in the shower, up against the wall. But the minute you zip up your pants and open your mouth, you're a rude, crass, insensitive asshole. So get out of my way."

She yanked open the office door and flounced out.

I stood there, staring at the door as it shut in my face, running through everything I'd said and done. I saw no fault lines. No red flags. No insults. What the hell had I said?

I'd been sucker-punched. This was not fair. And it was definitely not over.

I slapped the door open. Down the hall, the elevator was closing. I sprinted for it, but the doors pinged shut before I could wedge my fingers in. The other elevator was creeping up around the fiftieth floor. Screw that.

I dove for the stairwell. Enough guessing games. Enough bombs going off in my face. This woman wasn't getting away from me until I knew what I'd done to piss her off. That was not too much to ask

Fuck this stress-inducing bullshit.

Chapter Eleven

Nell

I stumbled out onto the street, my knees wobbling. With anger and dismay and everything else that had led up to this moment.

I wiped at my face with the back of my hands, smearing my tears into horrendous streaks. God, I must look like a Halloween horror.

Mutually beneficial arrangement, my ass. Hammer out the details? He might as well have asked for a fee schedule. Like a sushi menu. A combination platter. Four pieces of sashimi, maki roll, and miso soup. How much for a mind-blowing kiss, heart-pounding dry humping, amazing, drawn-out cunnilingus, and a long, hard screw on the conference room table? Should I give him a discount for all the orgasms?

Crass, arrogant asshole. Reducing it to that, after he'd laid me so totally bare. My heart, my fears and hopes, my deepest self, all stripped down and raw, live wires carrying a lethal charge.

Maybe I'd overreacted, but it took all the self-control I had not to scream like a banshee and swing my purse at his head.

Or maybe that had been my last lingering remnant of common sense. All I had to do was look at the guy to know I wouldn't fare well in any sort of physical confrontation with him.

My legs shook as I stumbled down the sidewalk. My crotch was still wet, hot, flushed, and glowing with residual pleasure. As if all the lights had been turned on, and then just left on. Every step, every clench of my thigh muscles felt ... well, good.

Damn him. That had been so crude, so unnecessary. He should stick to professional sex workers, not amateurs like me, primed and programmed to fall like a ton of bricks. Embarrassing myself and everyone else in my immediate vicinity.

I bumped into people as I walked, muttering soggy, garbled apologies. The colored lights of the city blurred into a colored swirl. I stopped at a street corner and wiped my tears and mascara away with my sleeve. God knew this dress would need to be cleaned anyway. I might never wear the damn thing again. It was tainted now.

I glanced up at the street sign. Broadway. Good. Busy at all hours. Even as a faraway, disconnected part of my mind reminded me of my promise to Nancy and Vivi. Snake Eyes, out on the prowl. This wasn't safe.

But my wallet was practically empty, and my bank account was likewise tapped out from that stupid haircut this morning. I'd spent today's tip money on my break, paying down my hefty credit card minimum. Then there was the car service I'd taken to Duncan's building.

But hey, no worries, right? Salvation was at hand. High-end call girls pulled in a thousand an hour or more, depending on the services they provided, and the level of kink they were down for. Not that I could really boast of my sexual technique

—I'd had too little effective practice—but I could fake it. It was in my blood, after all.

All I had to do was whip up a stiff fee schedule for that ice-hearted bastard, and there was all the cash I needed. For cab fares, haircuts, dresses, rent. Hell, even tuition, if I wanted to spend that much time on my back. Or my knees.

All I had to do was eliminate something inside myself. Something shining and precious and delicate. Something I hadn't even known I had until that moment of astonishing connection with him.

Hope.

I was appalled at myself. I hadn't even known my stupid went that deep, but I'd actually been hoping for love. From him. I hadn't let myself admit it, but I couldn't deny it now. Not after the huge, embarrassing tantrum I'd just thrown.

I'd been walking for a long time. My feet ached. The busy, self-important city swirled around me, the wind sweeping down the street, cool against my tear-streaked face. Then I spotted it—a familiar sign.

A big bookstore. It was a place I loved to hang out when I had time. I'd spent hours in there, standing in the aisles, devouring books I couldn't afford to buy.

If anywhere could offer comfort, it was there. Maybe I'd go in and buy something extravagant. Like the complete works of E. E. Cummings.

I'd stay there until they physically threw me out.

Chapter Twelve

Duncan

I dropped a few meters farther behind, keeping the pale flash of her dress in my field of vision. I'd charged out of there all fired up, ready to confront her face-to-face, right in the street, and demand to know—exactly, in every particular—what her fucking problem was. Then I got close enough to see that she was crying.

And I lost my nerve and hung back again.

Goddamn it. I should have known I'd pay in blood for anything that good.

So I went into surveillance mode. Emotions flat-lined. Attention locked on the target. Projecting a don't-see-me vibe. I was nobody, just a faceless suit in a sea of suits. Though at this hour, there was no sea of suits on the streets. The suits were vegging in front of their TVs or packed into bars, managing their stress with excessive amounts of alcohol. Not a problem, though, since Nell wasn't noticing me. She was stumbling along the sidewalk, hand over her mouth, clutching her purse.

Attracting attention. A beautiful woman, sobbing right out on the street? Christ. She was making herself a target.

That made my emotional flat-line twitch, with guilt and anger. What the fuck? Why? What had I done, anyhow? I hadn't intended any of this. The last thing I wanted was to hurt her feelings. All I'd done was make her come. So fucking shoot me, already.

Of course, seducing her hadn't helped with her current off-the-charts stress level. But I hadn't been able to stop myself. It just ... happened.

Now I was compounding my asshole status by stalking her. That was super intelligent. Yeah, just razor sharp.

But my feet didn't hear the sarcasm, didn't get the message. They just kept carrying me along, keeping her a safe thirty meters ahead. Watching that mane of springy black ringlets sway and swirl with every gust of wind.

Then I felt the tickle. Like the whispery brush of a cobweb breaking across my mind. An instinct that said, 'something's wrong with this picture.'

I looked closer. Since snapping into surveillance mode, part of my mind had been tracking not just her, but everything around her. That gray sweatshirt had been around for a while. Too long. Behind her, but not far enough behind. Gray sweatshirt, jeans. Long blond hair. Dirty white athletic shoes. Nell paused to wait for a light. The guy slowed and gazed into a cosmetics shop window. Yeah, right. Like that skank was interested in aromatherapy bath salts or orange blossom body butter.

I got in line at a streetside bank machine, watching out of the corner of my eye as the guy sauntered across the street and kept going, still in the same direction as Nell, staying parallel to her.

I flash-analyzed the data, tracking everything from the moment I'd given up confronting her. That guy had been in my field of vision the entire time. Might have been there since we walked out of the building. Might have been lying in wait.

Thirty-five downtown blocks. Too far to walk voluntarily, to not take a subway or a cab, to not have some other business or detour along the way. Nell crossed the street again. Gray Sweatshirt strolled after her. She disappeared into a big, brightly lit bookstore. The guy stopped, muttered into his collar, and followed her in.

A thread of ice congealed deep inside me. This guy was wired. He was reporting to someone, in real time. So this wasn't some random sicko obsessed with Nell's tits. This was a coordinated team of random sickos. A team meant organization, financing, an agenda. What the fuck was going on?

I eased to the back of the line for the bank machine again and waited, single-minded as a cat watching a mouse hole. Crunching data, speculating, presenting and rejecting hypotheses. It had to be the people who tried to get the sister.

Time warped. People swirled by like a sped-up film. I stood motionless in the middle of it, a laser-focused eye of contemplation. Just waiting.

Customers began trickling out. I glanced at my watch. The store was about to close. My adrenaline revved up as Nell stepped outside, swinging a plastic shopping bag in her hand. She looked around, like she was trying to get her bearings, then took off in the direction of the subway station.

Three seconds later, Gray Sweatshirt followed her out. I forced myself into a casual stride. No sprinting. No roar of primordial rage. My heart thudded. Blood roared in my head. I had to clamp down hard on the urge to leap on that piece-of-shit dickhead and take him apart, just for thinking about laying his hands on her.

I turned onto Lafayette and Gray Sweatshirt muttered into his collar again. Urgency pricked at me. Something was going down, and I was the only one around to stop it. Just me. One guy. I pulled out my cell and speed-dialed Gant.

"What is it?" Gant snarled, with his usual foul humor. "You again? Got any more unreasonable demands to make, Dunc?"

"Yeah. Remember the chick I'm obsessed with?"

"Yeah, the daughter of Lucia D'Onofrio. What about her?"

"I'm tailing her right now," I said. "Stalking her, you might say."

Gant hissed something obscene in Pushtu. "And you're burdening me with this embarrassing, extremely personal information about yourself exactly why?"

"Because I'm not the only one who's doing it," I said.

Gant was gratifyingly speechless for a moment. "Come again?"

"She's under surveillance," I explained. "At least a two-man team. I'm a half a block behind the guy tailing her. We're on Lafayette. Just past the Public Theater."

"Holy fuck," Gant muttered. "I'll send someone."

"Do it fast. They're gearing up for something. I can feel it coming together."

"Dunc? Do not engage." He paused. "Did you hear me? Hello?"

"I heard you," I said, noncommittally.

Gant snarled another curse in Pushtu. "Are you armed?"

"No, but I'll be careful."

He hung up without a farewell, and I hurried to catch up with Gray Sweatshirt.

I didn't like Lafayette. It was darker than Broadway, more deserted, fewer storefronts, everything closed. I wished she'd stayed on crowded Broadway, where I could afford to stay closer to her. As it was, it was a miracle Gray Sweatshirt hadn't made me yet. The guy was stupid. Incompetent.

That, however, didn't make him any less dangerous to Nell.

Alarm flickered in my gut. Gray Sweatshirt's demeanor was changing. He looked more focused and was walking faster, like he'd been released from some imperative, or else given a new one.

Beyond Nell, coming toward us in the opposite direction, was another pedestrian figure. A tall, rangy Black man with a shaved head. He looked at Gray Sweatshirt, then looked away and kept coming. They had her in a pincer grip.

Then the car pulled up, driving slowly. It passed me ... and its brake lights flickered—on, off—for no good reason.

Then it sped up. So did Gray Sweatshirt. So did the other guy.

I didn't remember starting to sprint. My legs pumped, closing the gap. The car door swung open. The guys grabbed Nell, wrestling her into the car, headfirst. She struggled and screamed.

I flung myself at the closest of the two men, the tall Black guy. He hit the side of the car with a grunt of surprise. Gray Sweatshirt's head whipped around.

"What the fuck—"

I slammed a fist into his nose, knocking him against the car door. In that split-second opening, I grabbed Nell by the waist, yanked her out of the car, and flung her in the direction of the sidewalk. She hit the ground with a yell, rolling into the gutter.

I surged back as a boot whipped past the tip of my nose. Blocked Gray Sweatshirt's swing with my forearm and rammed an elbow into the Black guy's neck. Turned to the side to take Gray Sweatshirt's knee-jab to my thigh instead of my groin. An uppercut to the Black guy's chin sent him bouncing heavily against the car. I whirled just in time to meet Gray Sweatshirt's renewed attack.

People had noticed now. A woman screamed nearby. Not Nell.

Block, duck, lunge, retreat. I caught Gray Sweatshirt's fist, twisted it up, over, around, and sent the guy flying over the hood of the car.

The Black guy came at me again with a length of pipe. It whipped down and I lurched aside. It whooshed past, displacing air, and shattered the passenger-side window. Pebbles of glass flew.

I darted in, grabbed the end of the pipe before he could work up another swing, twisted it up, torquing his arm, and sent him bouncing over the hood of the car. The car surged forward, pitching him off and onto the street. He rolled, howling.

Tires shrieked. The car peeled around the corner and sped away. The Black guy dragged himself up and fled, limping, the heavy, irregular slap of his rubber-soled shoes retreating into the distance.

Gray Sweatshirt came at me with a spinning back kick. I ducked, but my balance was off. I stumbled back, dropped to my knees. *Fuck.*

The guy leaped at me, eyes lit up with joy at the opening— *Crack.*

Nell had swung her plastic shopping bag, and whatever was inside connected with the guy's face. He let out a hoarse shout and stumbled back, hand over his nose, blood streaming.

I rolled to my feet, lunged to grapple—
Gun.

I stopped cold, reeling. Fought for balance. Hands up. Open.

Gray Sweatshirt held a pistol on us, a shaking, sideways two-handed grip—straight out of a bullshit action movie, but at point-blank range, even with that dumb grip, his aim wouldn't matter. A Glock 9mm would leave a big hole.

I scooped Nell behind me. "Easy," I soothed. "Easy."

"Fuck you, you fuck." His trembling voice was thin and high, bubbling and phlegmy with blood running down his throat. "Back off, or I'll shoot you like a fuckin' dog. And then I'll shoot the bitch."

He backed away, gun wavering, swinging wildly. The gathered onlookers screamed, scattering like startled pigeons.

"You don't need to shoot," I said. "Who hired you?"

"Some stupid fuck. Shut up. Don't talk to me." He backed up farther. "Back off. Everybody! Get the fuck back!"

Then, suddenly, he turned and ran, his legs a blur, like a double-jointed cheetah.

Nell sagged down onto the sidewalk. I dropped to my knees to break her fall, held her up. Fished my cell phone from my pocket—only to realize my fingers were shaking too much to enter the number.

Damn. I must be getting soft. Going civilian.

It took me a few tries, but I finally got Gant's phone ringing. At that moment, his car pulled up, and he unfolded his long, lanky self from the seat, holding up his ringing phone.

I stopped the call and dropped my phone back into my pocket. The asshole was long gone, but I relayed the info with weary precision.

"Three of them. One's rabbiting down Great Jones Street. Blond, six-one, jeans, gray sweatshirt, goatee. Armed and dangerous. Glock 9mm. The other two are long gone. One was a Black man, tall, thin. He ran, too. The car was a silver Jeep Cherokee. Busted front passenger window. Didn't get the plates. Didn't get a look at the driver."

Gant relayed the info into his radio. He was a square-jawed guy with cold blue eyes and sandy hair, buzzed off short. He looked down at Nell, still curled up on the sidewalk. "This is her?"

I pulled Nell to her feet. "Nell, this is Lt. John Gant of the NYPD."

She swallowed, coughed. "Ah, hi. Good to meet you."

"You okay, miss?" Gant asked.

"Been better," she croaked. "I'll be fine. I think."

"Did he hit you? Hurt you?"

"She broke his nose," I announced in ringing tones. "She broke that fucking son of a bitch's nose. Saved my ass doing it, too."

Gant blinked at the fierce pride in my voice. "Uh, wow. Hot damn. How'd you do that, miss?"

Nell held up the plastic shopping bag and fished out a massive volume that she could barely hold in one hand. "The complete works of E. E. Cummings," she said. "Just bought it." She started to giggle. "I had no idea what a good deal I was getting."

Her face crumpled, and she covered her face with her hands. I stared at her in helpless dismay. Fuck. Again. Gant gave me the hairy eyeball and jerked his hand toward Nell, snapping his fingers sharply.

Hug her! Asshole! he mouthed.

I flipped him the bird behind Nell's back and pressed my nose into her perfumed curls again, inhaling her scent.

The next couple of hours were long and grueling at the police station. She spent a long time on my cell phone, pouring her heart out to her sisters, first one, then the other. Hashing the whole thing out and filing the report took forever, and after a while, I started eyeing Nell's pale, stiff face and staring eyes. I wondered uneasily if I'd been stupid not to insist that she get medically evaluated. She'd told everyone she was fine—maybe a bruise or two at most—but I hadn't considered psychological damage. I was as tough as boot leather myself. I was used to rough treatment. I'd forgotten what a tooth-rattling, shocking insult that violence was to normal human beings.

Her hand was icy cold. I rubbed it between mine. "I need to get some food and a good stiff drink into her," I said to Gant. "Can we finish this up another time?"

Gant studied Nell with narrowed eyes. "Miss D'Onofrio, do you have someone to stay with tonight?" He shot me a keen glance. "A family member, maybe?"

She looked lost, chewing on her soft, cushy lower lip. "Ah ..."

"She's staying with me," I blurted.

Nell blinked at me, startled. I stared back, willing her not to fight it. It seemed so obvious to me, so inevitable.

She let out a long breath in short, jerky segments and nodded. "I'll stay with him," she murmured to Gant.

A jolt of hot triumph shook me. Urgency, too. I wanted to get her home now. Trap her in my lair. Before she changed her mind.

I made sure the car service was waiting before I let her leave the building. There could be snipers after her, for all I knew. I bundled her hastily into the car and gave the driver my address.

"Wait," Nell said. "My place, first."

I rounded on her, ready for battle. She put her fingers over my mouth. "Shhh. Don't start. I need to touch base. I need fresh clothes."

"I'll buy you clothes."

"Not at one in the morning, you won't," she said. "And I need to check my answering machine. And pick up my laptop."

"Those guys know where you live," I growled. "I don't want to come across like I've got no balls, but I wouldn't mind avoiding any more mortal combat this evening. If it's not too fucking much to ask."

She tapped my lips again, gently. "Don't be sarcastic. I am very aware of your big balls. But I doubt very much they'll be lying in wait for me there tonight. We'll park right outside the door, we'll see if anyone's there, we'll only be inside for a few minutes. Please, Duncan."

I settled back against the seat, defeated but disapproving. Her hand was no longer on my mouth. I missed it. It was almost worth it to me to goad her, just to see if she would try to silence me again. I could feel that soft, silky pressure again.

Then another possibility occurred to me. I reached down and took her hand. A long and cautious minute later, her fingers curled around mine. The city slipped by, but we were fixed in space. We were the hub—the unmoving center of the universe—and the rest of the world was a shifting illusion swirling around us. But she was so warm, so soft.

"Thank you," she said. "For saving my life."

"Any fucking time." I punctuated that statement by sliding my thumb into the warm recesses of her hand. I thought about the conference room table, and blood pounded in my ears. I fought it down. "I was, ah, wondering something."

Her fingers tightened around mine. "Yes? What?"

"If that earns me enough points to cancel out whatever the hell it was I did to piss you off before."

I braced myself, but she didn't freak out. She just made an impatient gesture with her free hand. "That's it, Duncan. That's exactly the problem—this reductionist idea that you have, that everything can be reduced to an economic exchange. Human emotions don't run on a point system."

I sighed. "It's a goddamn figure of speech, Nell," I ground out.

"No, it's not. Not with you. And not with me." Her voice was soft but stubborn.

Aw, fuck. I drew comfort from the fact that she was still squeezing my hand.

"It's been a hard night," I said wearily. "This shit is complicated. Show me some fucking mercy, already."

She grabbed me and gave me a quick, awkward hug. "Okay," she whispered. "I can be merciful. I hereby grant you points—lots of points. Are you happy now?"

"Very," I said. And I was. Hard, too. Like a diamond. I wanted to roll her onto the cushy leather seat and just have at her.

"One question," she said. "How did you happen to conveniently be there when they attacked? Were you following me?"

Tension gripped me. Here was where I tiptoed over blown glass.

"Yeah, I was," I admitted. "I, uh, wanted to apologize. But I'm not great at it. And you were crying, and that intimidated me. I didn't even know what the hell I was apologizing for. So I stalled—until I saw that asshole in the gray sweatshirt."

"And then I got attacked," she said.

"You have to admit, it was a great opening," I offered. "Works like electroshock therapy. The woman just forgets what she's mad about."

She snorted with laughter. "Uh, yeah. Right."

"No, really," I said. "If not for those guys, you'd still be pissed as hell, and I'd still be as confused as ever." I paused. "I'm still confused," I admitted. "And you're probably still pissed. But at least you're talking to me. That's progress."

She harrumphed. "Talk about looking on the bright side."

"I might as well," I said.

The car stopped outside her door. I told the driver to wait and got out, peering around the street before I let her out. I blocked her body with mine as she unlocked the door, then scanned every twist of the echoing stairwell before letting her proceed.

Her apartment was crammed with books, leaving barely any space to move. The bathtub in the kitchen was covered with a wooden top. A tiny water closet sat in the corner, and a half-sized refrigerator was tucked beneath the counter. A two-burner gas range and a toaster oven completed the picture. I'd never seen a place so small.

While she hustled around, pulling a suitcase from her closet, I studied the photos on the wall. Most of them were of two young women and a distinguished-looking elderly woman in different combinations and settings.

"This is your mother and sisters?" I asked.

She glanced up from where she knelt in front of a small chest of drawers. "Yes."

I studied them. Pretty, like Nell, but in different ways. "They don't look anything like you," I observed.

"We're all adopted," Nell said. "Lucia took us in as foster children when we were teenagers."

That information made me curious about what had shaped her—what had made her so smart, so difficult. But not tonight. There would be other chances. I hoped.

She looked exhausted, staring down at two different T-shirts in her hands as if she couldn't decide which one to bring.

"Pack both," I advised. "You're not coming back for a while."

She shot me a narrow glance. I walked over and knelt beside her. She swayed back slightly, her eyes going wide and wary as I pulled open her first drawer. My fingers closed around a fistful of silky fabric. Panties, stockings. I dropped the tangled wad into the open suitcase.

"Pack a lot," I said softly.

Her eyes dropped, color rising in her face. Her nipples

tightened against the stretchy fabric of her stained, rumpled dress.

That white-hot episode in the conference room hovered between us in the silence, complete in every delicious erotic detail. She licked her lower lip until it gleamed. The look in her eyes was cautious, but a hint of a smile played there.

I scoped the room with my peripheral vision. The bed, piled high with books, didn't look promising, but the beanbag chair behind her had possibilities. I could wedge her into it, pin her down with my weight, rock against her, slide into her—her body squeezing around my cock every time she came. Yes.

I reached out, letting my fingertips glide down her cheek, her soft throat. Over her breastbone. I spread my whole hand over her, feeling the quick, hard throb of her heart beneath my palm. My other hand slid up her thigh, gripping where the fabric of her stockings ended and soft, hot skin began. The energy built between us, swelling into something inevitable. She bit her lower lip, her breathing uneven.

Then it happened again—just like on the street. That ghostly sensation. Like a cobweb breaking across my mind. My guard slipping.

I froze, my grip tightening on her thigh. My eyes swept the small apartment. Nothing moving. Nothing changed. Just the sounds of the street outside.

"What is it?" Nell asked.

"Shhh," I hushed her, reaching out with my senses.

Two steps took me to the barred window overlooking a blind courtyard filled with garbage cans. Empty. Just a couple of rats scrounging. But the feeling remained. And by now, I trusted it blindly.

I was being watched. The hairs on my neck stood on end.

My gaze landed on the smoke detector attached to the low ceiling. I reached up and carefully detached it.

"Duncan, what are you—"

"Shhh." I didn't want to talk. Not with unfriendly eyes watching, unfriendly ears listening.

It was almost too easy. A tiny video camera was taped to the side of the black smoke detector, nearly invisible. The device had been gutted, its interior used to house a transmitter. I stared at it, cursing myself for touching it.

Finger-fucking the evidence.

Gant would lecture me. He never wasted an opportunity to give me hell.

"What on earth is that thing?" Nell's voice was thin and high.

"A video camera," I said. "Someone's been watching you."

She made a strangled sound and put her hand over her mouth.

Shit-eating bastards, violating her hard-earned private space. Watching while she undressed, bathed, ate, slept. Probably watching her now—seeing her hurt and scared. That infuriated me.

I laid the thing down on her table. "Don't touch it," I warned. "It might have prints." I looked around the room again, trying to imagine where I would plant spyware if I were one of them.

She had an old-fashioned phone. I grabbed the horn, unscrewed the mouthpiece. Bingo. I shook the listening device onto the table without touching it, then answered the question in her eyes.

"A drop-in bug," I said. "They've been monitoring your phone conversations."

Her eyes were huge. "I ... but I talked to Vivi just this morning—"

"We'll discuss it later," I cut her off. "Not here. Let's just get the fuck out of this place. It makes my flesh creep."

"Ah, y-y-yes," she stammered, flustered. She looked around wildly. "Um ... what was I—"

"Laptop. Clothes," I reminded her. "Fast. Oh, and that phone? Leave it. It's probably compromised, too."

Her eyes widened. "But ... my sister's numbers are—"

"Write them down. I'll get you a new one. The laptop is probably—"

"I can't leave that," she said. "It has all my scholarly work on it."

"Fine. Tomorrow I'll go through and make sure there's nothing planted in it."

She gave me an eloquent glance, but was quickly distracted when I started helping her, scooping stuff out of drawers at random. That perked her right up. She shoved me away with an irritated sound and finished packing her clothes. Then came the shoes, the toiletries bag vials, bottles, tubes, packets of this and that.

And then it was the books. Fuck a duck. She heaved eight of them into the huge suitcase. Big motherlovers, too. The suitcase wheels were probably going to collapse.

I dragged her and her bag out the door after that, scanned the stairwell landing, then stuck my head back inside her door. I made an obscene gesture, for the benefit of any hidden cameras I hadn't found.

"You're not getting her," I told the bug on the table. "Fuck off and die, shithead." I slammed the door for emphasis.

The driver stowed the suitcase in the back, and took off. I was starting to feel the effects of the adrenaline crash, and I was grateful not to be driving myself. Nell was alarmingly quiet, throat bobbing. The silence was heavy.

I reached for the first thing I could think of to break it. "Do you have a copy of that letter your sister found?" I asked. "The one you told me about yesterday?"

"I have it scanned onto my computer," she said. "Why?"

I shrugged. "I'm just—"

"Interested. Yes. I've noticed. I'll show you anything you want to see."

I stared out the window, wondering what my next move should be. A Korean deli was coming up on the corner, with banks of multicolored flowers on display. "Stop the car," I told the driver.

Nell looked startled as the car braked and I flung the door open. "Don't worry," I assured her. "This'll just take a second."

I stared at the flowers, at a loss, then grabbed a bunch of the best-looking long-stemmed roses out of a bucket. I handed the boy sitting next to the flowers a handful of cash and got back into the car.

"Here." I handed her the flowers, realizing too late that the long, thorny stems were dripping all over her lap. I hadn't even had them tied, wrapped, trimmed. But she looked at me, wide-eyed. Cautiously charmed. She sniffed them, sighed with pleasure.

She smiled at me. It had worked. Praise God.

After a moment, she reached for my hand. "I'm sorry," she said. "I appreciate the fact that you're interested. I'm probably still alive because of it. I just don't get it. Why is this happening? It's senseless."

"Money," I said.

She looked over at me, blankly. "Huh?"

"Money is why this is happening," I repeated. "Money is always the reason."

She looked doubtful. "Huh. Maybe you haven't noticed this yet, Duncan, but I don't have very much of it. Practically none, to be honest."

I shook my head. "Even so. There's a short list of motivations for crimes like this. Insanity, revenge, or money. I doubt you girls have pissed anyone off that badly—"

"We haven't. Not one of us. We're a pack of goody-goody pussycats."

I nodded. "Right. And there's the murdered jeweler and his family, too, so I'd strike personal revenge as a motive. We could consider revenge against your mother, but that falls pretty flat since she's passed on. Insanity's a possibility, but there are the references in those letters, to maps, searches, keys, secrets. Whoever this dickhead is, he's invested a lot of time and money watching you and your sisters. Whatever Lucia wanted you girls to find? It means big bucks, and they won't stop till they have it."

Nell massaged her temples. "It's so ironic if that's true." She sounded exhausted. "We don't need this money. We don't give a shit about money. None of us do. All we want is to do our thing and live our lives in peace. There's so much to freak out about, so much to be scared of. I'm ... I'm in tilt."

"Don't think about it," I suggested. "Just put it out of your mind."

"Neat trick." There was a smile in her voice. "And just exactly how do you suggest I manage that?"

It had been such a weird evening, I decided one more crazy risk wouldn't change anything. I lifted her hand and gave it a long, lingering kiss.

"I've got a few good ideas," I said.

She laughed behind her hand, and the vibrations in her shoulders went on for so long, I got nervous that she might actually be crying again. But when she looked up, she was smiling, even though her eyes were wet.

"Wow. I had no idea I was so damn funny," I said. "Who knew."

She threw her head back and wiped her eyes. "It's not you.

I just can't believe it. I felt safe in my place after I put the alarm in. The thing cost a fortune. And the whole while, they were watching me. God, it makes my flesh creep. How did they get in there?"

"They probably wired the place before you even put the alarm in." I handed her my phone. "Call your little sister. If she's told you where she's going on that telephone, tell her to change her plans."

"Oh, God, you're right. Vivi."

She called, and I listened to her garbled, one-sided conversation for the rest of the drive to my Upper West Side condo. The driver pulled over at the lobby entrance. She was still talking as I paid him.

"... can't stay with me there any longer, Viv. Haven't you been listening? They've been watching us all along! We can't go near the place until we fix this mess. Go to Liam and Nancy's ... yes, I know, I know, but please, be a grown-up, Viv. Being a fifth wheel is better than being stuffed into the backseat of a car ... oh, no, don't worry about me. I'm staying with a friend."

Her eyes flicked to me. Her voice got defensive. "No, you don't know him ... yes, it is a him, okay? And so? What of it?"

I heard a shrill burst of female verbosity from the phone, and Nell snorted. "If you must know, he's the one who clobbered the kidnappers for me ... Yes! Of course I knew him before! He's my new boss."

Another impassioned burst from the phone.

"Look, Viv, I know it's crazy, but can we thrash this out another time?" Nell pleaded. "Come to the seisiún at Malloy's tomorrow night with Nancy and Liam, and we'll talk there, okay? ... Of course. Of course I will. Okay. You be careful, too."

She ended the call and handed the phone back to me. "She's staying with an old art school friend that she met at the crafts fair by chance, and we never discussed that on the bugged phone or my cell, thank God. Snake Eyes has no line on her there."

"Could you folks work all this out once you're outside the car?" the driver asked, his voice plaintive. "I got another call. I gotta go right now."

I led her into my building, dragging her huge suitcase behind me into the elevator. It whooshed up thirty-five floors, and I closed the apartment door after her, engaging the chain, the deadbolts, and the alarm.

I let out a long, relieved breath. Finally, I had her right where I wanted her.

Whoever would've thought it would take this goddamn much effort.

Chapter Thirteen

Nell

I looked around, impressed. His apartment was huge, and almost empty. Austere to the point of chilliness. Blond wood on the wide expanse of gleaming floor. Three gray couches, grouped in a square around a low table with a vast plasma TV and entertainment console. A big, shadowy kitchen sat in a distant corner. Picture windows framed stunning, brilliant cityscapes on two sides. A big terrace. A scattering of black-and-white photographs hung on otherwise blank walls.

"Wow," I murmured. "Is this place, uh ... yours?"

He nodded.

Um. That answered any questions I might've had about how lucrative the business of intelligent data analysis program design had been for him. It beat academia all to hell. Not that it mattered. God knows, I hadn't chosen academia for money.

He disappeared into the kitchen. Lights flipped on. I heard water running, clattering, and clinking. When he came back out, he was holding out a big glass of wine to me. The wine was so densely red it looked almost black.

"This stuff will knock you out on an empty stomach, so sip slowly," he said, taking the roses I still held. "I'll find a jug for these. And I've got water on to boil for some artichoke ravioli, and some red sauce. That work for you?"

I accepted the glass gratefully. "That sounds like heaven."

I savored the complex, aromatic wine as I gazed at the photographs. They were stark, dynamic, full of high contrast. One showed a young man diving off a cliff into a lake. He was still upright, his body starting to jackknife, his face a mask of concentration.

I looked more closely and realized that it was Duncan's brother, Bruce. A younger version.

I studied them all, moving down the hall. There was a young girl curled up asleep, her mouth open. The same girl again, older, laughing, swinging on a rope swing, hair flying like a banner. She was pretty, with the same narrow face and uptilting eyebrows as Duncan. Then a photograph of a handsome older woman in profile, staring off a porch, smoking a cigarette. She looked like Bruce. Mother. Family.

There were landscapes, too. Deserts and mountains, barren and stark. Cruelly sharp contrasts of light and shadow made them almost like moonscapes. They were lonely, aching, extremely personal. I called to the kitchen. "Did you take the pictures?"

"Yeah."

"They're beautiful," I said. "Are there any pictures of your father here?"

He came out of the kitchen and leaned against the entryway, sipping his wine. "No. He's long gone. Haven't seen him in years. Off in California, working on his fifth wife. She's welcome to him."

"Oh." I stared down into the cup of blood-red wine. "I think I can one-up you on that one. I doubt my father even knows of my existence."

"No? Your mom kept it a secret from him?"

I stifled a snort. "In a manner of speaking. Are these landscapes Afghanistan?"

His brow furrowed. "What do you know about Afghanistan?"

"Bruce told me you were stationed there. Said you were a spy."

He grunted. "Bruce babbles a lot. About things he knows shit about."

"So? Did you take them there?" I prodded him, staring at a picture of jagged mountain peaks, the sun a blazing halo behind them.

"Yes, most of them," he said.

"Was that where you learned to fight like that?" I asked.

He hesitated. "More or less."

"Amazing photos," I offered. "I wouldn't have dreamed you had an artistic side."

He looked uncomfortable. "I wouldn't call it that."

"Heaven forbid that you engage in something as frivolous as art," I teased.

He crossed his arms over his chest. "Are you busting my balls?"

"No. I just like your pictures. I like what they say about you."

He looked alarmed. "What do you mean? What do they say?"

"Relax," I soothed. "I couldn't tell you in words. I can't discuss visual art intelligently. I don't know how. I just like the way they make me feel."

A cautious smile started in his narrowed eyes. "Thank you." Duncan lifted his glass.

I lifted my own in response, toasting rare, delicate moments of connection. The very kind that got me worked up and longing for things I could not have. The dangerous kind. The tinkle of crystal was a chime, sweet and faint as a blown kiss. The sound of an unspoken pact, delicately sealed.

Stop it, D'Onofrio. Stop it right now.

I had to stop projecting wishful fantasies onto every single interaction that I had with him. It was stupid and self-destructive.

I'd been privately dubious about the wisdom of eating a plate of pasta at two in the morning, but when Duncan set the plate loaded with plump ravioli, red sauce, and a generous dusting of savory pecorino, something inside me stood up and cheered.

We ate in silence, consuming every last bite. Afterward, he quietly watched me finish my wine. His unwavering gaze made heat rise in my face.

"I expect you're going to want a shower, after a day like this," he said.

I nodded.

"The best one is off my bedroom," he said. "Come this way."

Ah. Well, he could hardly be blamed for assuming, I thought wildly, as I followed him and my suitcase down the hall. Was this what I had intended? And if not this, then what? Get real. Calm down. Go with the flow. Don't be a baby.

He showed me through a vast, minimalist bedroom with a wall of glass that revealed the entire island of Manhattan, and from there to a huge, fabulous en suite bathroom—the shower big enough for an orgiastic army, jets of water pointing in ridiculous directions. He found me a couple of big, fluffy towels, indicated the shower soaps and shampoos, gave me my own personal scrubby sponge—and left. Not joining me in the shower.

Part of me was relieved. A stronger, louder part of me was flatly disappointed. Where was his overbearing alpha male vibe when I needed it?

But he'd gotten all careful and respectful. Probably treating me like blown glass because of my trauma. It was a good sign, actually. He was a good guy. He had self-control. Yay, him.

I stayed in the pounding hot water, wishing sharply that he'd joined me. Looking at him naked and wet would be the most potent distraction I could imagine.

Duncan Burke was all wrong for me. I'd known it even back before he ever spoke to me. His mind was wired in a way that was alien to me. He would annoy, insult, and disillusion me. He already had, and he would do it again. It was a sure thing. A death-and-taxes sort of sure thing.

This, set against the fact that he aroused me to a screaming pitch of excitement. The man was an incredibly gifted lover. There was also the fact that he'd saved my life tonight. He'd used his own body as a shield. That guy had been pointing a gun at us, and Duncan had shoved me behind him. That was something important to factor into the equation—that he was a heroic guy beneath his blunt edges. Brave, valiant, self-sacrificing. Incompatible with me or not. Insensitive to my silly romantic notions or not.

I wanted him. By the time I got out of the shower, my decision was irrevocable. I toweled off, shook my hair free of its clip, and shook it loose.

I hung the towel back on the rack and looked at myself in the mirror, naked but for my ruby pendant Lucia had given me, hanging between those large, full breasts that had always embarrassed me. I'd felt since I was twelve as if my curvy body were flaunting itself against my will, demanding attention that I did not actually want.

But Duncan seemed to like my figure. Finally, the boobs were good for something.

I reached up, touching them gently. They were much more sensitive than usual—goosebumped with delicious anticipation at the thought of what lay ahead.

My nipples tightened in excitement, and I walked out into his bedroom naked.

Duncan had showered in another bathroom and wore a terrycloth robe. He glanced over at me, and gasped.

"Holy God," he said hoarsely. "You're just ... look at you."

"Did I get around to thanking you for saving my life?" I asked him.

He looked alarmed. "I don't think we discussed it, but you certainly don't have to thank me by—"

"Hold it right there," I cut in. "Not another word. There is no exchange being made here. No trading. No payment. This is just me, asking something from you that I want, and hoping I get lucky. So make love to me. Before I lose my nerve."

"You don't have to tell me twice." He took a step toward me.

"I know this is a mistake," I said.

He stopped short, looking perplexed. "What? Why? How do you figure?"

"It's a mistake," I repeated. "But I don't care. Life's too short. I realized that when those guys shoved me into that car, and I thought it was over for me. Everything could go away so quickly. And I like the way you make me feel. I want to feel this."

He reached me, touching a gentle finger to my lips. "Don't work yourself into a state," he said. "Hey. How much wine did you drink?"

"This is not about the wine I drank!" I said savagely. "I know exactly what I'm doing, Duncan Burke! Don't you dare condescend to me!"

"I would never dare," he said forcefully. "You are terrifying."

"Oh really? Do I intimidate you?" I put my hands on my hips, striking a pose.

He blew out a breath, shaking his head. "Some parts of me." He tossed off his robe, displaying his naked body, his huge erection. "Other parts of me are fucking fearless."

Oh, he was perfect. I'd spent all that time admiring his face, but there were riches untold underneath all his clothes, with all those lean, defined, capable-looking muscles, just the right amount of hair, beautiful thighs and flanks, long, narrow feet. And his thick, broad cock. I wanted to touch him all over. Squeeze him. Lick him like a lollipop.

He tossed the comforter back and pushed me until I tumbled backward onto the silvery gray sheet. It was cool against my damp skin. I scrambled up, curling my knees beneath me.

He stood there, erection bobbing right before my eyes. I reached for it, but he grabbed my hands, holding them still. He started to speak, then stopped himself.

"What?" I demanded. "What is it? What's wrong?"

His throat bobbed. "I just don't want to fuck this up again. I don't know what I did wrong the last time."

The raw tone in his voice startled me into a rush of awkward tenderness. I had been so carried away by my own feelings, it never occurred to me that he could feel vulnerable, too. The thought gave me a somewhat unwelcome sense of power.

Elena had wielded power over men whenever she could.

And yet, she had died all alone. There had been no one but me at her funeral, besides the funeral home staff.

I pushed that thought away. I would not let it take any more from me than it had already taken. "You won't fuck up," I told him. "Your instincts are great. You did fine earlier today, in the conference room. You rocked my world. You almost made my heart stop."

"As long as I kept my big mouth shut." He had a rueful tone. "But now things are different now. Those assholes attacked you. I have an adrenaline hard-on. My hands are still shaking. I am not in control. I don't like not being in control—and I'm afraid you wouldn't like it either."

I wanted to smile, but sensed he wouldn't appreciate it. Instead, I ran my finger around the swollen tip of his cock, swirling the slick drop of pre-come until it gleamed.

"Strange," I mused. "This ravenous, howling-at-the-moon beast managed to buy me flowers, bring me to his fancy home, cook me a nice dinner, pour me wine, chat about art, express complex self-observation. Brrr. Such savagery really chills the blood. Besides, I thought sex was all about losing control. Isn't it?"

"Nope," he said flatly. "Not when you're as big as I am. Besides, I can't afford to make more wrong moves with you. You are a goddamn minefield, Nell D'Onofrio."

I swirled my whole hand around his cock, making the tendons stand out on his throat as he swallowed hard. "I'm sorry I'm so difficult," I offered. "Maybe I can make it up to you somehow."

He clambered onto the bed, dragging me close until our bodies touched. His heat was a sweet shock against my skin. The sheer mass of him, the crackling energy, his male scent overlaid with the perfumes of his soap and shampoo—he made my mouth water. I moistened my hand with more of that slick of pre-come and began milking the long, broad stalk slowly, enjoying the hot, pulsing feel of him under my fingers.

"It would be exciting to make you lose control," I whispered.

"Not happening." He slid his hand between my legs, teasing my tender folds open, sighing when he found me already wet and slick.

"No?" I caressed him with both hands—long, tight, sliding strokes while his fingers delved. We stared into each other's eyes. I squirmed around his fingers, my breath catching.

"I'm not afraid of you," I said breathlessly, for no reason I could understand. That was why the sex was so good—apart from his very considerable talent, of course.

He reached down and trapped my hand at his cock, holding it motionless. "Do not provoke me. I'm walking a knife's edge as it is."

I swirled my fingertips teasingly on that thick, pulsing shaft, and with my other hand, I gave his chest a tiny shove.

"What's that about?" he demanded. "How do I read that? You pushing me away?"

I smiled mysteriously up through my lashes. "That's just me, pushing you off your knife's edge."

He let out a rough laugh and shoved me onto my back. "You asked for it."

"I sure did." I wound myself around him. "Don't make me ask you twice."

I wiggled beneath his big body while he rolled the latex onto himself, lungs locked with excitement. He settled between my legs, stroking his hands wonderingly over my body, then inside my thighs. Petting and stimulating the sensitive nub of my clit, until I was gasping and lifting against him. I was so primed, I came almost instantly.

As soon as I could breathe again, he nudged his cock inside

me. The pressure of that his thick cockhead caressing my sensitive inner flesh was delicious, intense. He hooked my legs up over his elbows and began to move.

I gripped his arms, bracing myself against each deep, jarring thrust. I was melting for him, shimmering, liquid. He took his time, finding every sweet spot, tormenting me by stroking it, stimulating it, until I came, and long, sobbing spasms of delight wracked my body. And then he would start again. Over and over, until he finally let go, in a hard, pounding, thundering finish.

I could barely move. He got up at one point, got rid of the condom. Then he slid back between the sheets and wrapped me in this arms, holding me tight against his big, hot chest. It felt wonderful. I snuggled against him, suspended in a liquid dream.

But a needle-thin part of my mind stayed apart, wondering how long this sweet dream could possibly last.

Chapter Fourteen

Duncan

I was disoriented when I woke. I'd trained myself to wake at a quarter to five a.m., used to having my eyes open while the sky was still dark, my mind clear and sharp, already generating a streamlined plan of attack for the day's work.

But the sky wasn't dark. The room was flooded with light. And my mind was soft, floating, full of an intense, glowing sensation of well-being. The flower-like scent of silky dark ringlets tickled my nose, and the startled rush jolted me fully awake.

Nell. In my apartment, in my bed, in my arms. I still couldn't get over how soft she was. Her skin beneath my hands was as fine as a baby's. She slept with her back to me, her round, perfect ass pressed against my hips. And predictably, my body reacted.

The urge to roll her onto her belly and slide into the hot grip of her luscious body took all my mental strength to resist.

Too dangerous. I had no idea how she'd feel about being here with me when she woke up.

Better that she didn't wake up with my cock already inside her.

So I nuzzled her neck, and memorized the graceful angle of bones and tendons under her soft skin, that little brown mole on her neck, the way the grain of her hair swirled in wild vortices at her nape. The responsive skin there, perfumed and decorated with fine downy hair. The gold chain of her pendant.

I scooted back, just enough to let her roll onto her back, so I could admire her tits. World-class—luscious, plump, and perfect—the way they swelled out, the tight brown nipples. The glittering pendant lay on her collarbone, catching the light.

My self-control snapped. I cupped her breasts in my hands, pressing my face into that perfect, silken softness, and something inside me gave way, like a landslide.

I went at her, licking and sucking ravenously, and she woke with a gasp, stiffening beneath me. The startled sounds she made soon turned into a whimper of pleasure. Her arms wrapped around my neck, offering herself.

I rolled over, settling between her legs, and she opened them, arching and wrapping her thighs around mine in mute invitation.

I grabbed my rigid cock, petting the slick, tight silken folds of her perfect little pussy until I found the right spot, the right angle, and slowly pushed my cock inside her.

The slow, excruciatingly naked slide into her slick warmth was going to kill me. "Oh, fuck," I gasped. So much for eloquence. Poetry.

Her half-lidded eyes popped open as we both remembered latex at the same time. But it was too fucking good to stop. I rocked, sliding deeper. So tight, so wet, so impossibly hot. Like she was clutching me, sucking me, licking me with her pussy.

I struggled to speak. "I won't come inside you," I promised.

"But I ... we haven't even discussed—"

"I'm safe," I told her. "I've tested negative for everything in my last physical. Swear it. And I never do it without protection. I won't come inside you, I swear. It just feels so good with you. You drive me out of my fucking mind."

She laughed, a wispy, breathless sound. "Um. Same here." She wiggled beneath me, her eyes dazed. "I'm safe too, disease-wise," she said slowly. "And, um ... I'm on the pill. I use it to keep my cycle regular. So, that's not an issue. So, ah ..."

I slid deeper, letting her take all of me, silently jubilant. "So? So what?"

She lifted her hips. "So give it to me."

And we were off at a wild, hard gallop. My body had its own agenda. The scalding heat of her—the raw immediacy of naked skin to skin—was like nothing I'd ever known or imagined. It opened up parts of me I hadn't known were there.

It was Nell. She was magic. She was poetry. She was music. She was red-hot, honeyed, writhing perfection beneath me, around me.

I lifted myself up to see it all—the base of my cock gleaming with her slickness, her tender pink pussy stretched around my shaft, hugging and caressing as I plunged and surged. Her soft, shapely thighs open for me, the lush curves of her body, her tits bouncing with each hard thrust.

The look in her eyes made something break open in my chest, but I didn't have time to be afraid of it because my body was charging forward, desperately chasing the beacon of her impending orgasm. Like I'd die if I didn't overtake it and make it my own.

She tightened, trembling, and I cried out, as pleasure obliterated me.

Panting, still reeling, I collapsed beside her, pressing my

face into her neck, feeling the golden chain of her necklace against my lips.

After a few minutes, she pulled away and slid off the bed, mumbling something about a shower.

"I'll make you breakfast," I called after her before the bathroom door clicked shut.

I yanked on some sweatpants. My eyes slid to the small silver digital clock on my dresser. I was so startled to see it read nine thirty-seven, I checked my phone to see if it was true. I was usually up at a quarter to five, and out the door by five-fifteen on my way to the gym. In the office by seven. Seven-ten at the very latest.

Well, hell. So I was late today. Being the boss had to be good for something.

Who knew? Maybe I'd get lucky again. The thought floated me right into the kitchen, where I started rummaging for breakfast.

Then the phone rang. Nobody on earth called this landline but my mother.

Of all times. Christ. I picked up. "Yeah?"

"Duncan, honey! Thank goodness! I called the office, but you weren't there! What on earth?" She paused, significantly. "Are you sick? Is anything wrong? You never stay home from work!"

"I'm fine. Just working from home this morning. What's going on?"

"It's Elinor. You will not believe what she's done!"

I sighed. "What about her?"

"She's switched her major to theater arts! She dropped all her business courses and signed up for theater history and dance! She wants to be an actress!" My mother's voice cracked with horror.

I stared at the scabbed-up scrapes on my knuckles, flexing

and bending them to keep them from stiffening up. "So?" I said. "What's the problem? It's her decision."

"Oh, not you, too, Duncan. Bruce said that too, but it's madness to go into theater! You have to talk sense into her!"

Hah. Me, talking sense into anyone on a day like today was comical. I glanced toward the corridor, waiting for my problematic, sexy siren to appear.

I was no longer the poster boy for doing the sensible thing. But I also didn't want to get into it with my mother today. "I'll talk to her, if you want," I offered.

"Oh, thank you. She'll listen to you. It's not too late to change her major back." My mother's voice was relieved.

"Okay, Mom. Gotta go. Later, okay?" I hung up and went back to the fridge.

Nell appeared in the doorway just as I was laying out French toast, grilled ham, and orange juice on the table. She looked damp, rosy, and fragrant. She gazed at the food-laden table, her eyes big. "Whoa," she said. "Look at that. So you cook, too?"

"I like to eat, so yeah," I said. "I hope you're hungry."

She sat down with a murmur of appreciation and tucked into a gratifying amount of the breakfast that I'd made. Afterward, we sipped our coffee and stared at each other across the table. Neither of us could hold the other's gaze for more than a few seconds without looking away or laughing. Jesus. Look at me. Giggling. Touching her toes under the table with my own bare feet, like a goofy kid.

But it was getting on toward ten-thirty now, and I had to get my shit together. "I have to get down to the office," I said reluctantly.

She glanced at the clock. "I have to hurry, too. I'm going to be late for lunch prep as it is."

"You're going where?" I grabbed her wrist. She let out a small gasp and stared at my hand.

I didn't let go. "You are going where, you said?"

Her eyes got big and wary. "Duncan. Let go of my arm."

"Answer my question," I insisted.

"I'm going to work," she said crisply. "At the Sunset Grill! Remember?" She yanked at her wrist again. "I work there six days a week! As you should know, since you eat there six days a week!"

"Not today," I said. "You're not working there today."

She jerked in vain at her arm. "Excuse me? Why not? I'm just supposed to stop everything I do?"

"Yes!" I snarled. "After what happened to you last night, you think I'm going to let you just walk out onto the streets? Like nothing even happened?"

"Let me?" Her voice was soft and dangerous. "Duncan, watch yourself. You aren't going to 'let me' do anything. Because I don't have to ask your permission for anything I do. Not now. Not ever. Is that clear?"

"Wrong," I said.

She stared at me, and slowly shook her head. "That will never fly," she said. "You would have to genuinely sequester me, like a criminal. I'm talking, with rope, duct tape, and a gag. I really don't think so. That's not who you are."

"Goddamn it, Nell! If I hadn't been there last night, you'd be dead! I changed the course of the way things went for you last night, and that gives me some responsibility. That gives me a say. So deal with me. You don't have any choice."

"Let go of my arm, Duncan," she said quietly. "You're scaring me."

"Fine! It's about fucking time you were scared!"

I let go of her wrist, and she rubbed it, avoiding my eyes. "You don't seem to understand my situation," she said. "I am broke, Duncan. The Snake Eyes situation ate up all my savings. I spent so much on that damned alarm system, and so much on taxis and cars, and I'm already a month behind on my rent. I don't even have money for cab fare today, if I don't get out there and go to work. And Norma depends on me. I won't just bag on my employer with no warning, unless I have a broken limb or a contagious disease! It's irresponsible. I was raised better than that."

"I'll give you money," I said. "As much as you need."

Her mouth tightened. "That's not a solution, Duncan."

"Why not?" I demanded. "You, waltzing out into the street, into your stalker's arms? You call that a solution? Those assholes picked you up off a main thoroughfare, Nell. In downtown Manhattan, in front of multiple witnesses! By now, they know who I am and where I live. They'll watch this place, too. They will nail you down eventually. They will find a way, when your guard is down. You can count on it. You have to change your mindset if you want to survive. So does your little sister, incidentally."

She blew out a sigh, looking exhausted and lost. "Duncan, that may be true, but it doesn't matter. I don't have any choice but to work. I have to pay my rent, and I—"

"Oh, you mean that place with the bugged phone, the compromised alarm, and the hostile video cameras?"

"I still have to pay for it!" she said. "Unless I find some other place to—"

"Here," I cut in. "Stay right here. With me."

Her face was blank, her mouth open. "I ... ah ..."

"It's the best solution," I said. "There's plenty of room. The security's excellent."

Nell threw up her hands. "Duncan, no!" she wailed. "No! I can't! That's very sweet, but it's premature, and in any case, I still have to work!"

"No, you don't. Norma will manage. She doesn't want you to get killed, either. And it's not premature. Not after last night. Work on game texts, if you have to work on something." I gave her a hard, direct stare. "I don't need help with rent or the groceries."

"I noticed that." Her voice was acid. "So what does this mean?"

I shrugged. "What does it sound like?"

She fixed me with a piercing gaze. "It sounds to me like I'd be kept."

"It sounds to me like you'd be safe," I countered.

"Safe, yes. And sexually available to you, twenty-four-seven?"

Anger uncoiled inside me, hot and red. "Would that be so terrible?"

She flicked that away with a sharp wave of her hand. "That's not what I mean," she said. "The sex is not the problem. On the contrary. The sex is great. It's not that."

"Well, thank God for that," I said. "So what is your fucking problem, Nell? Is it that I have a lot of money? Big fucking deal. I worked for it. I have highly remunerative skills. You want to punish me for that?"

"No," she snapped. "It's not that."

"Then why are you so uptight about accepting help from me? Because it is starting to mortally piss me off!"

She cleared her throat. "My mother was a prostitute," she said.

Of all the things she could have told me, that was the last one I expected. "Huh?" I floundered. "Who? You don't mean ... the lady who got ..."

"No. Not her. That was Lucia, my adoptive mother." Nell's voice was colorless. "I'm talking about my birth mother. Elena Pisani. She wasn't a streetwalking kind of prostitute. She was always kept in style by rich lovers. Nice apartments, beautiful clothes, jewels, spas, spending money. But in the end, that part's just window dressing."

A heavy silence followed her words, and I struggled for something intelligent to say. "Why are you telling me this?" I asked.

She fixed me with her blazing look, the one that intimidated and aroused me all at once. "I remember her hammering out the details of each new mutually beneficial arrangement. As soon as she was done, off I'd go to another boarding school. Until the guy got bored with her, or she found a richer client."

I searched for a way to contextualize this new and dangerous information, but it wouldn't stick to anything. "Oh. I, uh, see."

"Do you?" She looked away. "It looked all right on the surface, I guess. We were safe, fed, clothed, provided for. But her whole existence revolved around her patrons. Their schedules, their egos, their convenience, their tempers. She didn't have any energy to spare for me. She didn't dare prioritize me. Ever. Then she died and I was absolutely alone. It was so fucking sad, it practically destroyed me."

"I ... ah ..." I floundered for something to say that wasn't stupid or offensive.

"I don't want a man to be the center of my life. I don't want to circle around him, dependent on him, subject to his whims, anxiously scrambling to please him. Fuck that. I've got plans and ambitions of my own. I will not get anywhere near that slippery slope, Duncan. Under no circumstances."

"I never meant to imply that," I said helplessly.

"It kind of implies itself," she said. "I'm sorry this embarrasses you. You're trying to be kind, and help me, and keep me safe. And I appreciate that. I really do. But I have my issues about it, and this is why. Since you were curious."

I closed my eyes for a moment to calm myself down, let my thoughts settle, and then walked over to her. I took her hands, and held them. Then kissed them.

"You misunderstood me," I said. "I would never, not in a million years, think that you were for sale. You, of all people." I lifted her hands to my lips again. "What happened between us is precious, and magical. Like a unicorn. It can't be bought."

A flush reddened her cheeks. I was heartened by that.

"Thanks for saying that," she said. "But I still have to go to work."

I let out a slow, very controlled breath. It was compromise or die, and I wasn't ready to die. "Then I'll drive you," I announced. "But we'd better get moving."

Chapter Fifteen

Nell

I listened to the shower through the bathroom door, thinking of his amazing, powerful naked body in there under the pounding stream, water and soapsuds cascading over his contoured muscles. I was so tempted to just peel off my clothes and join him.

But no. He was never quick. It would be long and wet and steaming and soapy and marvelous, and we would both forget all practical issues, getting to work on time, making money, safeguarding my self-respect, meeting my professional obligations. I was already missing the lunch prep. He had completely disarmed me, charmed me, bamboozled me. He'd wrapped me around his little finger.

Or, well ... maybe something a little more substantial.

I stared at the suit he'd slung upon the bed. I didn't know much about fashion, having remained deliberately ignorant of it, but I recognized the elegant cut and fine finishing of costly, bespoke men's clothing when I saw it. Many thousands of dollars lay there on that rumpled bed, in those smooth, graceful silver-gray garments. He looked so good in his clothes. Though it was more a function of his gorgeous body than skill on the tailor's part. Having seen him naked, I could bear witness to that personally.

I went back out into the front room. The roses had been stuck into a jug with some water, but the stems were too long for the vessel. I rummaged around, with the half-formed intention of looking for a vase in the kitchen. Such a sweet thought, last night, for him to stop and get me roses, after everything.

Some of the roses had wilted, bruised petals scattering over the gleaming wood floor. I gathered them up, carried them into his bedroom and on impulse, slipped some of them into the pockets of his suit jacket, and went out for a final cup of coffee.

He came out into the kitchen, fully dressed, clean-shaven and fragrant.

Our cautious truce lasted all the way down to the Sunset Grill, but as I was getting out of his car, he pulled me toward him and gave me a hard, possessive kiss.

"One more thing," he said. He pulled a smartphone out of his pocket, one of the extravagant, ridiculously expensive ones. "Take this. No arguments."

I rolled my eyes at him. "I was going to buy a fresh flip phone today anyhow. I don't need one with all the bells and whistles, Duncan."

"No way," he said. "You swore a blood oath that you would not leave the restaurant until I came to get you. Remember?"

That made me laugh. "A blood oath? Really?"

"Take the phone. Don't fight me on this. My number's programmed in."

I looked down to his big hand, clamped around my wrist, and realized that I could not win this fight. He would not let me go unless I gave in, and for God's sake, why didn't I? I was fighting just on principle. I couldn't afford this bullshit.

I slipped his phone into my purse. "Thank you," I said primly. "I hope I manage to use it. If I don't answer, it's because I can't figure out how, so don't take it personally."

"You know how to answer a damn phone," he said. "Keep it in your apron pocket at the restaurant. I'll call to check on you. And I'll give you holy hell if you're not reachable."

I laughed out loud. "Don't bug me while I'm working, Burke."

Chapter Sixteen

The guy worked fast. He was fucking her, already.

John chewed the inside of his cheek until he tasted blood. Antonella disappeared into the Sunset Grill, smiling, her face rosy red. Saddlesore from being fucked all night long. That dirty little slut.

Burke's silver Mercedes pulled out into Eighth Avenue traffic.

He was already chronically angry, dealing with that pinheaded dipshit Haupt night and day. John was starting to consider resorting to recreational murder just to unload some fucking stress, or he was going to start having panic attacks.

Nell had been celibate all those weeks that John had been watching her. Such a good little girl. Sleeping alone, with her piles of books, like a sexy, succulent little nun in her maidenly scholarly chamber. Not anymore. She'd spoiled his fantasy.

She would pay for that. And that scenario was its own pleasant fantasy. He was good at making the best of situations. Turning them into opportunities for satisfaction.

He'd have to punish her severely for soiling herself. Just like her sister, cheating on him with that randy carpenter, Knightly. That dumb fuckhead was slated to die a slow and ugly death himself, as soon as it was convenient for John to organize it. Same with this rich computer prick.

The list of possible targets for recreational murder was growing.

He wondered idly if the youngest girl was as much of a slut as her sisters. Probably more so, with the tattoo, the nose ring, the painted van like some relic from the sixties.

They were all misbehaving bitches. He'd punish them all. Thinking about it made him hard, but speed dialing Haupt's number wilted him fast.

He gritted his teeth, resigned to the scolding he was about to receive.

The geezer picked up with no salutation and just waited for a report, line open. Telegraphing his disgust his flat silence.

"She's back at the restaurant now," John said. "Burke brought her in his own car. Looks like he's fucking her."

"And upon what do you base this deduction?"

John's lip curled. "The way he stuck his tongue down her throat before she walked into the restaurant was my first clue."

"Tell me more about Burke," Haupt demanded.

John rifled through the documents he'd spent the night collecting. "He could be trouble," he admitted. "Ex-undercover field agent from the NSA, turned successful businessman. Designs software for the NSA, the CIA, Homeland Security, and various others. Close connections with various law enforcement agencies. I had difficulty getting info on him. Most of it's top secret."

"I see. Then you must be happy, John. Now you have a plausible justification for your incompetence, eh?"

John tapped on the console of his car with his fingernails and considered various options in killing this old shitbird after he'd gotten paid. In fact, he was starting to consider fucking the old goat out of the entire prize. At this point, that was the only outcome that could make this constant, grinding humiliation worthwhile.

And if it ruined his professional reputation, who cared? He'd be so rich, it wouldn't matter. He would retire. Live high on the hog. Kill for fun when the pressure built up.

"It does make things a little bit more complicated," he said evenly.

"Does it? And the idiot carpenter with his violin was complicated for you too, eh? The carpenter was no fucking NSA secret agent. Did Turturro have any luck with the younger sister?"

"No," he said reluctantly. "He combed that crafts fair for hours. Apparently she never showed up. Or maybe she left early."

"Of course. She is not an idiot, unlike others I could name. Stay right on Antonella, John. Do not delegate. Do not lose her again. Your hired muscle has, so far, failed miserably to help. Did she take any of her bugs when she went to Burke's apartment?"

"Just the laptop. I put a listening device in it."

"Good. Stay on her at all times, no matter where she is. Failure is not an option."

Haupt hung up, and John's teeth ground until his jaw ached. He needed to kill someone, and soon. The asshole who was fucking Antonella was the perfect choice. He was still smarting from Burke's brazen challenge, through the camera.

You're not getting her. Fuck off and die, shithead.

Oh yeah? Burke would die for that. Antonella would, too ... but much more slowly.

First, she would pay for everyone's sins.

Chapter Seventeen

Duncan

It was the oddest sensation. I observed it as I drove to the parking garage, parked in my spot, and tipped the bewildered garage attendant. Like a helium balloon was inside me, lifting me up. Floating me along. People were giving me strange looks.

Of course, I realized. I was grinning like a fool. My face hurt, for fuck's sake.

But damn, was it so abnormal to be in a good mood? Was I that bad normally?

The middle-aged lady behind the coffee counter in the building lobby gave me a strange look when I tossed a few bucks in her jar and told her I liked her as a redhead. It was the truth. She'd looked like hell as a blonde.

Damn. It was like nobody'd ever seen a guy in a good mood before.

I headed up to the office. The grizzled divorce attorney in

the elevator gave me a dark look and harrumphed. Maybe dealing with divorce all day gave a guy gastritis.

I strode into the lobby. Derek was there with piles of paper on his desk, briskly collating something. He dressed for a Saturday, in jeans and a T-shirt.

"Morning, Derek," I said.

Derek looked at me as if I'd sprouted wings. "Uh, hi, boss. Everything okay? You're, uh, later than usual."

"It's all good. By the way. I really appreciate you working Saturdays," I told him.

Derek's big eyes bulged even more than usual. "Uh, it's no problem."

I clapped him on the shoulder as I passed his desk. "You get paid extra for Saturdays, right?"

"Time and a half." Derek's face was almost fearful.

"Good. I'll tack on a bonus. You deserve it. Keep it up."

The hell? Derek didn't blink an eye when I snapped and barked at him, but a simple compliment scared him to death. Come to think of it, all of my die-hard Saturday employees were giving me a nervous look and a very wide berth. I started glancing down to see if my shoes were mismatched or my fly unzipped. Everything seemed to be in order.

I shrugged inwardly. Fuck it. I was having too good a time to worry about it.

The phone began to ring the moment I walked into my office. My private line. A fully formed fantasy leaped into my mind, that it was Nell calling to tell me she was in a good mood, too. This daydream was quickly deflated by the recollection that Nell did not have my office landline number. Answering the phone became suddenly less appealing. I sighed and grabbed the phone. "Burke here."

"So you finally came in to the office!" My mother's voice

sounded even more chirpy than usual. "What on earth is going on?" She paused expectantly.

"Nothing at all," I said blandly. "Same old stuff. Business as usual."

"Well, if you don't tell me, I'll just have to find out some other way. Have you talked to Elinor?"

My good mood was about to be put to the test. "No, Mom. I haven't had time yet."

"Duncan, it's so important that she change her mind before she makes decisions she can't go back on! She's determined to rebel. Please, you have to back me up on this—"

"I'll call her," I said. "As soon as you get off the phone."

I extricated myself from the conversation as quickly as I could, and punched in Elinor's number without even thinking about it. Might as well get this over with quickly. My mother was a piece of work if not managed carefully.

Elinor's roommate, Mimi, picked up the phone. Loud, incoherent music pulsed in the background. "Who is it?" Mimi shrieked.

"It's Elinor's brother. May I speak to her?"

"Elinor's brother? Like, which one? The bodaciously cute one, or the stuffed-shirt one?"

"The stuffed-shirt one," I specified patiently.

"Yo, Ellie!" Mimi screeched, as I winced and held the phone away from my ear. "It's your bro! The stuffed-shirt one!" Mimi listened to some muffled yapping, and said, "She's coming. Hang on." There was a loud, rattling clunk, and I leaned back in my chair, started to shrug off my coat, and stopped myself. I couldn't take off the coat. I was wearing the SIG. Shit. I put my hand in my suit pocket and yanked it out with a gasp, startled by the soft, silky texture.

Rose petals scattered, fluttering, all over the desk, my chair, my lap, the floor.

I laughed out loud, and a graphic designer and a junior accountant to peer through my open door, eyes big. They thought I was losing it.

"Hello? Hello?"

I yanked my attention back to the telephone, and Elinor's voice. "It's Duncan."

"Hi." Elinor sounded guarded. "Did Mother tell you to call?"

I paused for a second. "Ahhh—"

"You're supposed to convince me to change my major back to econ, right? You want me to consider my retirement plan, split-level suburban home, station wagon, and cemetery plot, right? Not! Forget it. I'm not going to embalm myself before I even start to live! So don't even try, Dunc. Just don't even start."

"That's great," I said, without hesitating. "Congratulations. Go for it."

There was an uncertain pause. Elinor pressed on. "You can't make me change my mind," she said, more uncertainly. "I really think that I've got what it takes to—"

"Of course you do," I agreed. "I never doubted it for a minute."

There was a confused silence from Elinor. "Ah ... what the hell?"

"You'll be great. Give it your best shot. I'll cheer you on." *And probably pay for your grad school myself,* I thought, but even that prospect could not dent my buzz.

"You're not being sarcastic, are you?" Elinor sounded bewildered.

"Jesus, Ellie." I sifted the soft, bruised petals through my fingers, marveling at the glowing depth of the crimson color. "Am I that much of an asshole?"

"Nah, I was just, you know. Wondering if an alien took over your body."

"Not lately. That I know of." I buried my nose in the petals. Like Nell's skin. So soft.

"Mother's gonna kill you," Elinor predicted cheerfully.

"I don't doubt it," I agreed.

Elinor explained her epiphany about following her heart at great length, and it all seemed completely reasonable in my current mood. We wound up our conversation, and I stared at the crimson mass of rose petals as the balloon inside me steadily reinflated.

Well, that was that. I was officially done being the designated buzzkill and wet blanket of the family. Why had I ever taken on that role to begin with? A psychologist would probably say something about being the oldest son in a family with no father, blah-blah-blah, but I was not interested in thinking about that right now. Talk about a buzzkill. I entered the number of the phone that I'd given Nell that morning, stroking a petal while it rang, savoring the anticipation.

"Hello?" came her low, musical voice. "Duncan?"

"I found the petals," I announced.

In her pause, I could actually feel her smiling that secret little smile that drove me totally wild with lust. "And? I hope they didn't embarrass you."

"Nothing could embarrass me today," I told her.

She let out a snort of laughter. "Look. Um, Duncan? It's great to hear your voice, and you're sweet to call, but I'm sort of in the middle of the lunch rush, so could we—"

"Do rose petals go bad, like vegetables, or do they dry out?"

"They dry out." There was laughter in her voice. "Do you think I would've filled your pockets with something that turns to slime?"

"I can't wait for your shift to end," I told her.

"Me neither. Bye."

I tried to concentrate, but all the urgent, pressing business that grimly occupied me on every other day seemed trivial today—a whole lot less interesting, too.

And I called Nell so often, she started to snap at me and hang up on me—but always with laughter in her voice. I'd never been the type who had any luck making girls laugh before, but I finally understood why guys worked so hard at it. It was an irresistible feeling. I'd do any crazy thing to get that gurgle of laughter out of her.

Meetings, conference calls. Seconds ticked by—heavily, laboriously. My employees were acting strange, too. I caught several whispering conversations, cut off when I walked by. Smothered bursts of laughter. Bruce had a shit-eating grin plastered all over his face. It would've bugged the shit out of me if I hadn't been in this altered state.

Gant called in the afternoon, and that snapped me right into razor-sharp mode. He was with his buddy Braxton, another ex-agent from our NSA days, a guy who now ran a security outfit. He was expensive as all fuck, but I arranged for Nell's apartment to be bug swept as soon as I got access to a set of keys.

Not that I intended for her to spend any more time there. Not safe. Or particularly comfortable, either.

I had a nice big extra room in my apartment that was still empty. All her bookcases would fit into it, plus a desk, a chair—a couch, even. Nell's studio. I loved the very thought of it.

Anything Braxton could reveal would inform us about our opponent's resources and agenda. That made it well worth every penny. The thought of having that conversation with Nell made me nervous, but hey. I would be as charming as I knew how to be. Which wasn't saying a lot, but hell, a guy could try.

At ten to five p.m., I just gave in to it. It was hours earlier than I usually left, but I wasn't getting a damn thing done around here. I might as well head to the Sunset Grill, park my ass there, and make sure she didn't leave the place alone—personally.

Nell was scheduled to work for three hours on the game texts with Bruce, from six until nine. That was ridiculous, considering that she'd just come off a long shift of waitressing. She pushed herself way too hard. I could pull rank, tell Bruce it wasn't happening tonight. Insist that she cut out early, considering all of last night's drama. We could grab dinner somewhere before we met her sisters at the Irish pub. That was an encounter I tried not to think about. I didn't want social anxiety to kill my buzz, and it absolutely could. I wasn't great in groups. Hell, I wasn't great one-on-one either, most of the time.

And I had to shut down this line of thought right fucking now.

I was kissed by the gods and found a good parking spot not too far from the Sunset Grill. I went in, heart thudding, and scanned the place until I saw her, swathed in her sunset orange apron, hair twisted up and corkscrewing around her face. She looked pale, tired, harassed. And freaking drop-dead beautiful.

She glanced over at me and promptly bumped into a table. I was at her side in two steps, reaching to steady her tray, but she pulled back with a hiss of warning, spilling half a bowl of French onion soup.

"Nope! Thanks, but I can manage. What the hell are you doing here? It's early!"

"It's a restaurant, right? Don't I have the right to come in here?"

"Yes, of course," she said, biting her lower lip. "But all the tables are full. You can wait fifteen minutes for one, or you can sit at the counter."

I seated myself at the free stool at the end of the counter. The place was hopping, with late lunchers and early diners everywhere. Nell and a red-headed girl were the only servers, and both were running frantically. I watched Nell grace her clients with her luminous smile, carrying loaded trays that looked far too heavy for her. She sneaked the occasional glance at me, and some minutes later she made it back to me with the coffeepot.

"Stop staring," she whispered. "It's making me nervous."

"What's with you?" I asked as she poured my coffee. "You seem tense."

"Oh, am I?" She snorted. "Hah. It's nothing. Business as usual. Money problems. Credit card debt. A bugged apartment. Armed kidnappers shoving me into a car. Nights of wild monkey sex with a hot but overbearing man who's practically a stranger to me. Then I get to work and discover that not only does Kendra have one of her weird illnesses, but Pete broke his toe, so we're short-staffed. And now you're here, staring at me the way a hungry cheetah stares at a zebra. Other than that, I'm fine. Let me take your order. Strip steak, I presume?"

"No. Actually, I ordered out for lunch a few hours ago," I told her.

Her eyebrow lifted. "Oh. Then why are you here?"

"I wanted to see you," I said. "I couldn't wait anymore."

Nell bit her luscious lower lip, a blush warming her cheeks. "Well. That's lovely, Duncan, and I appreciate it, but we have an eight-dollar minimum during the dinner shift."

"More coffee," I said. "And my usual dessert. I fully intend to burn it off later."

She gave me a disapproving look. "You should try something new. I think today I've earned the right to insist on it." She marched away.

"So. You're the one, eh?" a gravelly female voice said.

166

I looked across the counter into the clear gray eyes of a strong-jawed, wide-hipped lady of about seventy, the one who was usually in the kitchen. "Excuse me? What one?"

The woman smartly dressed a tray of salads and passed it across the counter to the redheaded waitress. The waitress leaned over my shoulder from behind, popped fragrant strawberry gum in my ear, and studied me as if I were some strange species of mold in a petri dish. "Not bad," she commented. "Big. I like 'em big."

"I'm Norma," the older woman said, examining me over the lenses of her glasses. "I own this joint. And you're Strip Steak."

Being defined in terms of my lunch choices was a new experience for me. "Duncan Burke, at your service," I said.

"Duncan Burke. So you're the one," Norma said again, wrapping silverware in napkins and stacking them on a tray with machine-like efficiency.

I took a cautious sip of my coffee. "What one am I?"

"The one who's taking away my right-hand woman. At the worst possible time."

"Nothing personal," I said. "Sorry, ma'am, but it's a dog-eat-dog world out there."

"Don't I know it," Norma replied, her voice steely. "And in light of that specific fact, I'd like to take this opportunity to tell you what a prize you've got in her."

My coffee cup stopped halfway to my mouth.

Norma went on. "I heard about that kerfuffle last night, see. You, saving her from those guys on the street. Very good. Bravo. I like that you can handle yourself in a tight situation. That's a good quality in a man. Very useful. But it's not enough."

I blinked. "Uh ... it's not?"

"No. Not for Nell. Nell's special. Sensitive, brilliant, empathetic, kind. She deserves an absolute top-shelf experience. She has more to give than you could possibly imagine."

I started to feel hunted. "How do you know what I can imagine?"

"Sorry, honey, but any guy who orders the same lunch every day for six weeks in a row has serious issues with his imagination," Norma told me, not without sympathy.

The redheaded waitress swooped by and leaned over my shoulder again. "But don't despair, big guy," she said, popping her gum in my ear again. "You can make up for a lot of that intellectual imagination stuff in bed, if you treat her good. And I mean, like, really, really good, get it? Life's a series of trade-offs, see. So work to your strengths."

"An excellent point," Norma agreed. "Keep it in mind. But beware. If you don't treat her like a goddess, you'll have me to answer to."

I forced my mouth to close, and coughed to clear my throat. "Just what are you implying, ma'am?"

"That depends entirely on you," Norma said crisply. "You see, unfortunately, our Nell is an orphan twice over. There aren't parents around to judge you, interrogate you, and generally break your balls." She pointed at her chest. "But here I am, Strip Steak—ready and willing to pick up the slack. I can be worse than the very worst mother-in-law you could imagine. More unreasonable, more demanding, more critical, more nitpicking. Beware. That's what you're up against. Stay on your toes. Don't get lazy. Don't get complacent. Mind your manners."

"Yeah," the redhead piped up. "And there's me, too. And Monica. And don't forget her two sisters. Mess with Nell, and Nancy and Vivi will rip you open and toss your entrails into the gutter. And I'll be right there with 'em, knife in hand."

I considered that startling image for a moment. "So, uh, what exactly are you getting at? Do you want me to formally declare that my intentions are honorable?"

Norma's smile turned approving. "Well, would you look at that, Carla. He's quicker than he looks. I like the way your mind works, fella. You're on the right track."

Nell appeared with a plate. "Here's your dessert. Carla, table five needs a slice of Black Forest and a Key Lime, and they're in a rush, okay?"

Carla gave her gum a final loud pop and sashayed away as Nell set down the dessert. It was not apple pie with ice cream. It was a fluffy, quivering yellow-and-white confection with towering whipped cream, cradled in a buttery, crimped crust.

"I decided you needed a change of pace." There was a note of challenge in her voice. "This is a house specialty. Banana cream pie. You must try it. I insist."

She stared at him, her soft mouth stubborn. Norma stared, too, from behind the counter, her chubby arms crossed across her voluminous bosom. Seconds ticked by.

This was not about pie. This was some subtle test that I could not afford to fail. And besides, God knows, I was doing plenty of insisting myself lately, so it was only fair.

Aw, what the fuck. It was just pie. I forked up a bite. "It's good," I said automatically. Then I took another bite and realized that it was true. It was amazing.

Nell's face relaxed. Norma harrumphed and stumped away to serve a customer at the other end of the counter.

Nell leaned down to my ear. "What did those two maniacs say to you?"

"I was just informed that I should declare my intentions," I told her. "I was warned that if I don't treat you like the shining goddess you are, I'll be sliced wide open by all your soul sisters and my steaming viscera tossed out into the street."

"Oh God." Nell turned a delicate pink. "No. They didn't."

"Verbatim," I said solemnly. "Swear to God."

"I'm going to kill them."

"It's fine," I said. "I actually like that you have friends who'll make death threats for you." With no warning, I was laughing. Then she was laughing, too. People were looking—and I didn't care.

It felt great.

Chapter Eighteen

Nell

He kept catching my eye, giving me that wicked grin that scrambled my brain. Those deep dimples, carving sexy lines into his cheeks. He'd done it in the restaurant and made me screw up a bunch of the dinner orders. He'd done it on the drive back to his office building. And now he was doing it again, right now, from behind his desk, while I was trying to concentrate on Bruce's game texts. I crossed my legs and tried to catch my breath. That bad bastard. It wasn't fair.

"Nell? Earth to Nell? Do you have any of them finished yet?"

I jerked my gaze back to Bruce. "Uh, do I have what finished?"

Bruce was hanging on to his patience. "The manuscripts for the goblin caves! Did you get those done? I need to submit them to the graphic artists! Soon!"

"Ah ... um ..." I winced. What with last night's attackers, and the police station, and the protracted bouts of incredible sex, I hadn't had a second to work on the game. In fact, I'd forgotten about the existence of the game. "I'm so sorry, Bruce, but I—"

"She's been busy," Duncan said.

Bruce's eyes narrowed. He looked from Duncan to Nell. "Busy? With what? More than usual?"

I felt myself begin to blush. "My life's been kind of crazy lately. If you want, I'll try to whip something up right now."

"Okay, but I was hoping to brainstorm about the octagonal tower and the magic mirrors right now, to get a jump on those for next week. And how about the prophesies for the cursed tomb of the lost kings? Have you started in on those yet?"

I resisted the urge to excuse myself for slacking off. "Not yet, but I have some ideas," I said. "They'll all need to be encrypted, though. Is the program ready?"

"I roughed out a Rosetta stone last night." Bruce looked like he was on the edge of pouting. "We'll be here till midnight if we want to have a chance in hell of finishing—"

"No," Duncan cut in. "She's been waitressing all day, and last night, she got attacked on the street."

Bruce looked at me, shocked. "Attacked?"

"Yeah. I was, ah, mugged," I mumbled. "Fortunately, Duncan was there. He scared them off."

Bruce looked at his brother. "Dude! You didn't say anything about a battle with the forces of evil on the streets of Manhattan! Mom is going to freak!"

"Not if you don't tell her," Duncan said. "In any case, Nell needs dinner and rest. Plus, she has an appointment at nine in Queens. It's not happening tonight."

Bruce looked from him to me, and back again. Slowly, a grin spread across his face. "I see," he said. "Does she need her beauty rest, then? So that's the way the wind blows. That's interesting as hell. Inconvenient. Poorly timed. But, ah ... wow. Who knew."

"Shut up, Bruce," Duncan growled.

"I'm sorry about you getting attacked, but we have got to get some more material churned out by Monday," Bruce fretted. "I don't know how you expect us to—"

"Tomorrow," Duncan said.

Bruce rolled his eyes. "Tomorrow's Sunday, Dunc."

"Who cares? Work doesn't care what day it gets done."

"I'm free tomorrow," I piped up quickly. "We can absolutely work tomorrow."

Duncan looked at his brother. "See? Problem solved. We're done here for the day. Let's wrap it up. We'll talk tomorrow morning about when to meet."

Bruce got up and backed toward the door. "Fine, then. I'll just go on home and slave away on my Rosetta Stone while you two lovebirds—"

"Out, Bruce!" Duncan's voice lashed like a whip.

"I'll just, ah, engage this lock for you. To save time, you know." Bruce flicked the lever and ducked out the door. It snicked shut behind him.

"Duncan! That was unnecessary!" I said hotly. "You embarrassed me to death! I promised him that I'd get those goblin cave manuscripts—oh!"

He pulled me up onto my feet and led me around his desk, then settled me onto his lap, straddling him. I struggled, twisting.

"Hey! Are you nuts? The conference room wasn't kinky and inappropriate enough for you? You have to up the ante?"

"Always." He stifled my protest with a persuasive kiss that stole my breath.

I grasped his wrists for balance, gasping for air.

"It's just a kiss," he murmured, nuzzling my throat. "About

that conference room. Every time I pass the door, my dick gets hard. No, no, don't panic. The door's locked."

"That makes it worse!" I protested. "Everyone is speculating!"

"No they aren't," he said. "Everybody's gone home but Bruce, and he's already drawn his own conclusions about us. Forget all of them." He gripped my hips, pulling me tight against that hot bulge, and kissed me hungrily. "I did a crazy thing today," he said, between kisses. "And it's all your fault."

"Oh, really?" I quavered, thighs clenching. "My fault? How's that?"

"I was supposed to convince my sister Ellie to see reason, and change her major from theater back to economics." His arms tightened, grinding his erection against my melting, quivering sweet spots. I could hardly breathe, it felt so good.

"I called her," he continued in a low, wondering voice. "I was about to do my spiel, just like a fucking robot when someone pushes the button. And then I found your petals."

"Really?" I said. My panties and his trousers were a whisper-thin barrier between the scorching heat of his erection. "And?"

"I just stopped. And I told her to go for it." He sounded bewildered.

I was so surprised, I laughed. "Really? Just like that?"

"Just like that. Out of nowhere. There I was, rose petals all around me. I just couldn't do it. I couldn't bring her down. The program crashed. And it's all your doing, Nell."

My heart swelled. I cradled his face in my hands and kissed him. "Congratulations," I whispered. "You did a great thing. You did the right thing."

He cupped his hand behind my head and deepened the kiss.

My long sweater skirt was rucked up high on my thighs,

over the same beige gartered stockings I'd worn the day before, and his erection pressed against the gusset of my panties. I tried to pull away, gasping for breath. "I'm going to give you a great big wet spot," I warned him. "You won't be fit to be seen."

"Only one solution." He lifted me up, cupping my bottom, and swiftly yanked his belt loose and his pants open. His cock sprang up, empurpled, stiff, and hard. I cried out as Duncan slid his finger delicately inside the crotch of my panties and into that hot, liquid well of pure sensation, swiveling and stroking. A sharp tug against my hip, the fabric strained, and ripped. He pulled me back down, and I gasped with pleasure as he slid his thick, stiff cock slowly, completely inside me.

I braced myself against his chest, arching and wiggling. "Hey! Hold on! I've been spoiling you, but don't you start thinking your masterful alpha bullshit is how it's going to be with us," I warned. "Now you're ripping my clothes?"

He slid relentlessly deeper, then rocked tenderly inside me. "But my masterful alpha bullshit always seems to make you come," he pointed out, his voice a low, velvety rumble. "And I can buy you more clothes. Anything you want."

"That's not the point," I said fiercely, though my body was betraying me. I could barely speak. I was swaying on top of him, head thrown back, gasping for air, my pussy squeezing eagerly around his cock. "It's like I said that first night. Just because you can turn me on doesn't mean you control me. That you run the show. Remember that."

His fingers clutched my hips, lifting, pulling, pulsing. "That's way too deep for a guy like me. Especially when all the blood in my body's been redirected to my dick."

"Playing dumb is a cheap excuse," I shot back.

"Only one I've got," he admitted. "Your waitress friend told me I could make up for my intellectual shortcomings by being good in bed."

That snapped me out of my sensual daze, and I jerked upright. "No! She didn't!"

"She absolutely did," he said solemnly. "Ask her, when you see her next. She'll corroborate with pride."

"Oh, my God." I covered my face with my hands and started to laugh. "I can't believe them. I just can't believe it."

"I have to admit, I found it kind of comforting," he mused. "I figured, maybe there's hope, you know? Even for a lumbering, fist-dragging, Neanderthal meathead like me."

"Oh, you just shut up!"

"Good thing you like 'em big and stupid, right?"

I swatted at him. "Stop it! You're making it worse!"

"Not worse. Better," he said. "It feels fucking amazing. Those little fluttery clenches around my dick every time you laugh. Laugh all you want. I'll keep you laughing as long as I can."

I pressed my hand to his mouth, chest hitching, eyes watering with shaky giggles. "Shhh. Really. Please, Duncan, damn it. I'm serious. Stop."

"Fuck, no." He pulled my hand down, grinning. "So this guy walks into this bar—"

"Shhh!" I stared fiercely into his eyes. "I. Am. Serious. Acknowledge it!"

He nodded, and kissed my palm. "Okay, okay," he soothed. "I'll be good. I won't do my alpha thing. I won't even move. I'll sit here like a statue. Your life-sized sex toy. You just squeeze me, ride me, do whatever you want until you've had enough. Sound good?"

Oh, boy, did it ever. I did exactly as he offered, squeezing him inside me until my lower body was flushed and glowed with intense, shuddering pleasure, shaking with firecracker jolts. He kept his promise, though I could it cost him. It took a while for me to get where I needed to go, with him so motionless. He trembled, gripping my arms tightly, staring at my face as I writhed and whimpered, too lost to pleasure to be self-conscious. It was a long, slow climb, but the outcome was inevitable. And explosive.

He caught me as I arched back and plunged into free fall, his growl of satisfaction vibrating through me.

I collapsed over his shoulder, breathless and limp—blushing and damp with sweat as the aftershocks rippled through me. I could feel his heartbeat in his cockhead, throbbing deep inside. A deep, steady, pulsing rhythm. So close to me. I loved it.

I lifted my head and the look on his face took me by surprise. Not that taut, tense mask of self-control he wore while I was pleasuring myself with his body. This expression was very different. Soft. Almost wistful.

"What are you thinking?" I asked him.

He touched my eyebrow, then my cheekbone, then my lips. "I was just wondering what a kid of ours might look like."

Those words pierced me with a strange mix of emotions—joy, fear, fury, hope. That bastard. How dare he. Playing me like a fucking violin.

"Don't say things like that to me," I forced out. "It's reckless."

He shrugged. "You asked what I was thinking. I told you the truth. I always do."

I dismounted, my breath shuddering out in a low sigh. The sweet, tight, delicious friction as his cock caressed my sensitized inner flesh felt so good.

I stared down at his cock, which stood high and hopeful against his belly. Rigid, pulsing, gleaming with my own balm.

I had no intention of sinking to my knees, but that's where I ended up, grabbing his thick, pulsing cock, stroking smooth, hot skin. Licking him, and tasting myself. It was a classic thousand-dollar-an-hour call-girl scenario. Blowing the boss in his swivel chair in the high-rise corner office. From the outside, it looked pornographic.

But I wasn't on the outside. I was so far inside, I was in a whole new world—one where the rules had flipped on their head. I had changed, too. I felt softer. More joyful. More sensual. More powerful. I felt fearless, shameless, and burning with a desperate desire to give him pleasure. To show him my favor. My chest, my face, my throat, my pussy, were all hot, soft, wet, aglow.

Of course. I was crazy in love with him.

I let that thought slide. I didn't dare examine it—and besides, it took all my concentration to give a blow job to a man as well-endowed as Duncan Burke. He was hung like the proverbial horse. I wasn't an expert, but oh, so very motivated.

I petted and stroked, swirling my tongue around his cockhead, and tried to draw him deeper. I loved the sounds—the shaking grip of his hands in my hair, the shudders that rippled through him. I was just hitting my stride when his fingers tightened and he let out a choked shout.

His come spurted into my mouth in hard, rhythmic jets.

I staggered to my feet after a few minutes, holding on to the desk for balance, and wiped my mouth. Too shy to look at him. My face was so hot.

He dragged me over between his legs, hugged me around the waist, hid his face against my breasts. All my shyness evaporated, leaving only tenderness.

So he felt vulnerable, too. That eased my ambivalence somehow.

We swayed in a clinch for a long time. He looked up. "There's a private attached bathroom with a shower right off my office," he told me, pointing at the door.

I widened my eyes. "How luxurious and elitist of you. What, you can't bear to pee with the hoi polloi?"

His teeth flashed in the twilight. "There have to be some perks for being the boss," he said. "I like to run to work sometimes, and I also like to smell good. I keep a few sets of fresh clothes here. So we can clean up. If you want to."

"You ripped my panties," I scolded. "Beast. I don't have another pair with me. I'll be walking around with my naked lady-bits catching a breeze under my skirt."

He gave me a look of mock contrition. "And I'll be walking around with a huge hard-on every time I think about that," he said. "Sorry, but I was afraid that if I stopped to peel them all the way down your legs, you'd wimp out on me. It was a delicate moment and I just couldn't risk it. Too much was at stake." He caressed my ass through my skirt. "If we hurry, we've got time for dinner before we meet your sisters in Queens."

"What about the texts that I have to write for the game? I have to have something for Bruce tomorrow!"

He shrugged. "It's more important that you eat. Come on." He grabbed my hand and pulled me into a small but luxurious bathroom.

"I thought we were in a hurry," I protested.

He grabbed a fluffy white towel off a pile on a shelf, and dropped it in my arms, with a devilish grin. "Everything's relative. And I'm guessing they'll wait for you."

He shrugged off his suit jacket, and I froze at the sight of the gun strapped onto his shoulder. "Um, Duncan? What on earth are you doing with that thing?"

He slanted me an "are you kidding" look. "Just being careful."

"But ... carrying a gun? To work?"

He raised an eyebrow. "Yeah," he said. "Last night, those guys were armed, and I wasn't. It was just blind luck and timing that they didn't kill me and take you, because I wouldn't have been able to stop them if they'd been even a little more organized. They weren't expecting any resistance. They will be next time. Don't worry. I have a lot of experience with 'this thing.'" He unbuttoned my blouse and peeled my stretch lace chemise off over my head, then unhooked my bra.

"That's, um, not all that reassuring, actually," I told him. "What experience?"

"Afghanistan, mostly," he said. "Just trust me. Will you trust me? Please?"

I gazed at him through the wild mess of curly hair that had fallen over my face when he pulled off my lacy undershirt. "Yes," I said, with absolute sincerity. "I have no doubt about your ability to handle just about anything."

He herded me into the shower, pinned me against the wall, and proceeded to live up to my faith in him, to the absolute fullest.

Chapter Nineteen

Duncan

I looked around Malloy's, and concluded that there were too many people crowded together in the place. It wasn't safe for Nell here. Good thing I'd had jeans and a sweater to change into at the office, because I would've felt like a clown in the suit in a place like this.

I'd never been in an Irish pub. The loud, fast, noodling melodies played by the table of musicians made my brain pound, but I could deal with it as long as Nell's fingers were twined with mine. I would accompany Nell D'Onofrio into the bowels of hell if I had to. Complaining bitterly about hell's shitty security all the way down, no doubt, but I'd be there to the end, stuck to her like glue.

My attention had divided itself into independently functioning units. One unit was constantly scanning for attackers. Another was intensely anxious about meeting Nell's sisters, who might or might not want to toss my entrails into the gutter if I failed to adhere to some incomprehensible code of behavior toward her. A third was intensely aware that, thanks to my uncivilized sexual excesses, Nell D'Onofrio was wearing no panties. She looked decorous and ladylike, her tidy blouse stretching slightly across her tits, her long sweater skirt reaching to her ankles—but paradoxically, that made it even worse. It was her little sexy secret. If I slipped my hand under that skirt and slid it up over her stockings, I'd find just hot, velvety skin between her legs. Warm fuzz. Damp ringlets. Tender, moist pink folds inside her pussy lips. That hot, tight, slick well. If I stroked my hand up the petal-soft skin of her upper thighs, I could just pet her tender involuted folds, feeling that hot, silken inside flesh clinging tenderly to my finger.

Talk about distracting.

We were the last to arrive, since I'd insisted on stopping at a good steak and burger joint that I knew near the Midtown Tunnel, to get some serious protein into her. When we walked into the bar, two women leaped up and went straight for Nell, sneaking fascinated peeks at me.

I was grateful for the noise level, so I didn't have to hear what they were whispering to her, but whatever it was, it made her blush.

"Duncan, this is my sister Vivi," Nell spoke loudly into my ear, indicating the smaller of the two women, a slender girl with long red hair and big gray eyes. "And this is Nancy." She touched the shoulder of the other woman, a pale beauty with hazel eyes and curly auburn hair that reached her ass. "This is Duncan, my friend," she told them. "And that tall guy at the table playing the fiddle is Liam, Nancy's fiancé."

The tune ended with a flourish and a burst of hoots and hollers. The guy Nell had pointed at glanced over at us, laid his fiddle on the table, and excused himself, to unanimous cries of protest. He came toward us, sizing me up with sharp green eyes.

He had a strong grip and a clear, unwavering gaze. Nell had told me the story of how Liam had defended her sister Nancy from Snake Eyes. I was a good judge of men, after all those years as a field agent, and this Liam seemed okay to me. A guy I'd want at my back. That was good. Alliances were good.

The musicians launched into a new tune, louder than the one before. "Let's go sit at a table in the back!" Liam shouted over the din.

I was relieved at the suggestion. The back room was deserted and relatively quiet. We sat down around a table and I stoically endured their collective scrutiny.

"So, Duncan," the sister named Vivi finally broke the silence. "I'll just start things off by saying thanks for saving Nell's ass for us. We can never repay you."

"My pleasure," I replied.

"Yes, I'm grateful too," Nancy said. "But that brings us to something important. Nell, you and Vivi can't live in New York alone anymore. You need to go into hiding. I know it sounds dramatic, but so is getting jumped by three guys on Lafayette. It's happened to me twice, and to you once. How many times will it take to convince you?"

Sensible though that was, I was instantly unhappy about the prospect of Nell leaving town. But I need not have worried, because Nell was shaking her head stubbornly, true to form. As contrary with her sisters as she was with me.

"I am so close to getting my doctorate," she said, her voice rebellious. "It's taken me years having to work full-time while I work toward this degree, but I'm almost there. I'm not going to let this murdering piece of shit take that from me."

"But where will you live? You could stay with me and Liam, but you'd be exposed every time you traveled back and forth—"

"She can live with me," I cut in. "I'll make sure she's covered."

All eyes went to me for a long, startled moment. After a moment, only Nell's eyes stayed fixed on me, big and worried, while the others exchanged silent signals, significant glances, suppressed smiles.

Nell leaned over to me. "Duncan, do you mind?" she hissed. "This is not an issue for everyone to—"

"Actually, that is not true. It is our issue now," Vivi said. "You're my sister, and I don't want you snatched. How's the security in your building, Duncan?"

"Good," I replied. "Even better when I'm with her. Which I'll make a point of being, as much as possible. And if I can't, for whatever reason, I'll make arrangements for a professional bodyguard. At all times. No matter where she is."

Nell glared at me. I stared back, unrepentant. The sisters and the future brother-in-law exchanged nods of cautious approval.

"I'd like to be included in the decision-making process here," Nell snapped. "And who's going to pay for a bodyguard? They're expensive!"

"So Nell's covered," Liam went on smoothly, ignoring her protests. "Thank God. That leaves you, Viv. You can always stay with us. You shouldn't go back on the road. At least not unless you change your name, your car, your brand, etc."

Vivi looked forlorn. "You're sweet, Liam, but staying with you guys is not a long-term solution. I'm the only one of us with no pressing reason to stay in New York. But I can't do the crafts fair circuit if I don't use my own name, or I'd be starting from zero again. I can't afford that after working so hard to build up my brand."

Nancy looked worried. "But I thought you wanted to quit the circuit!"

Her younger sister shook her head. "Sure. I'm sick of it, but it doesn't make sense to stop now. I have to wait until I've saved enough to buy a little house someplace beautiful, in the middle of nowhere, maybe. Somewhere with lots of trees, where my dog can run free. Where I can have a big studio, do sculpture again, maybe open my own shop. But that's just a fantasy. I lost thousands of bucks in crafts fair registration fees when I came back for Lucia's funeral, and even more after the Boston adventure. So now I'm way behind, and playing catch-up with my credit card."

Huh. Trees, flowers, a big art studio, far from New York. I had a sudden idea. A fucking awesome idea. "I know of a place you might be able to go," I said.

They all turned. "What might that place be?" Vivi asked slowly.

"I've got this friend I met in Afghanistan," I said. "We were on an intelligence-gathering task force together. He got out of that line of work a few years ago, around the same time I did. Bought himself a place out in Oregon. He's into organic gardening, orchards, that kind of thing. He grows flowers, I think. I've never seen the place, but he told me it's all covered with forest, and that the guy he bought the land from was an artist who'd converted the barn into a studio, with a small apartment in a loft."

Liam and Nancy gave each other speculative glances.

"And why would this guy want to host me there?" asked Vivi.

I shrugged. "He owes me some favors. He's not an artist, so he doesn't need the studio. He doesn't raise animals, so he doesn't need the barn. He built his own house, so he doesn't need the apartment. And he likes dogs. Maybe he'd rent the place to you. Do you want me to talk to him?"

Talk, my ass. Bully and guilt-trip him was more like it. Jack owed me his life, like Gant. Actually, the truth was that we all owed each other, but I would bring out the big guns to help Nell's sister, in a heartbeat. And the best part was, Jack was a hard-core badass. If anyone gave Vivi trouble, Jack could handle it. That would be part of the rental contract too. Although no one but Jack and I would know about it.

Having Vivi someplace safe would comfort everyone and earn me big points. I'd take every opportunity I could find to do that. No matter who I inconvenienced.

Vivi's shrug was casual, but I read signs of stress in her face, the shadows under her eyes, the nervous movement of her hands, her mouth. She looked pinched, kind of the way Nell's beautiful face had been, just a couple of days ago.

Nell herself was looking better. Rosier, brighter, eyes sparkling. So damn pretty, it just kept knocking me on my ass. In fact, she was giving me a look of such shining, unmixed approval right now, it was almost disorienting. She grabbed my hand under the table, and my brain went haywire at the contact. My fingers curled around hers, and for a moment, I completely lost the thread of the conversation.

"... told us about the secret drawer," Nancy was saying when I tuned in again

"Like the many other things Lucia never told us about."

"Secret drawer?" I asked. "In what?"

Nancy glanced at Nell, and Nell gave her an eloquent nod, prompting Nancy to proceed. "Lucia had a priceless intaglio Renaissance writing table," she said. "It had been in her family for the past four hundred years. It was smashed in the second B&E. You do know about our mother, Lucia? What happened to her? The burglary after, and all the rest of it?"

"Yes, Nell told me the whole story," I said. "So what's with the table?"

"Liam's been restoring it," she said. "And in the process of doing that, he found a secret drawer. You push one of the flowers carved into the back, and a drawer pops out. It had a letter in it."

I waited for the punch line. "And? What's in the letter?"

Nancy smiled at my impatience. "We don't know yet," she said. "It's in Italian, and Nell's the only one of us who speaks Italian. I guess I could have typed it in and put it into a translator, but it's so much easier and more fun to just, you know. Hand it to Nell and watch her work her magic. We all love seeing her do it."

I looked at Nell. "You speak Italian?"

"And Spanish. And Portuguese. And French. And Latin. And ancient Greek," Vivi piped up, pride in her voice. "Our Nell, the linguist."

Nell looked embarrassed. "My birth mother was Italian," she explained. "I learned it from her. It was a second mother tongue. And I was in a foster home for a while with a couple of Venezuelan girls. I picked up their Spanish before they had a chance to learn any English. French and Portuguese were easy steps after that. So it's not like it's any kind of big accomplishment."

I grunted. "Right. Sure. Ancient Greek. No biggie."

"Can I see the letter, please?" she asked primly. Nancy pulled a sheet of lightweight airmail paper out of her purse and passed it to Nell, who scanned it briefly. "It's dated three months ago," she said, then began to translate.

> *Dearest Lucia,*
>
> *Perhaps you will refuse even to read this letter. It would be no more than I deserve. Be aware that my silence was not due to lack of sentiment. On the contrary.*
>
> *I have given up the search. I accept that I will never find what I seek, and yet possession of the map is still a*

torment to me. I have no right to destroy it, as it is not mine,
and your father paid the highest price a man could pay to
keep its hiding place a secret. I wish only to be free of it
now. It gives me no peace, and after fifty years of fruitless
searching, peace is all that I can hope for. Perhaps even that
is too much to hope.

I wish to bring the map back to you, my precious love.
You are the rightful owner. Dispose of it as you think best. I
beg you, take this burden from me. Your pure heart and lack
of avidity make you its perfect guardian.

I have a flight reservation that will bring me to JFK
Airport on May the 16th, if you will receive me. If you do
not wish to see me, or you do not wish to take custody of the
map, I will respect your wishes, and you will not hear from
me again.

I await news from you.
Marco Barbieri

We all stared down at the letter, chilled.

"May sixteenth," Nell said. "The day she died. So we have a name—Barbieri."

"Marco said that her father paid the highest price a man could pay," Nell continued. "But he didn't break. So whoever's coming after us must have tortured him. But how can that be? It would've happened fifty years ago. How could these assholes still be at it?"

"Maybe someone younger found out about it later," Nancy mused.

"So maybe Marco brought Lucia this map that day," Liam said slowly. "And he led them straight to Lucia. But they still didn't find what they were looking for."

"Just a map," Nell said. "The treasure's still lost. Marco

couldn't find it, and it sounds like he tried very hard. Then he came here and was murdered, still unsatisfied."

"And where's the map?" I asked. "I'm guessing the murderer took it, but didn't have any more luck with it than Marco did." I looked at Liam. "I assume you went over that whole table?"

"Centimeter by centimeter," Liam replied. "There were no other secret drawers. But there's still the safe. It's a big question mark. The bad guys haven't seen it. It wasn't found or forced, in either of the burglaries. I pulled the whole safe out of the wall and took it to my house in the meantime."

Nancy held her hand up to her throat. "But even if we figured it out, we can't open it without all three of the necklaces, according to Lucia's letter. And Snake Eyes took mine. That son of a bitch."

"Can't you force the safe?" I asked.

Nancy shook her head. "It's a tricky design," she said. "God knows where Lucia found the thing. There's a warning printed on the top. If you try to open the safe in any way other than with the numerical combination, a mini-bomb explodes and destroys whatever's inside. Keeps everybody honest. Too honest for our purposes."

"So we'll go at it from another direction," Nell said briskly. "We find out more about Marco Barbieri and whatever he's been looking for these past fifty years. Maybe someone in Castiglione Sant'Angelo can tell us."

"Let's go to Italy and ask them," I said, impulsively.

Everyone stared at me, mouths agape.

"Um, Duncan?" Nell began. "Hold on a second. Slow down."

"Why?" The fantastic idea was taking hold in my mind, driving everything else out. Castles, frescoes, fields of sunflowers, great pasta, thick Florentine steaks, liters of kick-ass red wine. Walking through winding cobblestone streets with Nell on my arm—her in a skimpy little sundress with lots of cleavage, getting a tan, eating gelato, relaxing, seeing lots of beautiful art and architecture that turned her on. Nell, naked in our rumpled hotel room bed, her eyes sultry, satiated. Yeah.

Nell snorted. "Please. Be reasonable. What about the game? And my summer school students? And your business?"

"The game will wait," I said. "The students will live. And I haven't taken a vacation since I started the business. It's hard to justify vacations when you're running your own operation."

"Tell me about it," Vivi said wearily.

"I cannot afford a trip to Italy," Nell's voice had gotten sharp.

"So we'll divide the labor," I offered. "You do all the talking in the hotels and the restaurants, and I wave my credit card around."

Vivi laughed with delight. "I like your style, Duncan."

I shrugged. "It's a perfect way to get you out of their sights."

"Not really," Liam said. "To my mind, it's the first place they'd expect her to go. She'd be noticed there, and watched."

I was somewhat deflated by that very sensible observation, but I still couldn't let it go. I tracked with part of my mind, taking in data while they brainstormed about the letter, the safe, Marco, the attackers, the map. The rest of me played with the Tuscan vacation fantasy like a dog with a bone. Gnawing it, licking it, loving it.

Nell began rubbing her eyes at about one-thirty in the morning, and I took her hand. "We should get back. You need some sleep," I told her. "We promised Bruce you'd be at the office tomorrow. But not until later in the morning."

She stifled a yawn and smiled. "Yeah, I'm whipped."

"Give them your new phone number," I said.

Nancy and Vivi looked at each other, mouths theatrically agape. "New phone?"

"Oh, shut up, Viv," Nell grumbled. "He bullied me into it." She scribbled the number twice on a cocktail napkin and ripped it into two pieces, handing one to each sister. Hugs and giggles, jokes and teasing admonitions followed among the three sisters, while I and Liam eyed each other.

Liam's face was grim. "Stay sharp," he said under his breath. "Those fuckers are motivated. They almost got me both times they tried. It was pure luck that saved us."

"Same here," I said. "I'm on it."

Liam nodded, looking cautiously relieved. "It's good knowing someone else has our backs from another direction. Let us know what your friend in Oregon says. When Vivi's on the road, we don't sleep at night."

"I hear you." We shook hands and made our way out.

Nell and I were silent on the way home. I was so heavy into my Italian-vacation-with-Nell fantasy that I was surprised when she spoke.

"They really liked you," she said.

That made me happy. "Yeah? Great. How do you figure?"

"They told me so. But even if they hadn't, I could tell, the way they talked about our private problems. Like it was a given that you were part of it. They would never have done that if they didn't like you."

"So I don't have to worry about being disemboweled?"

Nell stifled a giggle. "Not for the moment," she said. "You sure did throw your weight around, though. Your bank account, too."

I glanced at her profile. "I'm sorry if that was offensive to you."

"It seemed like you were trying to communicate to them

that you've got money. I think they got the message loud and clear."

I took a few seconds to breathe down the surge of anger and frustration. "You're hung up on the money thing, Nell," I said. "I was communicating to them that I'm willing and able to protect you. Money is protection, too, whether you like it or not. And they know it. In fact, I didn't hear anyone objecting to it but you."

She was silent for a moment. "Sorry if I'm being oversensitive," she said finally, her voice subdued. "And thanks for making that offer to Vivi—about your friend in Oregon. I hope that works out. She needs a break. We all do."

"I got that sense too," I said. "I'll get right on it."

The silence that followed was an invisible wall between us. She was lost in her thoughts behind it, hidden from me. It made me anxious and lonely. I wanted to break through, get inside. I needed more intel. She was so complex. There was so much going on in her head. I wanted her exact specs, a manual of her operating systems. I wanted to study her, absorb her. Master her like she was a math problem.

And she'd have my ass barbecued if I ever said anything like that to her. I had to watch my metaphors with this woman.

"Talk to me," I blurted.

She looked at me, startled out of her reverie. "About what?"

"About yourself. I want to know more. You're incredible. Unique."

She harrumphed. "Yeah. I'm so unique, I'm practically extinct."

I ignored that. "Tell me about your childhood, your mother, your sisters," I urged. "Tell me anything. I don't care what. Just let me in."

Her big eyes were wary of the need she felt emanating from me, a vibration I could do nothing to hide. "Duncan ..."

"You make me feel so alive. Just please, Nell. Tell me how it is to be the way you are."

My appeal touched her. She gave me a shadowy smile, and something relaxed inside me. Excellent. By sheer chance, I'd hit upon the exact trick to calm her down. Some judicious pity-mongering, a small, tasteful glimpse of desperation, and she'd melted. I hadn't calculated the strategy, either. It just came to me.

Maybe this incomprehensible emotional shit could be learned, after all.

Chapter Twenty

Nell

The note in his voice released the floodgates. I talked so much, I embarrassed myself. I told him things I hadn't let myself think about in years, things I'd pretended to forget. The boarding schools. The bad foster homes. That solitary afternoon in the funeral home, alone with my mother's coffin. That bleak memory still haunted me.

I had no idea there was so much to say about my childhood, but it tumbled out. I told him about Lucia finding me. About Nancy and Vivi, and discovering that I could have a family after all. I talked about stories, poetry. My magical refuge.

Duncan listened intently. His rapt attention was flattering, but the car clock said it was after three a.m., and I looked up at the street numbers and realized that he'd been driving in big, aimless circles around his neighborhood for the better part of an hour.

"Why aren't you parking the car?" I asked.

"I wanted to hear you talk."

"We could talk at your apartment," I pointed out.

"What I want when we get home doesn't involve much talking."

I crossed my legs with a shiver at the sensual promise in his voice. "Well. Be that as it may. I'm about talked out for now."

He turned at the next block and started back toward his condo. "This morning you told me that you've got plans for your life," he said. "Ambitions. Do those include a man? Or any room for one?"

I hesitated. There was a peculiar tone in his voice when he asked the loaded question. Something that made me vaguely nervous.

"You know, Duncan, I've babbled for over an hour, but you haven't volunteered one single thing about your own life," I said.

"You're evading my question."

"Why, what a coincidence. You're evading mine, too."

"I asked first," he said stubbornly. "And? So?"

I twisted my hands together. "Well, my plan is to finish my thesis, get my doctorate, and find a teaching job. At which point, I guess I'll attempt to have a normal life—Snake Eyes permitting and all that."

"Let me rephrase," he said. "By normal life, do you mean marriage? Kids?"

I stared at him. My heart had started to thud quickly, and my palms felt damp. He simply waited. I looked at the streetlights swooping by.

"Of course I dream about love," I said. "After all those novels and all that poetry, how could I not? But I don't take anything for granted. There are no guarantees. I'll do the best I can, try to get over my emotional baggage. Hope I get lucky." *With you* was the real ending of that phrase, but my lips and throat shook too much to say it.

He was quiet as he pulled into his parking garage and drove down two ramps to his own slot. He parked, killed the engine, and stared at the concrete wall in front of us.

"You're special, Nell," he said. "You should ask for more."

Warmth softened my chest. I touched his face with the palm of my hand and stroked his cheek gently. "So should you, Duncan," I whispered. "So should you."

This was the moment. It could make or break us. He looked like he was poised to say it. He covered my hand with his own. I was poised to hear it. I couldn't move or breathe. Seconds ticked by, stretched to a minute. Then longer.

But he didn't say it. I turned my gaze away, blushing hard, feeling like an idiot. Here I went again, projecting my silly romantic fantasies onto an unsuspecting man. And him—bumbling along. No freaking clue. It was too soon for this nonsense anyway.

I tried to cover my embarrassment. "So? I answered your questions, Duncan. Now it's your turn to bare your soul. Let's hear some childhood reminiscing from you."

He looked alarmed. "I don't know how to do that."

"You just saw me do it," I said. "Watch and learn."

"That's different," he said, his voice defensive. "You're ... you're *you*."

"Right, and you're Duncan—and that's what I'm interested in. Why don't you start with your parents? They're usually at the bottom of things."

He let out an impatient sigh, as if humoring a child. "My mom's a piece of work, but tough, and fabulous. She taught elementary school for thirty-five years before she retired. She raised us on her own. She's a real general. Tries hard to run our lives, and mostly fails. She's a pretty good sport about it. Usually."

["\n\n\n\n\n"]

"How did she feel about you going to Afghanistan? And being a spy?"

He grunted. "She hated it. She nagged and schemed and lectured and admonished. She never let up. But I couldn't hear her from the other side of the world, so it was okay. I know how to block and fake. I suit myself."

"I've noticed," I murmured. "And your father?"

His face changed, like a door slamming shut in my face. "I have nothing to say about him."

I took a deep breath, and tried again. "So tell me what there isn't, instead of what there is," I suggested.

He looked baffled. "What the hell?"

"Silence is as revealing as words," I said softly. "But you already know that. I see it in your photos."

"Don't go all poetic on me, Nell," he warned. "I swear to God, I'll devolve on you. I'll start to grunt and snort and scratch my tufts."

"Stop being ridiculous, and just tell me what happened," I said. "It can't be worse than my father. At least you know the guy's name."

He looked hunted, scowling down at the steering column. Finally, he started to speak, but his voice was flat. "He fell in love with some woman who worked for him," he said. "His accounts manager. Sylvia was her name. She was younger than him and my mother. I was thirteen. Bruce was nine, and Ellie was a newborn. Ellie was Mom's last-ditch effort to tie Dad to her. It was a bad idea." He shook the memory away.

"I'm sorry, Duncan," I said softly.

"He tried to explain it to me before he left. How love was this great force he couldn't resist. It was his dick that he couldn't resist, but his family paid the price."

I put my hand on his leg, stroked him.

"He divorced Sylvia seven years later," he said. "Traded her in for a younger model. He's done it a couple more times since then. There's the power of love for you." The bitterness in his voice chilled me.

"That's not love," I said. "I don't know what it is, but it's not love."

He made a low, harsh sound of negation. "Whatever it is, I don't want to talk about it anymore. It depresses me. Let's go upstairs." He got out of the car.

I flung the door open before he could come around and do it for me, and followed him into his building, miserably aware of having maneuvered him out of that closeness I had felt before. I'd managed to make him tense and defensive. Well, hell. There were ways and ways to sweeten his mood. I was not without my resources.

Duncan stood aside to let me in first and flipped on a small row of track lights near the entry space, leaving the rest of the apartment in shadow but for the glittering cityscape outside. The delicious imminence of sex trapped my air in my lungs. I drifted over to the couches. They were big, oversized. Gray, velvety, plush. An odd choice for him. I would've expected gleaming black leather, stainless steel, and glass. I sank into one with a sigh and stared at his perfectly proportioned black silhouette standing there.

A hot sexual energy pulsed off him—all the more potent for his silence, for how fiercely it was controlled. It made me hot, shaky. Unstable inside. I could hardly wait.

"All evening, I've been thinking about your bare ass under that skirt," he said.

I grabbed handfuls of the knit fabric and screwed up my courage. "Do you, um ... want to see it?"

"Yes," he said. "Show me."

I took my time pulling my skirt up. I drew it out, gathering up folds of fabric inch by inch, until I had an armful of jersey pressed against my belly, and the tops of my stockings showed. A strip of pale thigh above them. The curls of my pubic hair.

But my legs were still clamped together. Duncan sank to his knees in front of me. His hands settled on my knees, pushing them wide. I closed my eyes, my face hot.

"I love the stockings," he muttered. "You are so fucking beautiful, Nell."

He grabbed my hand and pulled it down, arranging my fingers so that my clit was gently clasped in the V between my index and middle finger. "Touch yourself," he said, his voice a husky rasp. "I want to watch you do it. You know ... watch and learn."

I laughed as I parted my slick folds for him. I was so aroused by his intense attention. The feeling of exposure was transforming into something pleasurable. I slowly relaxed into it, like a cat sprawled in a patch of sunlight.

"That's one area where you don't need any lessons."

"Thank God I've got at least one piece of the puzzle."

I ignored his sarcasm and stroked the jut of his cheekbone with my finger. His skin was so hot and supple.

"I've been fantasizing about you ever since the first day you started eating lunch at the Grill," I confessed.

He pressed a hot, lingering kiss to the top of my thigh. "Really? And what did I do to you in those fantasies?"

"Lovely things," I admitted. "Many varied things."

He grinned and caressed the crease of my groin. "Such as?"

He waited, but I couldn't speak. My lips were trembling. "My mouth is watering," he said, parting my labia tenderly, and slowly penetrating me. "Did I lick you in those fantasies?"

"Yes," I whispered.

"Was it good? Did I treat you right?"

"It was amazing," I said.

He bent lower and lapped the length of my labia with his

tongue, slow and voluptuous. "And how do I measure up to my dream fantasy self?"

"You surpass your dream fantasy self," I admitted. "There's more of you in real life. More of everything—more feelings, more orgasms. More problems, too."

"Oh, yeah." He chuckled silently, the laughter vibrating against my mound, his lips tenderly holding my clit, his tongue fluttering expertly—swirl, flutter, swirl.

"Never mind all the problems," he suggested. "Let's just stop at the orgasms. And linger there."

"Okay," I agreed.

"Forever," he whispered.

That word just set me off. *Forever.* It made my pleasure crest and then break in great, pulsing ripples of milky foam through the endless ocean of sensation.

After that, we both went wild. A frenzied, feverish blur, clutching each other, dragging, pulling demanding. No control, no need for it. His clothes came off, my blouse was ripped open, my bra unhooked.

He settled between my legs and slowly entered me, pressing me down onto the couch with his solid weight. Folding my legs high. It was hard, deep, driving. Demanding and wonderful. We struggled, twining and writhing and pumping. Struggling toward the release we both needed ... and exploding together.

His vital energy poured into me. I clung to him and took in the wonderful heat. I felt transformed.

A single, piercing thought formed in my mind. He lifted his face, and it just flew out of my mouth. "I love you," I said.

His eyelids went tight. His face went blank. Fear stabbed through me.

Oh God. I'd ruined it. Now he'd take back all that intense,

passionate attention—never mind that it wasn't love—and I'd proceed to shrivel up and die.

Then came anger. How humiliating, to be terrified just because I told a man I loved him. I had nothing to be ashamed of. He should be grateful. I shouldn't have to beg for any man's love.

"Nell," he said, sounding pained.

"No. Forget I said it." I tried to wrench myself free, but his full weight was pinning me down into cushions. He rolled off onto the floor.

"Nell, I'm sorry if I—"

"Shut up, Duncan. The worst thing you could do would be to apologize. It's the one thing I could never forgive you for."

"So what can I say?"

"Nothing," I whispered. A burning tightness filled my chest. It felt like my heart was imploding. I collected my clothes and marched into the bedroom.

He followed on bare, silent feet. "Nell, don't," he said, his voice rough. "Don't do this to me."

I fought the tears. "Please, Duncan. Just give me some space. I'm too embarrassed to talk to you right now."

"Don't be. Please." He slipped his arms around me from behind and squeezed. "Thank you for saying it. Thank you for giving yourself to me like you do. You're beautiful and special, and you make me feel awake and alive like nothing else. Please. Don't be embarrassed."

I covered my face. "You drive me crazy when you talk like that," I whispered. "Don't confuse me. Don't jerk me around."

"I'm just telling you how I feel. I'm just being honest. Isn't that what women say they want from men?"

"What I want and what women in general want are two separate things," I said haughtily. "Do not generalize me."

"Never," he said smoothly, fervently kissing my neck.

I sighed. "It's strange. All those things you say about how you feel about me? That's exactly how I feel about you. I just interpret those feelings to mean that I love you."

Duncan's arms tightened. He buried his face in my hair.

"But we define those feelings in such different terms," I finished softly. "And that shouldn't be so important. But it is."

I squeezed my eyes shut. Tears overflowed, and I let them slide down my cheeks. He jerked as a tear splashed his forearm. I stroked his arm, brushing the moisture away. "It's okay. I appreciate the truth. Honesty is better than lies, I guess."

"I'm giving you everything I have to give."

I turned in his arms until I faced him and rested my face against his chest. "You give a lot," I admitted. "I just asked for the wrong thing at the wrong time, that's all. I love our time together. Don't worry. Let's just let it pass and float downstream."

Maybe I should just relax. Try not to put this experience in a box.

After all, the feelings he described for me were more than most lovers had to brag about.

Chapter Twenty-One

Duncan

Dread was heavy in my gut. Something shining and
precious was slipping away from me, and I didn't know
how to stop it. I massaged the muscles in her shoulders and
back, but she couldn't relax—and I couldn't blame her.

I coaxed her over to my bed, stripping off what remained of
her clothes, and turned off the light, tugging her close. She hid
her face against my chest, and I stroked her back in long,
soothing strokes—my hand gliding over the perfect, fine texture
of her skin, all the way down to the curve of her ass. My dick
rose up, hot and hard, prodding her thigh, but I gritted my teeth
and ignored its throbbing demands.

Patience. This time was all about Nell.

I slid my hand down the cleft of her bottom. She didn't
recoil or stiffen, just nuzzled her face to my chest with a word-
less murmur and parted her thighs, letting my hand slide lower,
delve deeper. I slowly, tirelessly apologized for what I didn't
have to offer her by showing her what I did have. My other

hand joined in, caressing her clit from the front while I thrust two long fingers into her slick, hot pussy from behind, petting and stroking. Long and slow. I drove her higher until she was squirming, panting, thighs clenching, fingernails digging into me. Finally, a sharp, desperate gasp—and her tight little hole pulsed hungrily around my hand. She flopped onto her back, limp.

I rolled on top of her and filled her with a relentless thrust. I wanted to chase away the pain and unease of our last conversation. This was the only way I knew—to lose myself in the heavy rhythm of my body jolting against hers, her gasping cries, my harsh breathing. Somehow, I waited on that razor's edge for her climax—and my own release followed a split second after, her tight spasms prolonging my pleasure.

Then she burst into tears.

I was appalled. She disentangled herself and curled up with her back to me, sobbing. I wrapped my arms around her from behind until her sobs quieted. She fell into an exhausted sleep.

I lay there with her for hours, until the pressure inside me built up to the breaking point. I crept from the bed, tucked the comforter around Nell, and pulled on some sweatpants, wandering into the living room.

The ache of impending doom in my gut kept growing. I went out onto the terrace and stared out into the endless skyscrapers while the chill raised the hairs on my bare skin. It was almost dawn. The city below would wake up soon. I just stood out there, staring. Thinking, feeling. Afraid.

I was losing her. I was killing this somehow, and I was desperate not to. I put my head in my hands, trying to think it through. The weirdness had started when I'd asked her that stupid, ill-considered question about marriage and kids.

Marriage. I examined the concept. Was that what she wanted? Because if it was, well, hell.

The more I thought about it, the more I realized that it wasn't such a crazy idea. Not looked at from a logical standpoint.

I ticked off the positive aspects. Protection. I would have a God-given reason to stay stuck to her if we were newlyweds. There was work, too. If we were married, our relationship would not be fodder for rumor and scandal in the office. No one would have any right to judge or criticize. I would have a further claim upon her undivided attention and expertise for my company. I could easily pay enough so she could quit her other job and have more free time.

She was so smart, I knew I would never get bored with her, as I sometimes had with other women I'd dated. Sex was an important element for both of us, and we certainly had no problems in that area.

I would be faithful. No question about that. I would wake up every morning and find her there, beside me. The thought gave me a wonderful, spine-tingling sense of rightness.

Yes, marriage was the logical culmination of a partnership that worked. It was a win/win. So logical, I couldn't believe I hadn't thought of it before. I could hardly wait for Nell to wake up so I could tell her what an excellent idea this was.

I hoped it would make her feel better. That she'd see that I was trying to meet her halfway—as far as I possibly could. And this was pretty damn far. I mean, marriage, for Christ's sake. How much further could a guy go?

The ache in my gut had vanished at the idea. I was floating again.

I went back inside, intending to creep into the bedroom, lie down beside her, and watch her sleep. Then I saw the eerie blue glow of a computer monitor emanating from one of the couches. Nell sat there cross-legged, wrapped in one of my bathrobes, tip-tapping on her laptop. She must've felt the breeze from the door, but she did not look up. She just worked on, utterly absorbed.

I must've stared for ten minutes before she took notice of me. Her smile was brief and wan. "Hi. I woke up," she said. "Couldn't seem to get back to sleep."

I stepped in. "What are you doing?"

"I had an idea for the last level of the game," she said.

The freaking game was the last thing I wanted to talk about, but I wasn't sure of a smooth way to shift topics and get from here to there. And a proposal of marriage had to be a segue as smooth as oil.

I swallowed, closed the door, and strolled across the room toward her. "What's the idea?"

Her voice was strangely businesslike. "As it is now, the player rescues the princess only if he garners sufficient points and collects all the magical weapons necessary to defeat the Sorcerer. If the player is clever and ruthless and forgets nothing, he gets the princess. It's a very simple, banal, mercantile sort of exchange. It's cold."

The tension was back in my gut again. This was one of those conversations with undercurrents where a phrase like "pass the butter" could blow up in my face.

"Hardly simple," I muttered. "You have to sweat blood to make it through all those levels."

"I propose something different," she went on. "These tricks should get the player through the Sorcerer's defenses and to the door of the enchanted tower, but no farther. I propose one last barrier, at least, and maybe one at each level, too, with escalating intensity for each level. To win the game, the player must learn to make leaps of blind faith. He has to go against everything his senses and his past experience tell him. To break the last spell, he has to leave his weapons and spells behind. Dive headfirst into a pit of snakes. Jump into the mouth of a dragon. Walk into a wall of flames. He has to sacrifice everything for love."

My fingers bit into the couch cushion. So Nell was still pissed. And fucking with my head in this weird, oblique way. I fought with my anger. I had to be careful.

"I've been playing with a short text that could be inserted," she went on. "Something like 'Only empty hands and a full heart shall pass through the wall of flames unburned.' This way, it's not just cleverness that wins the game. It's faith, courage. Love."

"It would make the game impossible to win," I said.

"Not for everyone," Nell replied softly.

A muscle pulsed in my jaw. "What are you saying, Nell? That it's just impossible for me? Is that what you mean?"

"I didn't say that," she said.

"But you meant it. Come on. Just say it. No symbolism. No metaphors. Could I have it in plain English just this once?"

Nell wrapped her arms around herself, shivering. "I think we understand each other perfectly," she said.

I circled the couch and sat down next to her. This was probably futile, given her unapproachable mood, but I had to get it off my chest.

"You're cold," I said, grabbing the afghan off the couch. I wrapped it around her. "I don't want to talk about the game right now. We need to talk about us. I've been thinking."

"Me, too," Nell said.

"I've decided that the best thing would be for us to get married."

Dead silence greeted that statement. Her eyes were huge and startled. "What?"

I cracked my knuckles uneasily. "I was thinking about the situation after you went to sleep. And I decided that—"

"You decided?" Her voice was deceptively calm. I paused, sensing a pitfall.

"Well, uh, of course your agreement is crucial to the plan," I said cautiously.

"So I should hope," Nell murmured.

"After I explain my reasoning, you'll see that it would be the best thing for both of us."

"Oh, really. Will I?" Nell's voice sounded almost strangled.

"Yes. Let me explain." I presented my analysis, during which Nell was ominously silent. The chill in my gut was a lump of ice by the time I concluded my well-balanced, water-tight, foolproof case for marriage.

Nell tugged the afghan around herself and looked into my eyes. "Do you love me, Duncan?" she asked baldly.

I closed my eyes, sighing. Aw, fuck. She had to say it. She just had to insist.

"Goddamn it, Nell," I snapped, "that's not the point."

Nell shook her head. "I think it is the point," she replied. "In fact, I think it's the only point."

"Marriage is about partnership. Trust. The long haul. Not a bunch of stupid platitudes that don't mean a goddamn thing! If I had you on staff full-time, we could—"

"Duncan, you're not going to hire me onto your staff," she said wearily. "I've studied for years for my advanced degree. I want to teach literature, and write. It's what I've always wanted."

I threw up my hands. "You're being deliberately difficult. Tell me what you'd make as a professor. I'll top it."

"If I wanted money, I would've gone to business school."

"We're straying from the issue," I ground out. "We're good

together. If you would just loosen up a little with your lofty romantic ideas—"

"Marriage is not a merger. Love is not a stupid platitude. If I was as detached and cool as you are, it might work. But I'm not." Her voice faltered for a moment. "I'm in love with you," she finished.

Love. Jesus, all I wanted was to be honest with her. To be fair and completely on the level, to not lie or manipulate her with any kind of falsehood or facile bullshit. That took effort, it took rigor. It was a sign of deep respect and consideration. And this was what I got for it. My chest felt like it was in a trash compactor, getting squished into something small and cold and hard.

Nell rewrapped the afghan around herself. "And the worst part is, I think you love me too—but you can't, or won't see it."

"Don't tell me how I feel. I'm not talking about feelings. I'm talking about real things. Concrete things. Commitment. Fidelity. Protection. Support. Resources. Everything I have. And children, if you want them. I thought that if you cared for me at all, you'd be pleased."

It took her a while to respond to that. "I don't 'care for you,' Duncan," she said, her voice small. "I love you. Greedy Nell. Always asking for more. And besides, feelings are real. Mine are. What would it cost you to admit you love me? Is it just a control thing? You have to have the upper hand? You can't give in to strong feelings?"

"They're not necessary," I retorted. "None of this drama is necessary."

"This is about your father, right? You hated him for calling what he did love. You have to be his opposite. No matter what."

That froze me cold. "Don't talk about my father," I said.

The tone in my voice made her lean back, her eyes big.

"Sorry," she whispered. "I can't marry you. Not on these terms."

"I figured that out by myself, by context and inference," I said. "I'm not as intellectually stunted and backward as you seem to think."

"Don't be sarcastic," Nell snapped, dashing away tears. "It's one thing to wait around for a lover to admit to loving you. It's entirely another to wait around for a husband to do it."

I stared at her. "You would've waited a long time," I said. "I've offered you more than I ever dreamed of offering anyone. If it's not enough, then there's nothing more to be said."

Nell straightened up, stiff and dignified. "I understand."

A phone began to ring somewhere. I recognized the muffled ringtone of the cell I'd given to Nell. It was in her purse, which she'd left on the floor next to the couch.

She made no move to get it. I leaned over, fished it out, and checked the display. "It's an upstate area code," I said, handing it to her. "Maybe it's one of your sisters."

She stared down at the ringing phone in her hand, a perplexed frown between her brows, as if she wasn't quite sure what to do with it. That was my cue to get the hell out of the room. I walked back out onto the terrace and pulled the sliding door firmly shut behind me. Letting her take her goddamn phone call in privacy.

Since her affairs were no longer any of my fucking business.

Chapter Twenty-Two

Nell

I t took a long time to find the right button to push, since I could barely see, my eyes were so blurred with tears. I finally got it and held the phone to my ear. "Yes?"

"Nell? Finally! It's Nancy. Sorry I'm calling so early, but I couldn't stand to wait. I hope I'm not interrupting anything, you know, delicious?"

"No," I forced out after a pained little pause. "You're not."

Nancy was silent for a moment. "Um ... is everything okay?"

"Fine." I forced false brightness into my tone. "So what's up?"

"I just got off the phone with Elsie."

Elsie was Lucia's sweet but extremely nosy next-door neighbor. She'd been there decades before we'd come to live there. I was surprised to hear her name.

"I thought Elsie went down to the Jersey Shore to live with her daughter after what happened to Lucia!"

"Oh, but she did. She just spent a full half hour telling me the horrors of sharing a bathroom with her teenage grand-daughters. Alison brought her home last night. Elsie had the key Lucia had given her years ago, so this morning she decided to go over and check the place out for us."

I sucked in a breath. "Yikes. Did you ask her to do that?"

"Hell, no! I told her not to ever do it again. It could be dangerous. But you know how she is. Anyhow, she found a letter under the mail slot, from an Elisabetta Barbieri, in Castiglione Sant'Angelo. Elsie opened it—"

"Good God," I muttered.

"I know, I know, but I wasn't inclined to complain. And besides, it didn't matter—it's in Italian, and Elsie's Polish. So she called me."

"I'll go up there right away and get it," I said.

Nancy made a suspicious sound. "With Duncan, right?"

I squirmed, pressing against the ache in my middle. "We'll see," I hedged.

"You be careful," Nancy scolded. "Are you sure you're okay?"

"I'm fine," I lied. "Just really tired, that's all."

I closed the call, trying to sound cheerful, and stared through the glass doors at him, leaning over the railing. He'd asked me to marry him. I'd said no. I was nuts.

Could I risk it? I knew he had feelings for me—he just couldn't admit them or articulate them. Could I accept a cool, practical "partnership"? With protection, money, and lots of hot, excellent sex, and constant proximity with a man I was crazy about ... just hoping that someday he'd finally recognize his feelings for me as love?

No. I just wasn't made that way. Maybe I would always be alone. Maybe I was unrealistic. Or just stupid, letting my chance at passion go by for the sake of semantics.

I wanted my man to love me. Fearlessly. With an open heart.

I opened the door and stepped out onto the terrace. A gust of wind blew the terry cloth bathrobe open over my legs. I yanked it closed. I was nude underneath. Nudity that had abruptly become inappropriate. In fact, it had become an agony of embarrassment. "I, um, have to go," I said to his rigid, muscular back.

"Why am I not surprised," he said, without turning.

I told him the story of Elsie and the letter. Duncan stared out at the city. "I'll take you up there," he said, his voice was stony.

"No," I whispered.

"No?" He turned, and the fury in his eyes hit me like a punch. "What the fuck am I supposed to do? Nothing's changed. You've still got criminals prowling the city, waiting for your guard to go down. Am I supposed to cut you loose and let you get killed now? Just because I disappointed you again? Is that my punishment?"

I shook my head. "It's not your responsibility, Duncan," I said. "It never really was."

"What a crock of horseshit. I get it, Nell. You can't stand to be with me—"

"That's not it!"

"—so I'll arrange for a car service and a professional armed escort to accompany you. When you get back with your letter, you'll check into a suite at the Hilton. Twenty-four-hour bodyguard coverage. No more Sunset Grill shifts. Just your university work. And you'll be covered anytime you leave your room."

My mouth dangled, and my head shook helplessly back and forth. "Duncan. That's insane. You can't do that."

"I can do whatever I want. I'll finance it until you've

written your fucking thesis and gotten your precious Ph.D. At which point, we'll reassess the situation."

"But I—"

"Consider my position, Nell. Cold and detached as you think I am, I don't want you to die. Even if you're blowing me off, even if I'm not fucking you, I don't want you to get hurt. If you got hurt, or died, I'd feel like it was my fault for dropping the ball, and that would suck, to the point of ruining my life. I can't allow that. Is that clear? Are we on the same page here?"

I scrubbed my eyes with the back of my hands and nodded.

"Good. Then stop arguing. I'm sick of it. And I no longer need to bother trying not to piss you off. Wow. What a fucking load off my mind."

He stood there like some sort of raging, thunderous pagan god in the chilly morning air, the towering cityscape as his backdrop. His face was rigid with fury. He made a sharp gesture for me to precede him inside. "I'll make the calls. Come on, let's get moving. This shit is killing me. Get dressed and packed. Fast."

I dragged my suitcase out of his room into the living room, overhearing snippets of Duncan's conversation with someone named Braxton as he arranged for the bodyguard. He turned, frowning. "What's the address of this neighbor?"

"Twenty-one thirty-one Fairham Lane, in Hempton," I said.

Duncan repeated the address to Braxton. "Put this one on my personal account, not the corporate account," he said into the phone.

His personal account? Dear God. I'd be in debt to this guy for the rest of time.

Well, in essence, I already was.

Chapter Twenty-Three

Duncan

I escorted Nell down to the parking garage, where the car service was waiting, and bundled her into the vehicle. I lectured the bodyguard— a burly guy with long arms and a low, bulging forehead—about the mortal danger Nell was in for about fifteen minutes before I let them take off.

I watched the car pull out of the garage, turn, and disappear. I wanted to run after the car, screaming and waving my arms. Something had been wrenched out of me, leaving a bleeding hole.

I stumbled upstairs like a zombie and dropped onto the couch. The sun got higher. My landline phone rang. My mother, probably. Calling to give me hell about Ellie. I could give a shit. It went to voice mail. There it would stay, unheard.

The square of sun on the floorboards inched along. My phone rang. I checked the display. It was Bruce. He was probably wondering what the hell was going on, since Nell had stood him up. I tossed the phone onto the couch, still ringing. Later for Bruce.

Odd that she hadn't contacted him herself, though.

The only reason I didn't turn it off altogether was because Nell was out there in the world without me at her side. With just some random mercenary bodyguard to protect her. That phone was my last and only link to her.

Some time later, the phone rang again. This time Braxton. I pushed "talk."

"What happened?" I barked. "Is she okay?"

Braxton was taken aback. "Ah ... yes, as far as I know," he said carefully. "I haven't heard anything from Wesley, so I assume things are fine."

My lungs released, allowing me to inhale. I felt stupid and hysterical. "Oh. Good. So, uh ... what's up?"

"Just letting you know that Teiko and Sam just presented their report about the apartment they bug-swept yesterday."

"Yeah? What about it?"

"It was riddled with stuff," Braxton said. "High quality, foreign made. Amazing stuff. There were cameras behind both air vents, and bugs and traces everywhere. Teiko's convinced that they didn't find everything there was to find."

"Fuck," I muttered. "Did you have them deliver the material to Gant for the evidence techs to look over?"

"Of course, as promised. One last question. Did she bring any stuff with her when she came to your place? Suitcases, electronics?"

"Who told you she was at my place?" I snapped.

"Word gets around," Braxton said patiently. "So? Did she?"

"She brought a suitcase," I said. "But she took it with her again. It's in the car— with her and Wesley." A cold chill began to prickle up my back. "Oh my God. Shit."

"Yeah, it was probably tagged," Braxton said, his voice not without sympathy.

My eyes fell on her laptop, which lay right where she'd forgotten it on the couch. The chill transformed into an icy cramp, squeezing my guts.

"Fuck me," I whispered, my voice a thread. "Her laptop. It's still here."

"Check it," Braxton said.

I grabbed it. It was a big, clunky dinosaur of a thing, at least eight years old. I found a screwdriver and pried the case open. There it was. A listening device. It was transmitting in real time, as I watched. Everything we had said had been heard, clear as a bell. Including the address where Nell was headed right now. Where she might have already arrived.

I yanked the thing out, detached its power source with a yank. "Bugged," I said.

"I just tried Wesley." Braxton's voice was grim. "He didn't answer."

"Fuck," I hissed. "Call the cops for me, right now. The local ones. Have them check the place out. I'm on my way."

"Wait! Dunc, don't go alone. I'll organize a—"

I ended the call. No time. I shoved the phone into my pocket, sprinted for the bedroom. Tossed on a T-shirt, army-issue pants, shoes for sprinting. Shoved my gun into the back of my pants, buckled on my ankle sheath and knife. Dug out the drug-treated throwing stars from my weapons stash, filled my side pants pockets with them. Grabbed the laptop with the software to triangulate the GPS signal implanted in the cell phone I'd given her.

I ran to my car.

Chapter Twenty-Four

Nell

I kept my face averted so I didn't have to see the bodyguard Wesley's sympathetic glances. My stores of dignity and restraint had been completely exhausted by the last scene in Duncan's apartment. Now all I wanted was to crawl into a hole.

Funny. That was exactly the scenario I had in store for myself, once I collected this letter—if I accepted Duncan's help. Huddled in a hole. Cloistered in a hotel suite with the blinds drawn. I supposed I should be tough and brave and refuse to do it—but that would mean fleeing New York, starting over. Abandoning everything I'd worked so hard for in the last decade.

But once I got my degree, what could I do with it, if Snake Eyes was still out there hunting me? Even if I changed my name and ran, I would still be barred from teaching literature. Colleges and universities would be the first place any fool would look for me. Snake Eyes was no fool.

No, it would be waitressing for me if I had to go into hiding. Or being a cashier, or an office temp. I'd survive, of course. I always had. But oh, God. All those years of study. All that work. Up in smoke.

I swallowed back my tears. I had to be practical. Break this problem into pieces, and tackle the pieces one at a time. I could not control the future, but I could do something useful right now.

Finishing my thesis. That was within my power. Maybe this mess could even be an inspiration. The poets I studied were all heart-hungry, lovelorn. Bleak despair was the very stuff of creativity. Look at Emily Dickinson, the Brontës. There's a long, noble literary tradition of hunger for love and sex being sublimated into deathless art.

Perhaps, like them, I could salvage something from the wreckage of my emotional life. Transmute pain into work. I was unemployed, homeless, rudderless. Too scared to walk out on the street by myself. My days would be long, silent, boring. What excuse did I have now not to hunker down and write a kick-ass thesis?

I grabbed my black shoulder bag and unzipped the central pocket where I kept my laptop. It was not there. I'd forgotten it.

Shit, shit, *shit*. I blew out a shuddering breath through trembling lips at the idea of having to face Duncan's rigid face, blazing eyes, and cutting remarks again in order to retrieve it.

Maybe I could have it sent over by courier. Uh-huh. With what cash? The cost of that courier would go right onto Duncan's personal account. Ka-ching, ka-ching.

And my debt to him was already crushing.

My laptop was gone, but the cell phone he'd given me was there. He wasn't going to call me on it. I slid it into the side pocket of my pants.

Onward. I dragged out the folder where I kept my tattered

notes, outlines, and ideas. I turned to a fresh sheet in my note-book and dug out a pen. I could scribble on paper the old-fash-ioned way.

By the time we pulled up in front of Elsie's house, I'd roughed out a pretty acceptable main thesis paragraph for "*Sex, Desperation, Despair, and Death in Nineteenth-Century Women Poets.*"

Wesley got out and opened the door for me, peering around the deserted block. Nothing moved on the narrow lane. We climbed up Elsie's porch, which was nearly identical to Lucia's. I rang the bell, and waited. And waited. I rang again, then knocked. "Elsie?" I called. "Are you in there? It's Nell!"

Still no answer. Wesley muscled me behind himself, holding up a very large pistol.

"Nell?" It was Elsie, all right, though her voice was muffled behind the door. It sounded higher and thinner than usual.

"Elsie?" I knocked again. "Is everything okay?"

"Ah ... yes, honey, everything's fine," Elsie quavered. "Come on ... come on in. The door's unlocked."

I reached for the door handle, but Wesley gently pushed my hand away and pushed the door open himself.

I stood on my tiptoes and looked over his bulky shoulder as he peered into the dim interior, through the foyer.

Elsie stood across the room, in the entryway to the kitchen. Wesley started inside just as I registered the look on the old lady's face.

The pallor. The stiff, frozen expression. The staring eyes.

I knew that look. Oh, God. Oh, no. "Wait!" I lunged after Wesley's coat, trying to yank him back—

Thhhpt—the clap of a silenced gun. Wesley grunted, spun, and crashed heavily to the ground.

The room boiled with black-clad masked men, leaping for me. A burlap bag whipped down over my head. I struggled and screamed in airless darkness that stank of mold and rot, arms and legs flailing—

A sting, like an insect bite in my arm, a sickening weakness swept through me with horrible quickness—

And it all went away.

Chapter Twenty-Five

Duncan

I kept the car between 95 and 105, depending on the sharpness of the curves. I was lucky that the road leading away from the city was clear. Traffic going the opposite direction was clogged with rush-hour traffic. My phone showed the map with the icon representing the phone I had given to Nell.

So far, the signal was stationary, fixed at Elsie's address in Hempton. I wanted desperately to call, but the fact that Wesley no longer answered was reason enough to be terrified. Maybe they'd already discovered the phone and left it, since GPS traces in phones were so common. Maybe they hadn't. If not, I didn't want it to ring and give her away. That trace was my only hope.

The signal began to move.

The fear made me want to retch, but at least I knew where she was going. The signal moved along the main drag in Hempton and took a highway heading north and east. I had to change routes if I wanted to intercept them.

It was like walking a tightrope—driving at that speed while monitoring the phone, calculating possible shortcuts. A minute later, my smartphone rang, adding another ball and hoop to my balancing act.

Fortunately, I had my earpiece. "Yeah," I barked.

"The cops are there," Braxton said. "It's not great. The old lady was hit on the head and tied up on the ground. Wesley's shot. He's bad, but still alive. No sign of your lady friend at all."

My gut cramped. "Her signal's heading northeast," I said. "Keep me informed. Later."

"Dunc. I'm sorry about this, man. I let you down."

"Not your fault," I said curtly. "I miscalculated. She should've had a team. She shouldn't have been let out of my apartment at all. Gotta go. Later."

"Gotcha." Braxton hung up.

I pressed the accelerator harder, glancing over at the map. I had to close that gap. More speed. I let the powerful motor open up, humming at 115 mph.

Play it cool. Like a glacier. As long as she was moving, they probably weren't hurting her.

But when that signal stopped, I could fucking forget about playing it cool.

I was going to be twisting in the flames of hell.

Chapter Twenty-Six

Nell

S tabbing pains in my head woke me. I was confused.
Terrified. It was horrifically dark, and I couldn't get any
air. I was buried alive—dirt and rot in my nose. Air. God, I
needed air.

I started struggling. Found that my arms were wrenched
back, wrists bound. I was curled in the fetal position. I couldn't
move. My own weight made my hyperextended shoulders burn
and throb. The vibration confused me. A bump slammed my
head against the floor.

Ah. Yes. I was folded up in the trunk of a car.

Panic would not help. I tried to relax, took the slowest, shal-
lowest breaths I could. Lack of oxygen explained the headache.
Carbon monoxide, maybe. Or both.

The car began to rattle and bump. We'd left the asphalt and
gotten onto a rutted dirt road. It stopped. A muttering of male
voices. Car doors popped open. The vehicle's weight lifted and
shifted as men got out.

I tried to remember how many I'd seen at Elsie's. Four, maybe.

Elsie. A fresh wave of emotion jolted me. Oh God, poor Elsie. And Wesley, too. They'd shot him and just left him there.

The trunk opened with a hollow *pop.* Daylight filtered through the filthy, stinking burlap that shrouded me. Rough arms grabbed me under the armpits, giving my shoulders an agonizing jolt. I was jerked out, legs bumping over the lip of the trunk. The ground whipped up and smacked me a blow that loosened every sinew.

"Take her into the building," said the harsh, cracked, aged voice with a thick accent. "And tie her to a chair. Tie her carefully. I'm tired of rude surprises."

I was hoisted up and dragged—feet bouncing over rough ground—into an enclosed structure. The sunlight I'd felt outside didn't penetrate here. It was humid, and cold, as if I were in a cave.

The man dragging me dropped me onto a straight-backed chair. My arms were jerked tighter, fastened to my ankles, twisting me into an agonized pretzel around the chair back. I gasped from the pain.

"The rest of you, out. Go keep watch," ordered the man with the accent. There were mutters, tramping feet, and a large door creaked and banged shut. The light filtering through the burlap diminished sharply.

A latch fell into place. *Clunk.*

Silence. My teeth chattered. I shook—huge, seismic shudders, as if I were freezing to death. I trembled so hard, the chair rattled against the floor.

The two remaining men stood there, watching me. I could sense their enjoyment.

"Take off the bag, John." The German-sounding man's voice oozed satisfaction.

The bag was wrenched off, whipping my head forward against the brutal pull of my tied arms. I coughed, dragging in big gulps of air.

My hair was over my eyes. I tried to shake it back, but the slightest movement made my head throb. I just stared through the veil of tangled hair, like a captured prehistoric cavewoman, face dirtied, mouth open, eyes staring and wild.

It wasn't bright inside that room, but it still took a moment for my eyes to readjusted. By some miracle, my glasses were still clinging to my face—askew, but still there.

Two men. One old and collapsed in on himself, with a flabby, jowly face. Watery blue eyes peered out from puffy bags of unwholesome flesh. His lips were an unhealthy, blotchy purple. He leered at me.

So did the other man—the one who fit Nancy's description of Snake Eyes. Burly, with deep-set eyes glittering with concentrated evil in the flushed, tightly packed fat of his heavy face. His lips were wet from being constantly licked.

Both were loathsome. Neither seemed concerned about me seeing their faces. They didn't expect me to ever have a chance to identify them.

I pushed that unhelpful thought swiftly out of my head.

The old man stumped forward, and tipped up my chin. "Antonella," he crooned. "In the flesh. And such lovely flesh." His hand crept down my chest, groping. He found my nipple and pinched.

I did not allow myself to yelp. "Who the hell are you?"

"My name is Ulf, my dear—Ulf Haupt. And this is my assistant, John, who your mother and sister have met before. But I am the one who will ask questions today. Not you."

"Wh-what do you want from me?"

The light in his eyes was pure insanity. "Information, my dear. Of course."

My stomach plummeted. That commodity of which I had so little. The other man, whom Ulf Haupt had called John, rummaged in my blouse, groping my boobs until he got his fist around my pendant.

He wrenched it until the chain broke. "We'll add this to our collection," he said.

"John's been eager to question you," Haupt said.

"Yeah, since this morning," John agreed. "When you broke up with the prick."

He waited for a reaction, laughing at my shocked expression. "Yes, I heard it all," he taunted. "I bugged your computer, you stupid cunt. You wanted him to declare his love, huh? Wanted him to grovel, suck your toes? I almost found it in my heart to pity the guy—if I hadn't had to listen to him fucking you for the last two days."

I recoiled. He leaned forward, until his face was inches from mine. "I heard it all. You dirty little slut. Heard you screaming and coming." He slapped me, rocking the chair so hard it teetered on two legs. "You love it, don't you? Filthy whore—"

"Enough, John!" The old man's voice was sharp. "Don't get carried away. She must not lose consciousness before we get the information we need. Play later."

John subsided, muttering something under his breath about cunts and sluts. His fists were clenched, his mouth open and wet, breath rasping fast. Irrational hate shone in his eyes. I was tied to a chair with a pair of raving maniacs.

Haupt patted the cheek that John had slapped, as if I were a little girl and he was a hideous parody of a benevolent grandfather. "So, my dear. Tell us what you know about the sketches."

Sketches? I seesawed frantically, wondering what would

get me killed the fastest—admitting ignorance or feigning knowledge. Either option looked bleak.

"I don't know anything about any sketches," I said.

Haupt's eyes hardened, and his fingers tightened on my cheek, pinching. "Do not lie. We read the Contessa's letter, you stupid girl. She said the three of you could solve the puzzle, so you must know something!"

"But I'm alone. I'm not with them." I shook my head to clear it, blowing hair up and out of my eyes. "And you took the letter, so we never got a chance to read it ourselves. And Lucia never had a chance to—"

Another vicious slap. My head rang. Tears sprang into my eyes.

"So the Contessa never told you how her father died?"

I shook my head, gulping. "No," I whispered.

"You want to hear the tale?" Haupt sounded eager to talk. "My father knew the old Conte de Luca, you see, back in their youth. In the thirties, before the war. They attended the art academy together in Rome for a time. They became close friends. Such good friends, the Conte even invited my father to visit his ancestral home. To show off the family's art treasures."

"Ah. I, um, see," I said, although I didn't.

"And then, the war. And the Reich," Haupt went on. "My father was a high-ranking officer in the SS. He arranged to be headquartered in de Luca's palazzo during the occupation. One of his duties was to appropriate the cream of the art pieces for the glory of the Reich. But the Conte de Luca was greedy. He kept aside his greatest treasures. He hid them, but drew a map describing where to find them."

I was hypnotized by the pale, mad eyes of the ruined old man. Spittle landed in my face as he talked. I silently willed him to go on and on. All day, all night.

As long as he was talking, they would not tear me to pieces.

"The war ended," Haupt went on. "My father fled to Argentina after the war, but he never forgot. He paid de Luca a visit fifteen years later, but the sketches were still hidden. Would you like to know what my father did to the Conte? In his efforts to convince him to reveal the hiding place?"

"N-n-no," I quavered. "Thanks, but no."

"Do not be insolent!" Haupt shrieked. "Perhaps if I tell you that you will share his exact same fate, it will spark your curiosity, hmm?" He slid his cold, puffy hand down over my arm, my breasts. "All that smooth, flawless skin. So pale, and soft and perfect. A pity, really."

Delay, delay. "And, ah, wh-what about M-m-marco?"

"So you know about the Marchese Barbieri? Worthless old turd. He had the map—little good it did him. My father, and later I stationed domestic spies in the Palazzo de Luca for decades, watching him search, but he never found the sketches. And then, one fine day, he climbs on a plane! And flies to America! What a curious thing, eh?" He rubbed his hands together. "John was there to meet him. That was how we finally located the elusive Contessa. But John has an impulse control problem. I call it, 'kill now, ask questions later.'" Haupt shot a poisonous glance at John. "The Marchese and Contessa were dead before we could find out what he brought, or where he hid it. So be a good girl, Antonella, and maybe John won't be so harsh with you, eh?"

I swallowed. "I will cooperate. As much as I can." Which wasn't very goddamn much. As they would discover soon enough.

Haupt held up both necklaces. Nancy's sapphire pendant, and my ruby one. They swung and glittered in the dim light filtering through the cobwebby windows.

"Tell me the secret of the necklaces," he commanded.

I winced. "I don't know. I only saw an incomplete draft of

the letter you took. It said that only the three of us, working together using our love of art, could open some sort of key, but we never figured out exactly to what. I'm sure she meant to tell us more before she—"

Crack, another slap. My nose was now dripping blood.

"Do not lie!" Haupt shrieked. "I know you know more! We have researched you, Antonella. The bitch Contessa had you study Italian and Latin. You were being groomed to take over the search! Admit it! Why else would you study a dead language? Have you seen the map? Have you read it? What does it say?"

"No! I-I-I haven't s-s-seen..." I floundered, stammering. My imagination was failing me. How could I justify a passion for language and literature for its own sake to subhuman monsters like this? They wouldn't understand it. They didn't even know what beauty was. How could they imagine loving it?

John stepped up, with a businesslike air. His next blow knocked my chair off balance. It teetered on one leg, tipped. The room swirled as I tumbled backward, onto my tied hands. *Crunch.* Wood splintered beneath me—and oh shit, oh dear God, my hands ... oh, that *hurt*—

A long broken shard of wood from a piece of junked furniture had stabbed into the pad of my thumb. I wrenched my thumb loose from the shard, again, groping with my fingers feeling blood flow, slippery and hot. Felt for the shard. There it was. My hand closed around it, and clenched.

Snap. I broke off the tip. Small, but sharp, hidden in my fingers. A few inches long.

John hooked the back of my chair and heaved me upright. "Let's try that question again, Antonella." He leaned down, the whites of his eyes showing, and slid the point of his knife under my blouse. A few sharp jerks, and the fabric gave, gaped. Buttons flew, skittering on concrete.

He dug the knife tip under silk cord that held my bra cups together, flicked the knife. This time, he nicked my skin. Blood welled up, trickled down my belly. Blood dripped from my wounded hand, as well. I clutched the splinter, hard enough to hurt, to ward off the squirming nausea, the waves of sick vertigo.

The knife gleamed in front of my wide, hypnotized eyes.

"Now, Antonella," he said, companionably. "Let's talk about art."

Chapter Twenty-Seven

Duncan

"Right on Connemara Drive, four point two miles. Hard left onto a dirt road, half a mile past the creek. Her signal's three hundred meters ahead of me—perpendicular to the main road and ten degrees to the right. I'm leaving the car. Tell the cavalry to hurry the fuck up."

"Dunc! Hold on! Don't just—"

I killed the phone and took off running. Glad for whatever instinct had prompted me to put on brown and olive drab. Her signal had been stationary for twenty minutes. Plenty of time to hurt her, if that was their intent.

I felt cold, my emotions flatlined. A virtual figure in a video game, sent out to earn points, defeat goblins, gargoyles, basilisks, to defeat the evil sorcerer, if I scored enough points and made no wrong moves. But in the video game, the player's life wouldn't be gutted if he fucked up. There would be no "Game Over" flashing on the screen. No invitation to try his luck again.

I had one chance. One. I hoped.

I ran onward, darting from bush to tree until the building came into view—and then the car. I hoped there were no infrared alarms, but I doubted there would be. This struck me as an improvised, last-minute snatch. This place was makeshift. Not their turf.

I hoped.

The building looked like an abandoned, crumbling barn. I spotted the first sentry and sank down into the bushes, recognizing the tall Black guy from Lafayette. I dropped to my belly and slithered around him, keeping beneath his line of vision. When I spiraled in closer, the guy was turned, pissing against a tree.

I leaped up behind him. The guy spun around, dick still in his hand. He sucked in air to yell, and took the heel of my boot to the point of his chin. *Crunch.*

He toppled, eyes rolled back, hit the tree and slid to the ground on his ass, slumped over, pants still open.

Voices. I followed them, slithering toward the hushed murmur in the clearing around the barn. It was the blond dickhead from Lafayette, smoking a cigarette and talking to a stocky, shorter guy. The blond had bruises beneath both eyes.

I crept closer, recognizing his reedy, whining tone before I could make out the words. I pulled out a couple of drugged throwing stars.

"... with this kind of shit! It ain't worth the fuckin' money to get treated like fuckin' dogshit," he bitched. "All I'm saying is, they better let me take my turn with the bitch after John works her over, because I mean to teach that cunt nobody messes with Curtis, man—hey!"

His monologue choked off to a shriek. He clawed at his ass and held up the throwing star I'd lobbed at him. "What the fuck?"

The second guy howled. A star protruded from his shoulder.

Curtis spun, and sprayed the woods with bullets from his Uzi. "Who the fuck are you, you fuck?" he shrieked. "I'll waste your ass!"

So much for stealth. Curtis was wavering, toppling. The other guy went down even faster. The points of the stars were treated with a high-power, quick-acting sedative. I waited for some reaction from the barn.

Sure enough. The door opened and a man poked his head out. A man who fit the description Nancy had given of Snake Eyes. Big, burly, close-set eyes.

"What the fuck is going on?" he snarled. He saw the unconscious men collapsed on the ground, and his face twisted with disgust. "Fucking jerk-offs," he muttered, and lifted his pistol.

He pumped a short burst of bullets into them both. The sprawled bodies jittered on the ground and lay still.

I stared through the foliage. The two men were torn apart, lying in pools of blood. Snake Eyes lifted his gun and sprayed the woods in a wide arc. Bullets sliced through grass and leaves, right above my head. Splinters of bark and earth flew, bullets thudded into the ground.

Snake Eyes laughed hysterically. "Fuck off and die, shit-head!" he howled. "It's my turn now! I got her now! You can go fuck yourself!" Another spray of bullets punched into the forest —*rat-tat-tat-tat.*

Snake Eyes ducked back inside. In the distance, police sirens started to wail.

I ran like a bolt from a crossbow across the carnage in the clearing and flung myself at the door. "Nell!" I bellowed.

"Duncan?" she called back, just as bullets pumped through the door.

One of them grazed my hip, like a sharp flick of flame. Another caught my pocket above my knee, ripping the fabric.

She screamed, a wrenching cry that froze my blood as I sprinted around the building.

Chapter Twenty-Eight

Nell

"They're coming," John said to Haupt. "We have to cut loose. Curtis and Turturro are meat. Didn't see Gerard. Probably dead, too."

"They're coming? Who is coming? How did they know where to come? How is it possible?" The man's voice rose to a shrill, querulous squawk. "You stupid, incompetent—"

"You want to berate me on our way to jail, or save it for later?" John snarled back. "Move it!"

He slashed the ropes that bound my arms. They fell free, numb and tingling. John yanked a handful of my hair, jerking until I cried out. "Be good, bitch," he hissed. "Or I'll gut you."

He hoisted me up and flung me over his shoulder, letting my head and arms dangle down over his back.

Something banged against the door. "Nell!"

Duncan. Oh, God. "Duncan!" I yelled.

"I said, shut up, bitch!" John swung up his gun, riddled the door with bullets.

Light shone through the pattern of holes, and I screamed again, in horror and despair, but John was running now, and my voice was jolting in my throat, my torso bouncing and thudding against his back.

They burst out the back of the barn. I couldn't see where they were going, just green leaves, the ground behind John's pounding heels, his loose belt, his T-shirt riding up to reveal pimple-spotted rolls of flab hanging over the waistband of his jeans.

The sound of his footsteps changed—a hollow thud on wooden planks. Haupt hurried along beside them, huffing and puffing.

A bridge. I saw weathered planks below John's booted feet, water murmuring and gurgling beneath us. John swung around, started shooting—a deafening barrage of bullets. My whole body jiggled with the jackhammer explosions.

My blood-slicked hand tightened around the splinter. I worked it down until the sharp part protruded a couple of inches, the blunt part clutched in my fist. The point was wickedly sharp. I gathered my nerve for the blow.

I concentrated everything I had to give into that sharp point: my love for Duncan, for my sisters, for Lucia, even my childish devotion to Elena. My reverence for beauty, for love, for art. My respect for effort, honesty, bravery. All the things that couldn't be bought.

John turned. The gun rose up. *No.* Because he had no right to hurt me, or Duncan, or anyone else.

He had ... no ... goddamn ... *right.*

I stabbed down, driving the splinter deep into the meat and fat that covered his kidney. He squealed, and his shots went wild.

Bam, Duncan's bullet blew John's gun out of his hand. It flew up, curling and turning in the air. John lunged to catch it one-handed, but it danced off his fingers and down. An eternity later, it splashed into the river.

"Put her down." It was Duncan's voice, cool and even.

John stared back, panting. He laughed. "Sure thing, shitbird."

He heaved me over the bridge railing.

I flew, fell, down, turning, spinning, and cold green water closed over my head.

Chapter Twenty-Nine

Duncan

I sprinted to the middle of the bridge and pitched myself over the side. The current was strong when I burst up for air, the river swollen from recent rains.

Nell bobbed to the surface, her face plastered with hair, gasping for breath. I fought my way over to her and pulled her close.

When I finally got us over to the shore, I scooped her out into my arms. Her cheek was swollen, her lips split. There was blood crusted in her nostrils. They'd been hitting her. Rage clawed at me, but the fuckers were long gone. No one to catch and punish. Yet.

Her eyes fluttered open and fastened onto me. Her lips chattered so hard, it took a long time for her to speak.

"Y-y-you c-c-came for m-me," she said.

She dropped her face against my chest and shut down. Shock. Her face was so pale. I struggled up the steep creek bank and broke into a heavy, stumbling run through the forest.

Hoping that whoever was blowing those police sirens had the presence of mind to bring an ambulance along.

They did. Soon, I was able to pass her into the hands of people whose business it was to make sure she'd be all right. But I had to struggle to let go of her when the time came. They had to pry my shaking, clawed fingers loose.

The period that followed was a murky blur. A lot of people tried to talk to me, to very little purpose. I'd just shut down.

I stared at myself in the hospital bathroom mirror. I stank of that bitter antiseptic foam soap in the squeeze bottle over the sink—the stuff I'd tried to clean myself up with. I supposed it beat the stench of river mud, but the blend of the two bad smells was uniquely nasty.

Nancy and Liam had brought me a change of clothes. Liam's stuff fit well enough, although the shirt was tight around my shoulders. My own clothing lay in a clammy, mud-slimed snarl on the hospital bathroom floor. I shoved the gun back into my jeans, covered it with the shirttail.

I was crashing. I felt icy cold inside, and my hands couldn't stop shaking.

The doctors and nurses had forced me out of Nell's room so they could examine her, hook her up to all the tubes, needles, and machines. I'd waited outside the door like a patient hound shivering on the doorstep until they took pity on me and let me back in again.

She looked so fragile. So pale. Only her hair had vitality, lying in great billows of fuzzy black ringlets over the pillow.

I was so afraid I could hardly breathe. I wondered if I'd earned enough points with this stunt to get another chance with her, after everything that had happened.

I'd seen how my world looked without her in it. I'd felt that to the fullest during that hellacious race against time. I couldn't face it.

I'd say any words she wanted to hear. I didn't give a fuck whether they were true or not, realistic or not. I no longer cared about honesty, dealing straight, any of that meaningless bullshit. She could write out a script for me, if she wanted, and I'd parrot it back to her, get it signed, witnessed, and notarized. I wasn't ashamed. I didn't have the energy for shame. I knew when I was whipped.

The only reason I'd left her bedside at all was because Liam and Nell's sisters were there, talking in hushed tones, giving me worried looks. Vivi had bought me coffee and a sandwich at the lunch stand in the lobby. I hadn't been able to eat it. My insides had turned to stone.

I kicked my stuff into the corner of the bathroom and walked out, braving the sympathetic glances. Vivi vacated the chair near the head of Nell's bed. I jerked my chin at it, indicating that she should sit again.

"As fucking if. Sit." She grabbed my shoulders and pushed me into the chair. "You're the one who's been out there being heroic, getting shot at."

I slumped into the chair and took Nell's hand again—the one that wasn't torn up, bandaged into a puffy white ball. Her hand was so cold. But so was mine. Clammy with fear. I had no heat to give her.

Vivi put her hand on my shoulder, leaned over, and kissed the top of my head. "Hey. Duncan," she said softly. "You did good. It's going to be fine. Try to relax, okay? You're scaring us."

I jerked my head and hunched lower over Nell's hand. Some time later, her fingers twitched inside mine. My heart jumped into my throat. Her eyes were fluttering open. Dazed.

Nancy and Vivi got up and came over to the other side of the bed. "Hey, sweetie," Nancy said, her voice thick with tears.

Nell gave them a tiny smile, like the corners of her lips were too heavy to lift. Her eyes flicked to mine. I stared back, mute.

A silence took over the room. An electrical charge that grew ... and grew.

"Ah, maybe the three of us can just go take a little coffee break," Vivi suggested softly. "Come on, you guys. Let's go."

They trooped out the door, leaving the two of us finally alone.

Chapter Thirty

Nell

I gazed up, so happy he was there. Both of us, still alive. How marvelous—and improbable—was that? My heart was swelling. So soft and full, it felt like a supernova in my chest. I was exhausted, limp. So soft. Just a fuzzy glow of light lying in the bed. Probably it was whatever they'd drugged me with. Nice stuff, whatever it was.

Duncan lifted my hand and leaned forward, elbows on the bed, rubbing my knuckles against his cheek. His beard stubble was a delicious cat's-tongue rasp of pleasurable friction against my skin. He didn't look good. His eyes were shadowed, and his mouth was grim. I tried to speak to him, but my muscles wouldn't respond.

"Don't talk," he ordered, frowning. "Rest."

I finally got words out, letting them ride on the outbreath. "Did I thank you for saving my life?"

A smile softened the grim cast of his face. "Not in the last thirty-six hours."

247

"Ah. Well." I squeezed his hand. "For the record. Thanks. You always come through for me."

There was so much to say to him it was bottlenecked inside me. Then suddenly, my memories coalesced—and with them, a clutch of fear. "Elsie?" I asked. "Wesley?"

"They're okay," he assured me. "Elsie was treated for shock and a knock on the head—your sisters told me—but she's already getting a huge charge out of being a local celebrity. She's in hog heaven, giving interviews to the local paper from her hospital bed. Wesley's pretty bad, but he's in stable condition. The bullet missed his vital organs. He lost a lot of blood, but he should be okay."

"Thank God," I murmured. My eyes drifted closed again. I felt like a radio, tuning in and out of the frequency of consciousness, but Duncan was always there, like a rock coming in and out of view in the mist. So comforting.

Another factoid popped to the top of my mind. "They're looking for sketches," I said.

He frowned. "Huh? Who is looking for what?"

"John and Ulf Haupt. Snake Eyes and his handler. The bad guys. Lucia's treasure. They're after sketches of some kind. Tell my sisters and Liam, okay? Haupt told me his name and a bunch of other random stuff, just for the fun of it. To taunt me. They were so sure that they were going to kill me, they didn't even worry about it. Hah. Funny, isn't it?"

His eyebrows furrowed. "Don't know if funny's the word I'd use."

"The Conte de Luca, Lucia's father, went to school with Haupt's father," I said. "Then during the second World War, the senior Haupt came to loot all the De Luca art treasures for the third Reich. But de Luca hid these sketches, whatever they were. Wild stuff. How did you know to come after me?"

"Found a bug in your laptop," he said. "I knew they had a bead on you. I followed the GPS in the smartphone I gave you."

"No way," I whispered. "Saved by a smartphone. The irony."

He pressed my hand against his cheek. "I couldn't let them hurt you."

I stroked his jaw. "You're cold," I fretted softly. "Why are you cold? You're usually so hot."

"I'm scared shitless," he blurted out.

My eyes widened, shocked. "Huh? You? Why?"

"I thought I'd lost you." The words rushed out as if they were under pressure. "Nothing's worth shit without you, Nell. If they hurt you, that would be it for me. I'd be finished. Dead meat. Worm food."

I petted his cheek, trying to soothe him. "Duncan. Don't—"

"I have to have you in my life," he said. "Have to. I don't give a shit anymore about all that crap we argued about. You want me to make a formal declaration of love, fine. You want me to memorize poetry and recite it to you naked and standing on my head, I'll do it. Any fucking song or dance routine you want—"

"No," I said.

He cut off the stream of words, alarmed. "Uh, no in what sense?"

"No, in the sense of no, it's not necessary at all. You don't have to stand on your head or do any song and dance routine. You don't even have to tell me that you love me. Because you already did."

He blinked. "I did? How do you figure? When?"

"Just now," I told him. "You were telling me all along, if I'd only listened with my heart. Then you saving me down on Lafayette, and coming to save me from Snake Eyes and Haupt today, that was another big fat clue for me. Then again, you are the heroic type by nature, so maybe I can't read that much into it—"

"The hell you can't," he said forcefully.

I smiled at him. "Okay, then. You get big points for that. And for the blazing originality in your manner of communicating love and passion. That's worth some serious extra credit."

His face cleared, but he still looked perplexed. "Great," he said doubtfully. "Hold on, here. Points? Extra credit? What's this? I thought talking in terms of scoring points pissed you off. That it was ... how did you say it? Reductionist?"

I laughed softly, petting his cheek again. I couldn't bear to stop. "There's something about staring death in the face that helps a girl get over her pet peeves. It cuts through big steaming piles of psychological bullshit like nobody's business."

"Ah. So I don't have to figure out how to get all poetic now? Do I have to tell you your eyes are like stars and your skin like lily petals? And your ass like a ripe, juicy peach?"

I shook my head. "Stars, lilies, peaches, pah. Overdone. Having a guy charge in to save you from torture at the hands of psychopathic sadists? That is deathless poetry, buddy."

"I think you're making fun of me," he said doubtfully.

"Oh, God, no," I assured him fervently. "I mean every word."

Duncan laid his head on my chest. His shoulders shook, but I couldn't tell with what emotion. I ran my fingers through his sweat-stiffened hair, again and again. I didn't want to break our physical contact for a single second. I wanted to cling to him. I wanted to be fused.

"So. Are we getting married, then?" His muffled voice had a challenging tone. "Is that what you're saying? Is it a done deal? Can we do it soon?"

I smiled up at the ceiling, euphoric. I was going to float up there and get stuck on the ceiling. "As soon as you like," I told him. "As soon as we can make it happen. It's the done-est deal that ever was. You are never getting out of my clutches."

He raised his head and fixed me with a narrow gaze, as if daring me to contradict him. "And we're having our honeymoon in Italy. Right?"

"Sounds amazing," I said softly. "Great idea. I've always wanted to go."

He hugged me tighter. "You are so beautiful," he muttered. "And by the way. Your ass really is like a ripe, juicy peach—smooth and downy and perfect."

"Thank you," I told him. "A lovely sentiment. I'm so touched."

"Oh, you will be," he promised. "At great length, as soon as you're up for it. But I'm not done with my spiel. I know you're tired, but I have to get all this out."

"Duncan—"

"Just let me say it," he said. "I know I'm stubborn, and resistant to change, and I tend to always order the same thing in restaurants. But the flip side is—I know what I like. Once I make up my mind, I don't change it. I'm talking about until the fucking end of time, Nell. I'm talking about to the ends of the earth. You get me?"

"I do now," I told him. "And I love that about you. I love the way you say it. To the ends of being and ideal grace. I'm melting. Keep going."

He looked worried. "Keep going? Oh God. You mean, I have to keep being poetic? Long term? Fuck me! I can't keep that shit going indefinitely!"

I giggled. "Oh, so that's the hard part? And the mortal combat was easy?"

"Maybe not easy, but mortal combat is more or less straightforward," he said. "You get killed or you don't. But love, man ...

that shit's complicated. I didn't know how to give you what you want. I'm still not sure I know. But I want to learn."

Love. He'd said it. He'd put it out there. Not that I had any more doubts, but still. It was nice to hear the word come out of his mouth, in that soft tone.

I traced his stern, sexy mouth with a fascinated finger. "I think we fixed it," I told him. "I think we were talking about the same thing all along. But now I see it. It took getting my ass properly kicked, but I see it very clearly now. We met halfway."

"Uh, thanks." He looked bemused. "So this is the halfway point?"

"Yeah." I pulled his face down and kissed him. "It's nice here, isn't it?"

"Best place in the world." He touched his lips to my forehead, as gently as if I were a newly opened flower. "Let's stay there forever."

I wrapped my arms around his neck and pulled him down. "Forever works for me," I whispered, as our lips met.

If you want more of the saga of the D'Onofrio stories, don't miss Edge of Ruin, Book 3 of The Edge Trilogy!

Excerpt: Edge of Ruin

The Edge Series, Book 3
Chapter One

Vivi

I had to just grit my teeth and face it. My van was stuck in the mud.

I'd been spinning the tires in the slop for over fifteen minutes now, and my poor old Volkswagen van was groaning and lurching with the strain. I had to come up with an adult solution, probably one that required spending money I could ill afford, and looking stupid and feckless and ridiculous in front of a bunch of people that I had never even met. Which made me wince and cringe. Alas, poor me.

I killed the engine, shoved my tangled red hair back behind my ears, and pounded on the steering wheel with a grinding shriek of frustration. I was alone, aside from my long-suffering dog, Edna, so I could afford a little tantrum. Edna would never tell.

It didn't make me feel any better, though. The world outside the rain-sluiced windshield was a wavering blur of greens. Lightning flashed. I braced myself for the huge crash ...

Chapter One

Edna yelped when it jolted us, and scrambled frantically into my lap. I petted the quivering dog. "Easy, honey girl," I crooned. "It'll be over soon. We'll get through it."

A hopeful thought, but I would still be in a very sticky jam when the storm was over. Perhaps an even stickier jam, depending on how much water was still in the sky, still getting ready to fall on top of me. This road could slide right off the mountain and bury us under tons of mud.

Which struck me as a train of thought to carefully avoid right now.

It had seemed like a good idea late last night, to just push on, rain and all. The truth, if I was being honest, was that I'd been simply too scared to stop driving.

Too much tragic, horrible, terrifying shit had happened recently. The most horrific being that my adopted mom, Lucia, had been murdered some weeks before.

That calamity had knocked me and my two sisters all onto our asses.

Then, to make matters worse, my two sisters, Nancy and Nell, had both been attacked, multiple times. We had finally managed to conclude, mostly based on the meager crumbs of information the attackers had let drop when they kidnapped Nell, that our enemies were looking for some mysterious art object, something hidden decades ago in Italy, before the Second World War. As far as we could tell, everyone who knew where it was, or hell, even what it was, had long since died.

The killers had tried to get information about it from Lucia, but they had failed. Lucia had died without giving it to them, because she was a boss. Fierce. Indomitable. My role model, my hero.

After that, infuriated, the murdering assholes turned their

sights on us. Lucia's clueless adopted daughters, who knew jack shit about any of Lucia's mysterious past.

It was hard to argue with stomach-churning fear when I was all alone, no one to act tough and fearless for. Only Edna knew the truth, and bless her sweet heart, she did not judge me. She just panted her hot, fishy breath heavily into my face and offered her solid, comforting presence like the very good, loyal girl that she was.

Edna's silky, chocolate brown fur had soaked up many tears I wouldn't show to anyone else. But even with my trusty dog at my side, I hadn't been able to face a roadside motel with a single door lock between me and the night, which was all I could afford. I was the only D'Onofrio chick left without a big, vigilant, protective guy, giving the hairy eyeball to every stranger within shouting range of his new lady. That made me the obvious soft target. Good old Vivi was on her own, as always.

Not that I begrudged my sisters their good fortune. They both deserved to have a tough, devoted, foxy guy worshiping at their shrines. In fact, Liam and Duncan still didn't know how lucky they were in their fabulous new fiancées. They were going to be discovering it for the rest of their lives. Those men had been tongue-kissed by Fate.

I was intensely grateful for those guys, and what they had done for Nancy and Nell. Both men were both tough, vigilant, battle-tested. My sisters were as safe with Duncan and Liam as they could possibly be in these strange days. But as for me, well. I was feeling very solitary and unworshipped. I had been feeling that way even before Ulf Haupt and John the Fiend, a.k.a. Snake Eyes, started attacking the D'Onofrio women. I was a generally cheerful person, and I made a real effort to keep it positive. But under these conditions, it was almost impossible to keep my chin up.

Chapter One

Both of my sisters had tried to persuade me to stay with them until we figured out what to do about our bloodthirsty enemies. But who knew how long that would take?

That solution struck me as nonproductive, unsustainable, and ultimately embarrassing. How long could a woman realistically sit around like a bump on a log in her sister's place, bored out of her mind, not working, not making art, being a financial drain and a big fat fifth wheel?

No way. I just couldn't. I would go mad. I would start to misbehave.

Besides, I really missed my dog. She'd been boarding with a friend of mine who lived out in the country since things got so weird, but my girl belonged with me. I'd never committed to anything in my life the way I'd committed to Edna. Every day I had made her wait for me had hurt me just a little bit more.

Nah, I just had to muddle on somehow. Even with all the grief and jealousy and confusion and stalking fiends. I was plenty stubborn. It was a D'Onofrio thing.

I stroked Edna's floppy, velvety soft ears, and buried my face against her silky fur. It calmed me down and let me breathe a little deeper. I peered out at the heavy, swollen gray sky. I supposed I could call my new mysterious landlord Jack Kendrick, Duncan's old friend from his stint as a field agent in the NSA. Kendrick liable to know how to begin solving my complicated logistical problems.

But how freaking embarrassing was that.

I checked my phone. Well, hell. There was no coverage here anyway. That settled that. I was utterly lost out in the ass end of nowhere.

Which was the whole idea, of course. To hide out somewhere remote, lost, trackless, where Ulf Haupt and Snake Eyes John would never think to look for me.

I'd made it to the town of Silverfish, Washington, around

two in the afternoon, if one could call it a town. Through the torrents of rain, all I had seen there on the main drag was a convenience store, a gas pump, a bait and tackle shop, and a boarded-up old Dairy Queen.

I had followed the directions, which I'd been advised to print out, since the place was out of the reach of GPS. I made my way onto progressively smaller roads, finally arriving at a dirt track with a hand-painted sign that read Moffat's Way. Nothing further in the directions. At that point, it was straight on til morning, evidently.

But Moffat's Way wasn't a driveway, but an old logging road, deeply rutted and frighteningly steep. By the time I had realized how rough the road actually was, those ruts had become streams, with no place anywhere that was wide enough to turn around. I had made a sharp turn into a deep puddle, sank into the mud at a terrifying angle, and that was that.

I leaned my hot cheek against the cool window, mind racing. Still procrastinating. Edna stuck her nose into my hand and gave it a sloppy, comforting lick, and then started enthusistically in on the side of my face.

Who knew how much farther this road went on before it came to Jack Kendrick's land? I hadn't bothered to inform myself about such nitpicky details. I just figured, I'd get there when I got there, since the road stopped at his house, the directions said. You couldn't go wrong, the directions said. Hah. If there was one thing I was unusually good at, it was at taking wrong turns. Everyone had their little superpower.

I spun the tires a few more times, just to torture myself. Time to take action. Self-sufficient, proactive Vivi D'Onofrio could rise to any occasion, I bracingly told myself. Psychopathic kidnappers? Bring 'em on.

A long shudder racked my body. Well. Maybe not.

The rain was no longer a torrent, just a regular shower, so I flung open the door of the van, looking around myself in vain for a solid place to put my feet. Edna crawled eagerly over my lap, and I clutched at her collar in alarm. "No way, babe," I said sternly. "That's all I need. A mud-covered dog. Get back inside. In!"

Edna shrank back, looking reproachful. I rolled my pants up, looked at my cheerful, bright-green high-tops regretfully, and jumped out. At least they were old, like most of my clothes at this point. Maybe a run through a washing machine would salvage them.

Cold, sucking mud swallowed my feet to the ankles. I slogged around the van, and realized that the tires were half buried. Chilly rain plastered my hair to my scalp and the green T-shirt to my body. I let loose with a stream of explicit profanity, the foul, biting kind I'd learned in the Bronx as a child, and punctuated by kicking a slimy tire. Hard enough to make a bolt of pain shoot up my leg.

Yeah, that's right, Viv. Check me out, yapping like a fishwife at inanimate objects. Very impressive. Very mature.

Farther back, I'd seen what looked like a collapsed shack. Maybe some planks laid down in front of the tires would give them purchase to get out of the muck. Beyond the puddle, the road looked almost drivable.

I would exhaust every possibility before limping to Jack Kendrick's house on foot like a cat left out in the rain. Fine first impression that would be. I knew only what Duncan had told me about the guy. That Kendrick was some sort of ex-spy commando who'd been on some top-secret intelligence gathering task force with Duncan years ago. Now, unaccountably, he grew flowers. Duncan had been vague about the details of that career change, his brain being flash-fried from being insanely in love with Nell.

So this mysterious Kendrick lived in the woods, and

evidently had an apartment in his barn. According to Duncan, he was cool with letting me huddle in his flowery bower like a quivering, nose-twitching bunny until we figured out what to do about our art-hungry, murdering psychopaths. Very nice of him, but it didn't say much for his smarts, though, or his sense of self-preservation. He must owe Duncan money. Only an absolute bonehead would take on a hard-luck case like me.

Seriously, though. I was still waiting for the other shoe to drop. Duncan had assured me that Kendrick knew the score, that he had agreed to the plan, that he wasn't intimidated by the risks. But no normal person would agree to something that crazy. The guy must have a screw loose. Yeah, sure, I'll invite the unknown girl with the deadly psychopath stalking her to crash in my barn. What could possibly go wrong?

It had sounded so perfect, back in New York City. Too perfect, in retrospect. Now that I was thinking about all alone, stuck in the mud.

Ah, yes. There it was, a stack of gray, weathered planks, rusty nails sticking through them at crazy angles. I wrestled and yanked until I'd extricated a few boards, along with some ugly splinters, then negotiated the slippery boards through the fir thickets. By the time I got back to the van, soggy, scratched, and panting, I was spewing a fresh stream of profanity. I hauled out my handy toolbox, hammered the nails flat, and started wrestling them into place. Mud oozed over the tops of the planks, and I was thoroughly slimed from chest to feet when I heard the deep voice from behind me.

"I don't think that'll work right now." A deep, calm voice.

I jolted up, knocking my head on the bumper. "Who is that?" I scrambled to my feet, looking frantically around myself. There was no one there that I could see.

I scanned the trees and reached for the tire iron stowed

under the seat, groping until my fingers closed over the bar of cold, hard metal.

"Where are you?" I called out. "Say something."

"Over here."

I spun, brandishing the tire iron. A tall man, stood there, half hidden in the trees. He was shrouded in a dull-green hooded rain poncho, dripping with rain. I would never have seen him if he had not spoken.

Adrenaline zinged through me. I gave the tire iron an experimental heft. "What do you think you're doing, sneaking up on me like that?" I demanded.

He took a step forward. I raised the tire iron with a menacing face, and he stopped.

"Sorry I scared you," he said.

Edna whined anxiously from the van, sticking her nose outside the door I'd left halfway open. "Stay, Edna," I snapped. "Who the hell are you?"

"I'm not going to attack you," he said, pushing back his hood. "You can relax."

Relax, my ass. Light, silver-gray eyes, cool and unreadable. His face was brown, lean. High cheekbones, a hooked nose. A scar on one temple slashed down into one of his straight, dark eyebrows, leaving a white line. He had a short beard, or maybe longish beard stubble. Dark hair, long and shaggy. He regarded her steadily. Drops of rain beaded his face. He did not look like Snake Eyes, as Nancy and Nell had described him. This guy was not loathsome, swollen, squint-eyed, or malodorous. Not that I could smell him from here. I would have to get much closer. And inhale. Hungrily.

This guy was oh-my-God fine. I tried to breathe. My terror was transmuting itself into utter embarrassment. An unfortunate development.

"Put it down, please." A small smile crinkled up the skin around his eyes.

"What?" I said, realizing that my mouth had been hanging open.

"The tire iron." He glanced at my white-knuckled hand.

"Oh." I felt foolish, panicked. Acutely conscious of the mud on my clothes, the hair stuck to my face, the way my wet, muddy shirt clung to my tits. Of how incredibly tall he was. Even if he wasn't Snake Eyes John, he was still a complete stranger, and there was nobody around here for miles. Just me and Edna, the world's friendliest dog.

I looked at the hand that clutched the tire iron. It was shaking.

"The boards aren't going to work," he said gently. "It was a good idea, but the mud is too wet and deep." He took a step closer. I backed away, then kicked myself, for acting like a scared, cringing kitten.

He picked up a stick, walking away from me. He headed around the back of the van, prodding at the mud with a stick he held.

Released from the spell of his eyes, I finally managed to exhale. *Get a grip.* He was not going to leap on me like a rabid dog. I had to at least try to be civil. My face felt so hot, raindrops should be skittering on it like water on a griddle. Insane. I never blushed.

"I asked what you were doing here," I said, trying to sound authoritative.

"This is my land," he said.

"Oh." I dropped my gaze, before his bright eyes could catch it and nail it down again. "Do you always walk around in thunderstorms?"

"I do, actually. Rainstorms, at least. The thunder took me

261

by surprise. But I like the rain. I like the way it smells. I really, really wish you'd put that thing down."

"I'll put it down when I'm ready to put it down," I said shakily.

He tossed down his stick. "Whatever. Just don't hit me with it."

"I wouldn't without provocation," I said.

His mouth twitched. "Oh, please," he murmured. "Would you just chill the fuck out, already? You are safe. Completely safe. I swear it. On my immortal soul. Okay?"

I felt ridiculous, and threw the tire iron back into the van in disgust.

"You travel alone?" he asked.

"No. With my dog," I replied.

Edna barked excitedly when her existence was mentioned, taking it as permission to bound out the door. She landed in the mud with a wet plop, shook herself, and trotted over to the stranger. She gave his large brown hand a cautious sniff, then panted up into his face, smiling. Then she stroked her mud-spattered head against his leg.

"Down, Edna," I ordered, startled. Edna had never cozied up to strangers without taking her cue from me first. It made me feel vaguely betrayed. "Get back in here!"

Edna trotted back, panting. "Sorry about that," I said.

"No problem." A brief smile lit his face. "Nice dog."

"Too nice," I muttered. I started to push back the tangled hair that clung to my face, but stopped short, remembering the mud on my hands.

He gazed at me, projecting a weird, supernatural calm. Maybe hanging out in nature did that to a guy. Look at him, walking through pouring rain because he liked the way it smelled. What was he, a freaking Jedi knight? Give me a break.

It made me feel embarrassed to be myself. Frantic, citified, stressed out, nervous, afraid. A shallow little squeaking hamster racing on a wheel. And the hungry, fanged tomcats were lurking out there, licking their chops. Waiting for lunch.

Oh, for Christ's sake, I needed a vacation. Or at the very least, a night's sleep.

"Your van's not going anywhere today," he remarked.

I suppressed a snarky comment and wiped my hands on the hem of my drenched tee-shirt. Good grief. He could see everything through that shirt. I hadn't worn a bra, being alone, and I wasn't wearing a jacket. And oh, shit, now I was blushing again.

"I figured that out all by myself," I said. "Can you tell me how might I get a tow around here?"

He prodded the mud with his stick once again, looked up at the lowering clouds. "That isn't going to happen for a while," he said calmly. "See how steep that hill is? No one can pull you out until this dries up." He stroked Edna's head. "What possessed you to drive a beat-up old vehicle like this out onto an old logging road in the middle of a thunderstorm?"

"This beat-up old vehicle is the only one I have," I shot back. "It's been my home for years, and it's a perfectly fine machine that's served me very well from the start. It's the damn road that's the problem!"

A frown appeared between the man's brows. "You live in this thing?" His tone was faintly incredulous.

"Yes, actually," I said. "I'm a craftswoman. I work the craft fair circuit, so I often end up living on the road. Up till now, that is."

"Interesting, but this road goes nowhere that's relevant to you and your crafts fair circuit. So it doesn't explain what you're doing on my land."

Why, that arrogant dickhead. "That's none of your business," I said.

"It is now," he said. "Since this thing is blocking my road."

I lifted my chin. "Wait a second," I said. "Didn't you just say that nobody's going to be driving on it until it's dry anyhow? Ergo, I'm not blocking anything, buddy."

His eyes looked me thoughtfully up and down. "True enough, I guess," he said. "But it's still my land." He wasn't ogling me, but my body still shivered, as if he were slowly checking me out, inch by inch.

I suppressed an urge to cross my arms across my breasts. I would remain nonchalant, or I would freaking die in the attempt. "Besides, I'm not trespassing," I said, with all the bravado I could muster. "I'm on my way to my new landlord's place. Can you tell me how far is it to Jack Kendrick's house?"

The man's face went blank. His brow furrowed as he stared at me, and then at the mud-splattered, fantastical painting on the side of my van. "Wait," he said slowly. "Hold on. Don't tell me you're Vivien D'Onofrio."

Tension started to tighten, in my belly, my neck. "Why shouldn't I tell you that?"

"You're not what I expected," he said. "I have to talk to Duncan."

"Oh, my God. You mean, *you're* Jack Kendrick?" I was appalled. I'd been expecting a stolid jarhead type, older, thicker, with a paunch, balding graying hair buzzed off. Maybe a long, bushy mountain man kind of beard. Gray, of course.

Not a foxy silver-eyed sex god who loved to walk in the rain.

If you want more of the D'Onofrio stories, check out Edge of Ruin!

Also by Shannon McKenna

Standing In The Shadows

Out Of Control

Edge Of Midnight

Extreme Danger

Ultimate Weapon

Fade To Midnight

Blood And Fire

One Wrong Move

Fatal Strike

In For The Kill

Standalones

Return To Me

Hot Night

Meet Shannon McKenna

Shannon McKenna is the NYT and USA TODAY bestselling author of over thirty novels, ranging from sexy contemporary romance to action packed, turbocharged romantic thrillers. She loves tough and heroic alpha males, heroines with the brains and guts to match them, terrifying villains who challenge them to their utmost, adventure, blazing sensuality, and most of all, the redemptive power of true love.

Since she was small she has loved abandoning herself to the magic of a good book, and her fond childhood fantasy was that writing would be just like that but with the added benefit of being able to take credit for the story at the end. The alchemy of writing turned out to be messier than she'd ever dreamed, but whatever, she loves it anyway and hopes that readers enjoy the results of her experiments. She loves to hear from her readers. Contact her by email at her website, http://shannonmckenna.com, or find her on Facebook at https://www.facebook.com/AuthorShannonMckenna/ to keep up with all her news! Follow her on Bookbub to get new release and discount alerts! https://www.bookbub.com/authors/shannon-mckenna

If you'd like to know when new books will come out, and hear about discounts, giveaways and promos, join Shannon's newsletter at http://shannonmckenna.com/connect.php. She has special goodies waiting for you there, exclusive bonus stories that are just for her subscribers, and a free Obsidian Files novella!

She hopes to see you there!